Angel
WITHOUT WINGS
An Old West Christmas Tale

LYNN LUICK

Copyright © 2023 by Lynn Luick

ISBN: 978-1-77883-030-3 (Paperback)
        978-1-77883-031-0 (Hardback)

All rights reserved. No part of this publication may be reproduced, distributed, or transmitted in any form or by any means, including photocopying, recording, or other electronic or mechanical methods, without the prior written permission of the publisher, except in the case brief quotations embodied in critical reviews and other noncommercial uses permitted by copyright law.

The views expressed in this book are solely those of the author and do not necessarily reflect the views of the publisher, and the publisher hereby disclaims any responsibility for them.

BookSide Press
877-741-8091
www.booksidepress.com
orders@booksidepress.com

CONTENTS

Chapter 1 1
Chapter 2 11
Chapter 3 23
Chapter 4 36
Chapter 5 45
Chapter 6 62
Chapter 7 75
Chapter 8 90
Chapter 9 104
Chapter 10 123
Chapter 11 138
Chapter 12 152
Chapter 13 168
Chapter 14 184
Chapter 15 197
Chapter 16 209
Chapter 17 224
Chapter 18 236

1

It is a nice day up here in the clouds. But it's always a nice day. There is always-new people coming up and bad people going down. You've heard that there is a silver lining in every cloud. Up here the clouds are lined with gold and the streets are paved with silver. I messed up my last assignment again but I hoped Peter would give me another chance to make good and get my wings. It seemed to me that the modern world is hard to deal with. I came from a time when life was hard and you had to rely on your mind more than machines. I sure don't want to be considered one of the bad people going down the stairs. Up here you always hear stories of what awaits you down there just like you hear on earth. I am waiting to hear of Peter's decision about if I get another assignment on earth.

"Peter, come to the main office!"

"Please wait Peter he'll be right with you. Have a seat."

"How you been Judy?"

"Busy as usual. They come and they go. It's going to be a madhouse around here with Christmas coming. Peter, he'll see you now."

"Peter good to see you."

"You too sir. You're looking well."

"I am. Except for this one little problem."

"What's that, sir?"

"Gabriel, I thought he would do better. That's why I named him after the arch angle. He's been a little disappointing."

"I know he's been on fifty assignments over the one hundred and fifty years he's been with us."

"Peter what can we do. He was such a good man. I hate to have to send him down to my rival. We need to come up with a plan so he can get his wings. You know I don't like to send anyone down if I can help it."

"Well sir, I've been thinking about this since he came back from his last fouled up assignment."

"Well, what is it?"

"I think he's been stuck in his past. I don't think he can adapt to the modern world. If we send him back to his time, I think he'll make it and make the future a better place."

"You have someone in mind?"

"Yes sir, three someone's in mind."

"Alright, you take care of the details. If he needs help, gave him what is allowed. No more."

"Yes sir, I'll get right on it. I know right where he is."

"Good luck you'll needed it."

"Judy, would you mind calling Gabriel to my office? Your P. A. system is better than mine. The boss doesn't seem to want to invest in my office."

"Sure I'll do that for you. She said. "Gabriel, please report to Peter's office. Gabriel, please report to Peter's office."

"Thanks Judy, I owe you."

"Non-sense."

"You want to see me Peter?" Gabriel said.

"Yes, I have a new assignment for you."

"Yes sir, I'm ready."

"Do you remember anything about your life before you came here?"

"Not much just tidbits now and then."

"Good, you know about the Civil War?"

"Yes sir, a bad time in the past."

"You're going back there to help a mother and her daughter save their ranch and help the mother find true love. All this by Christmas, you know that's the boss's birthday? That will be your present to him and get your wings at the same time."

"But, that's only three months. You know I don't have any powers yet?"

"I know I'll give you some limited powers at first. That's all I can do. Bosses orders. But as you progress you will earn more powers."

"Alright, when do I leave? And where is the assignment this time?"

"You leave right away. It's in Missouri near the town of Joplin. I'll put you down in eastern Missouri. Your name will be Gabe Owens. That's all you need to know except the mother is Emily Truman and the daughter is Lilly Ann Truman. You'll be dressed for the time period. You ready?"

"I guess I'll learn more as I go. Bye now."

Peter put me down in a nice green place on a beautiful fall day. I had forgotten what earth could be like out in the country without any of the noise of the big cities. I better get started west. At least I haven't lost my sense of direction. I was heading west down a dusty trail when a man came out of the blue. He pulled up his horse right in front of me. He looked to be about thirty-five or so with a black beard and hair. He had an old union blue uniform all torn in places and a hat to match. He was riding a mare that looked to need some food as much as he did.

"What you doing out here without a horse?"

"Had mine stolen last night while I was asleep."

"That's been going on since the war's been over. Where you from? From the way you're dressed you don't look to be from nearby."

I looked down and I had on a plaid suit, which were green and red and a bright purple bow tie around my neck with a brown derby hat on my head and a pair of black boots that buckled up the side. I thought. "Peter so much for being dressed in the time period."

"No, I'm from back east. My boss sent me out here to look into some things that are going on. By the way, how long since the war ended and what's the date? I've been out of touch."

"The war ended in April and today is September 25, 1865. Where you heading? My name is Jason Benning."

"I'm heading to near Joplin, Missouri. My name is Gabe Owens."

"Good to meet you Gabe. Haven't seen no-one in a few days. Getting kind of lonely."

As we shook hands I said, "Know what you mean. I haven't seen many humans for a long while."

"Maybe I can give you a ride into the next town, Polar Bluff. You got money to buy a horse and, no offend, some new clothes."

I reached in my pocket and out came three-hundred-dollar bills. "Thanks Peter."

"You give me a ride and I'll buy you and your horse some food and maybe some clothes. Those look pretty worn out."

"You know after you buy a horse, why don't we ride together. I'm heading to near Joplin myself. Hop on, it ain't too far to Polar Bluff."

As we rode along I could see that fall was in the air. The leaves were starting to turn yellow and red. I had forgotten how beautiful this time of year could be. We rode up main-street of Polar Bluff, if you could call it a main street. There were only five stores. Jason stopped in front of the stables. A man came out and led the horse inside.

Jason said. "Give him some oats and good hay. We've been on a long trip."

"He looks it."

"Mister I need to buy a horse."

His face lit up.

"You got money. Most people don't now days with the war just being over."

"Sure I do."

"Then come this way. I only have three. But they'll do."

I looked them over. For some strange reason I knew what I was looking for. I felt it deep inside, like I've done this before.

"This bay mare, she'll do. I need a saddle and bridle also."

Jason said, "Being from the east you sure know your horse flesh."

"No offense mister, but the way you're dressed I didn't think you would know the front of a horse from the back."

"I'm going to change that at your general store. How much for everything? The whole outfit for a hundred dollars."

"I need a hundred and fifty."

"How many horses have you sold lately? How about one-ten?"

"I haven't sold many lately but now the war's over I look for things to pick up and you were riding double. One twenty-five."

"Good point, it's a deal. Could you have her ready in about two hours."

"Sure can."

I paid him and me and Jason headed to the general store to pick up some supplies. Walking up the steps, there was an old man sitting in a rocking chair. He looked up from the newspaper.

"Any good news."

"Not much, it's a month old. I heard most of it from men like you returning home from the war like you. I don't know why I still take it. It's always a month late. Just something to do I guess. Can I do something for you two?"

"We're looking to buy some clothes and some food for the trail."

"You both look to need new outfits. That one I know he's been in the war but you I don't know where your dudes came from. Not around here that's for sure. Now I'm through funnin' you. You got cash money."

"Sure we do."

"Then go inside and pick what you need. I'll be in shortly."

We went in and looked around. Things were all put on the shelves neatly. The first thing that Jason went to was the guns and rifles.

"Gabe, come over here. I have a good gun but we're going to need a rifle. We may need to hunt for food or to protect ourselves. Sometimes a handgun won't do."

"Alright, put it on the pile."

"Don't you need a gun, just in case of trouble?"

"No, I think I would get in more trouble if I bought one."

We both tried on new clothes and finally found some to fit. We both found hats and boots. Then we got the entire foodstuff and some pans to cook with. That was it. The old man came in and the first thing he did was threw the newspaper in the trash. I hoped that this would fit on our two horses. He added up the cost of all we had on and what we had on the counter.

"We need shells for my gun and this new rifle."

"That a be forty dollars. You take the old uniform and these others whatever they are."

"No, you can do away with mine. I don't ever want to see those again."

"Mine too, you might give it to someone that needs it."

"I don't know anyone that's down on their luck that bad."

"Alright, I get the picture. My boss thought they would do."

We got everything packed on our two horses and were heading out of town to the west. We had four or five hours of daylight left and we made as many miles as we could. Now that we had two horses it was faster going and easier on the backside. It was so dry, that we didn't see many animals around but lots of wagon ruts along the trail.

"Jason, what are all the ruts from? They're so deep."

"That's from all the wagons of war pulling the canons. They're heavy and then if it rains the wheels sink deeper. These ruts will be here for many years to come, a reminder of a bad past. It was bad no matter what side you were on. But it was worse for the south. They lost but they were fighters. I lost one of my best friends near the end. I might as well tell you. The short time I've known you, I think you are a good man and can be trusted. My best friend was John Truman he was killed right after we heard the war was over by someone we didn't see. He had just come back from home near Joplin, Missouri. I promised him before he died I would help his wife and daughter with their ranch until they get back on their feet after the war. I have been wondering around but now I feel I'm bound to do this. I could use some help from a good man and friend."

"Who would that be?"

"You, Gabe? I don't know what we'll run up against. I could really use the help. There won't be any pay, but John said Emily is the best cook this side of New York. From what he said, the ranch is a horse ranch and is on good land and there would be people after it if she didn't have help to guide her. So how about it, maybe hard work."

"I'm not handy with a gun. But I can work. I think I'll come along and see what happens."

"That's good, now who's going to cook. Let's stop for the night."

"I'll try my hand. I may have the touch if the good Lord is looking down on me."

I went to cooking. I really didn't know what I was doing, but it looked all right. I didn't want to try it but Jason was downright hungry. He dipped his fork in it and the food was in his mouth before I could warn him. He didn't stop until he was done.

"The Lord must be on your side 'cause that's the best cooking since I left home. My ma was the best."

Then I dug in and it was pretty good. Then I said.

"Thank you Lord for the fine food I couldn't have done it without you."

"So, I see why you didn't want a gun. You must be very religious. I'm glad we might need some Divine help."

"Yes, I am. It happened the last few years you might say. It might help us on our mission."

"It sure couldn't hurt. You might pray for Emily and Lilly Ann."

"Don't worry that's already been taken care of. You might try it yourself."

"I wouldn't know where to start and what to say."

"It's not hard, just put your hands together and talk like you were talking to me. He will hear you. You could start by thanking him for being alive after the war and to see you through the time ahead. Whatever it might bring. And to help Emily and Lilly Ann."

"You really think it would help. My ma made me pray when I was little but with the war it just didn't seem that it would help."

"I'm sure it would. It might take some time but yes it will come with time. Even I don't know how much time."

We went to bed with our bellies full. The horses were staked out close by in a good stand of grass. I didn't need sleep but I pretended to be asleep. During the night I looked over at Jason and he was on his knees with his hands together and looking up at the starry sky. I would keep this to myself for that was for him and God to know. Now I knew I had met the man for Emily. After all he went through he still had time to pray. I had to find a way for Emily and Lilly Ann to see that goodness in him. The next morning, after a delicious breakfast we headed out on the trail again. He was driving the horses hard. It was like he couldn't wait to get there now.

"Why are you driving so hard now?" I asked Jason when we stopped for the night.

"I don't rightly know. I have a feeling in me that they need some help right now. I've taken too long. I should have been there months ago. Seem like since I've met you I've become driven to get it done."

We rode out the next morning as we had stopped the night before at a tremendous pace. We would stop and water the horses and let them rest, but they didn't seem tired at all. The days were going smooth and the nights were quiet. That night I asked Jason.

"Should we be getting there soon?"

"I judge about day after tomorrow. You said you had business in Joplin?"

"I'm going to stick with you for a while. Your business is more urgent than either of us knows. Your business is becoming mine. I have a feeling that we deal with yours and mine will be easier to accomplish."

All the next day we rode on and as it got near sunset we stopped. We had a fire going and were finishing eating when out of the night came three riders. I let Jason handle it for I was not use to the ways of the west. The one in the led spoke up.

"Who are you? What are you doing here?"

Jason said, "That's none of your business. Who are you to come in our camp and start demanding answers?"

"We work for the biggest cattle ranch around these parts and my boss wants to know about everyone that comes into his area."

"Are we on his land? If so would you kindly point us to a road that leads to Joplin."

"No you're not on his land, but it will be his soon enough."

"The road to Joplin?"

"Find it yourself."

They rode off, but the last man came back and told us.

"Mister you'll see a trail to your right about half a mile up then about a mile you'll see a sign that will tell you. The Truman ranch is about a mile pass that and then straight into town. I don't care for Ben's ways but it's the only ranch job around these parts my name is Jay Whatson."

"Thanks Jay for the help, my name's Jason and this is Gabe."

"I better catch up. They'll wonder what I'm doing, so long."

He went on down the trail fast to catch up with the other two.

"Looks like we'll pull in there tomorrow morning, if we don't have any more guests."

"Why didn't you tell the first man our names and who we were looking for?"

"He wasn't very friendly and the first thing he would do is go tell his boss who we were going to see. I don't think Jay will and I want to see what's going on before I let anyone know our business. He already gave us some information."

"What's that?"

"He said this land will be his boss's soon. Let's hit the sack; I have to tell Emily and Lilly Ann about John. I don't rightly know how to do it."

"Go to sleep thinking about it and it will come to you during the night or tomorrow before we get there. It will be alright."

"I don't know how you do that but I come to trust what you say. Then other things, like those men you know nothing. You're a mystery, goodnight Gabe."

We woke up and Jason got a razor out of his saddlebag and shaved his beard off and we headed down the trail to the Truman ranch. The trail was easy to follow just as Jay had said. Instead of going on into Joplin we stopped in front of a sign that read Truman Ranch, John and Emily Truman, Owners. The sign was faded and hung on the fence at an angle, but it was still readable. On the way up to the house you could tell the place had been neglected. There were parts of the fence lying on the ground with dirt almost covering them. Riding up to the front of the house a woman came out on the porch shading her eyes against the sun coming up in the east. She was wearing a light blue dress with her light brown hair tied back in a ponytail. I could see she was with child. My attention turned toward the barn, I could see it and the corral were in disarray. Then an older girl came out of the barn carrying a pail. She was wearing light colored pants and a red shirt. She hurried up on the porch next to her mother, for I know this had to be Emily and Lilly Ann. She reached inside the door and pulled out a shotgun and pointed it our way. Emily said something and put her hand on the barrel and pushed it down toward the ground.

I heard Jason say under his breath.

"Lord, nothing has come to me, please help me do this."

2

As we rode up to the porch, the woman spoke out.

"I'm sorry about my daughter, pulling out the shotgun but we don't get many strangers come up to the house. Can I help you?"

"Yes, you can Emily and I understand about Lilly Ann wanting to protect you both. John would have wanted it that way."

"How do you know my husband and our names?"

"I don't know if John told you about me. I'm Jason Benning and this is Gabe Owens. John didn't know him but I met him back on the trail a few days ago. Nowadays you learn about people fast and Gabe has become a good and trusted friend. John may have told you about me the last time he was here just before the end of the war. When he came back he told me about the ranch and how much he loved you and Lilly Ann."

"Are you trying to tell me that John is-------"

She dropped hard to the floor and Lilly dropped the shotgun and rushed to her.

"Mama, what is wrong? Are you alright?"

Jason and I were off our horses and on the porch in two seconds. Jason picked Emily up in his arms.

"Lilly Ann, show me the way to your mother's bedroom."

Lilly Ann was crying but she led us to the bedroom. Jason said.

"Gabe, go get some water out of that well I saw in front. Lilly Ann bring some rags. Don't worry she'll be alright, she just passed out."

Emily came to and started sobbing.

"What will we do Lilly, your father is dead and the bank wants to take the ranch if we don't pay it off by Christmas."

"Don't worry we'll do something. Stop crying, think of the baby." Lilly was hugging her mother and crying.

"Emily, I know it's hard. I was with John when he died. He made me promise to come and help you two get back on your feet. I didn't know how to tell you. I've been wandering from place to place. Then I met Gabe and something came over me and I knew I had to come. I felt you needed my help right away."

She sat up and Lilly Ann helped her to the chair in the front room. Now looking closer I noticed how well kept the inside of the house was. It looked to have two separate bedrooms and a large kitchen with a good size front room. This was her home and she took care of it and the fresh garden I had seen on the way to the well.

"I don't know what you can do? Sam has been so nice. He said if I ever need money he would buy the ranch so I could get back east to our family."

"Mother, you know I don't like that man. He's up to no good. Zack said he thinks the fence has been cut and horses may be missing."

"You shouldn't talk about Sam like that. You know he's brought things from the store that we needed. You know Zack can't fix things with one arm. He just does small jobs for room and board."

"You know Mr. Johnson just wants this land. I'm old enough I see the way he looks at your stomach. Just like the town's women. They don't think pa came home. They think the baby is someone else's. But, I know it's pa's I know he was here and no others."

"Lilly Ann, don't talk like that in front of these two men. You know better than that. We don't know them. Mr. Benning I can't pay you and Mr. Owens anything."

"Emily I know it's hard to trust us but John did or I wouldn't know all I do about this place. We don't want to be paid, room and broad is enough. Let us fix up the place and have a look around. You may have enough horses to sell and pay off the bank."

"I know John wouldn't tell all that you know to anyone unless he trusted him. So stay and see about the horses and help Zack fix up the place. We'll see what happens after that. If worse comes to worse I can sell to Sam. You'll have to stay in the barn with Zack. But you and Gabe can take your meals in here."

"Thank you, call me Jason."

"Ma'am, you can call me Gabe it's short for Gabriel. I hope we can get to know you and Lilly Ann better."

Lilly Ann spoke up. Call me Lilly, ma just adds the Ann when she's mad at me."

We laughed.

Jason and I headed to the barn and unsaddled our horses. There wasn't much hay in the loft and the inside of the barn was as bad as the outside. There was enough room for two or more beds in the room where Zack stayed. Jason said,

"We might as well get to work. Now that I've told them it's like a great weight has been lifted off my shoulders."

"Jason, I told you it would come to you. You handled that well. I'll make two beds and get hay for them. We need to clean up this room and the barn."

"While you do that I'll get started repairing the barn and corral."

Jason found John's tools. They were in good shape. So we went to work and got a good bit done when Zack came in the barn.

"Who are you? And what are you doing here? You have no business in here."

I said, "Calm down Zack, Jason and me are here to help you get this ranch back on the right track."

"And who are you? And what makes you think I need any help? I'm doing fine, and why you move things around? I had them where I could find everything."

"We had to make room for two more beds, see. I'll help you find anything that you can't find."

"I guess it's alright if missy knows you're here and little missy."

"They do, and you have no need to worry. We're not here to replace you just help you. They think the world of you. I know Lilly has learned a lot from you. They need all our help to keep this ranch now that John won't be coming back from the war. I was with John when he died."

"Mr. John died. It's hard to believe. Lilly loved her daddy so much. How did they take it? I don't know what missy will do with the baby coming."

"Hard at first. John told me about Emily. I think she can handle it if she's as strong as he said."

"She is, she held this place together these last hard four years. I've changed my mind glad to have you. We better get to the house missy doesn't like me to be late for dinner."

Jason said, "Then we better get going Zack." He slapped him on the back.

We walked in the house and there was a wagonload of vittles on the table. Emily invited us to have a seat. She said, "In this house we pray before we eat."

We bowed our heads and held hands.

"We thank you Lord, for the food on our humble table. Thank you for sending Jason and Gabriel to us. I know you had your reasons for taking our beloved John away from us. With your guidance we will make it. And as always thanks for Zack and all the help he's been over these hard years. Amen. Now pass your plates."

"Ma'am, that was a beautiful prayer. I'm sure he heard every word and more help will be on the way."

"Let us all eat, and I told you to call me Emily, Gabriel."

"I will Emily. Thank you. You know Jason looks like we came to the right place. We'll never starve, long as we're here. This is great food."

Lilly said, "What are you so quiet about Jason? Did the work tucker you out?"

"No, just pondering what to do next. I'll take any suggestions from any of you. I know we need to go to town and get some more nails and some white paint, tomorrow. The work felt good. My muscles are a little sore, but it will be alright in a few days."

"Miss Emily these two have done more work in one day than I've done in four years."

"Zack, you do what you can. I know that, you fought for this country to help free your people. I applaud you for that."

"If you don't mind me asking where did you lose your arm?" Jason said.

"Sir, I don't mind it was in the first battle of Bull Run. I still think that is the proudest moments in my life. Now that my people are free I will never regret what I lost. Jason you asked for suggestions. You watch out for that Mr. Johnson and his gunman Ben Warren."

"I didn't know you felt like that, Zack." Emily said.

"He brought you things we needed to survive on until our prayers were answered. I think these two are the answer."

"I told you mama, I didn't like Mr. Johnson."

"Jason, I don't have money for the things you need to fix this place."

"Emily, you don't worry about that. I have some money and as we need more I'm sure the Lord will provide in ways we could not imagine. Let us all keep praying."

"You were sure named after the right angel. I thank you, Gabriel."

"This was a great meal. But it's time for me to hit the sack. Just be ready to go to town tomorrow morning."

"I can't go, you know."

"Emily, I don't care what those old bitties think. That is John's baby and you should be proud of it. Stand up to them." I could tell Emily laughed under her breath.

"You're right Jason. Lilly and I will be ready."

"You to Zack."

"No sir."

"Now Zack you and I fought for your rights to go and do what you want to. I will be proud to have you come with us."

"Yes sir, I will be ready. Thank you, you're the first white men to say anything like that to me."

Gabe said, "I'll buy you all some new clothes. Goodnight."

In the morning we loaded up in the wagon, after some minor repairs, and headed to town. It was a nice ride. The leaves on the trees were turning different colors in anticipation of the winter to come. Then Jason said,

"This afternoon I'm going to take a ride along the fence line and find that brake in the fence. I'll check on the other side for any of your stock before I fix the brakes. What is your brand?"

"It's a T with a circle around it for the Circle T. But we hadn't did any branding since right before the war started."

"I'll check, but the ones unbranded I can't bring back through the fence, but it will be alright. I'll take the branding irons with me and build a fire by the brake in the fence. I know the irons should be in the barn somewhere."

Zack spoke up, "I know exactly where they are and I'll go with you and show you where the brakes are. We will have to be careful, that is Mr. Johnson land on the other side of ours."

As we came down the main street all eyes were turned toward us. I could see the women turn their heads toward the woman beside them and shield their mouth, so not to be thought that they were talking about anyone. The men would just put their hands on their hips and shake their head as if they were discussed with what they saw. They were rushing to judgment before they knew all the facts. They would get what they deserved in the end, but that was not my call. Only one can decide that. As we pulled up in front of the general store there was Jason sitting next to Emily driving the wagon and not even aware of the stares around us. He helped Emily down off the wagon seat as we got out of the back of the wagon. As we entered the store I notice two of the men that we had words with on the trail coming our way.

The storekeeper was pleasant enough, but the air was full of tension.

"Haven't seen you in town for a while Mrs. Truman. What can I do for you?" The storekeeper said.

"Mr. Jimson, this is Jason Benning and this is Gabriel Owens. They are helping me out at the ranch. Jason wants to buy some things for the ranch and Lilly Ann, Zach and me are going to buy some new clothes."

"Just look around and you can try the clothes back there. But not Zack."

Jason turned around and handed Mr. Jimson a list to fill and said.

"Why not Zack?"

"That's alright Jason, that just the way it is."

"No it's not. Why can't he?"

"You know he's black."

"I have you know that he fought for this country, just as I did so everyone could go where they want and do what they want. Fill that list, so we can get out of here."

"He can go in the back room and try on the clothes. But Zack try to get the right size because I can't put them back on the shelve."

"Yes sir, I understand."

"This will be cash."

As Emily, Lilly and Zack took the clothes to try on I stepped up to the counter and said.

"It will be cash Mr. Jimson."

"Fine!"

Everyone got what he or she needed and we left the store. As we stepped off the stores porch there was Ben and the other cowhand leaning against the back of our wagon. Jason helped Emily up on the wagon seat and then went to the back of the wagon. I helped Lilly in the wagon and then Zack and me got in. Jason put everything in the wagon. Then I heard Ben say to Jason as he came to the side.

"Why are you helping that knocked up bitch in the wagon?"

I don't believe what I saw. Jason hit Ben so hard he went flying on to the porch of the general store. Jason drew his gun and took two steps and his gun was in Ben's face.

"You better be glad that there are women and children around are you would be dead right now. If I ever hear of you talking about this woman or her family I will hunt you down and put you in the ground. I just spent four years hunting down rebels." He took Ben's gun and dropped it in the horse trough then jumped up on the seat and we left town. It was very quiet all the way to the ranch. As we pulled into the now fixed gate, Jason said.

"I'm sorry y'all had to see that but I will not let a woman be talked about like that. Emily, let me know if I ever overstep my bounds. We're just here to save this ranch."

"Jason, you don't have to be sorry. That wasn't your doing."

I said, "That was his doing. Don't talk about someone unless it's good."

"Dinner will be ready in an hour. Come on up to the house."

After dinner Zack and Jason headed out to check the damage to the fence. It was a ways but Zack knew right where it was cut. Now that they were off their horses it could be seen it had been cut on purpose. We had found the branding irons in the barn where John had wrapped them up in burlap. Not a rust spot was on them.

"Zack would you please get a fire going and get the iron nice and hot. I'm going thru to the other side of the brake."

"You be careful, that is Mr. Sam's land far as the eyes can see."

"Don't worry I'm only looking for our brand and the colts that may belong to them. The colts are the only ones we are branding."

Jason went thru the cut in the fence. That is one power Peter had given me, I could see what was happening to the people involved. He was going around the area looking for horses. He passed thru lots of cattle. Finally he came to a small herd of horses. I could tell he was looking thru to find the Circle T brand. He rode on and came to another bunch and looked around. He started driving them, along with the other bunch, toward the cut in the fence. Two riders were coming toward him. I thought really hard, and about that time Jason looked around and saw the riders coming toward him. He slowed down the herd, now about thirty, and waited for the two men to come up to him. They stopped right by him a ways off.

"What, you think you're doing with those horses and on this land?"

"I'm glad you stopped by. If you look closely you'll see a Circle T on all except the colts that are running with their mothers. We had a cut in our fence and I just came over to our goods neighbors to get our horses and repair the cut in our fence and brand our colts. Please look thru the herd and make sure I didn't get any of yours by mistake."

They looked the herd over.

"I guess you're right, we don't have any horses over this way."

"You tell Mr. Johnson and Ben Warren that we will keep a better eye on our fence line from now on, so this shouldn't happen again. Do you understand?"

"You trying to say we cut Mrs. Truman's fence?"

"No, just that we'll keep an eye on it. I'll be back to check for more of our stock."

"You wait until we talk to Ben. He'll let us know what to do."

"I'll be done by the time you get back to him. You tell him that you checked the brands and to come see Mrs. Truman and myself at the ranch house. Use the road, not by the way of the fence anymore, understand? Bye, now."

Jason droved the horses off, the cowboys just sit there puzzled. He drove them thru the brake toward Zack.

"Zack, you think you can keep these here, I'm going back for more. I don't have much time. They talked to me, but they're going to get Ben, so I have to hurry and then get the fence patched before he can get back. We'll brand the colts when I get back."

"Sure, I can but hurry. The ranch house is not too far."

"Got you. Be right back."

Jason went back to the Johnson's ranch and came back with about fifty more head. Him and Zack branded the colts and they put out the fire. Then they fixed the fence and drove the horse away from the fence line back a ways.

"Zack, get back to the ranch house and tell Emily what happened. I'm going to check some more of the fence along this side. I won't be long. Tell her that Mr. Johnson or Ben might come by."

"Sure thing, it's sure nice working with someone with some real guts."

I was there with Emily when Jason rode up. Mr. Johnson and Ben were talking to us.

"There he is the one my men said took the horses off my ranch."

"I did, and your men saw the Circle T brand on all the horses except the colts that were with their mothers. Zack and me only branded the colts. There was a cut in our fence and there was another one north of that one that looked like the horses had been driven thru not just wondered thru. You are welcome to check the brands, you'll find no other brands on Mrs. Truman's herd."

"Emily, you let this man speak for you. We have been friends for so long."

"I know, but Zack had said there were brakes in the fence. I had told you and you said that you would have your men fix them. You didn't fix the fence and Jason does speak for this ranch and me. Somehow I'm going to keep this ranch for my late husband. It was his and my dream. I hope we can still be friends. But Jason, Gabriel and Zack will be keeping an eye on all our fence line and there better not be any more cuts. I hope you understand."

"I too hope we can remain friends. I'll take your word that those were your horses."

They rode out, a little angry I think, as they reached the gate Jason said to Emily.

"As I told Mr. Johnson, after Zack came back I found another cut fence and some more of your horses about a mile in his ranch. They looked like they have been driven thru. I think someone is stealing your stock. At this point we can't be sure if it's on Mr. Johnson orders or not."

"Why weren't they taken and sold before you found them?"

"No offend Zack, but they hadn't had anyone to stop them up until now so they could wait as long as they wanted. Zack you couldn't have done it on your own. You would have gotten killed. It would have been to Mr. Johnson avenge to have your stock stolen. He wants the ranch, I'm sure of it. But we need proof to take to the marshal. How much is your loan at the bank? I've counted 350 head. At today's rate, I think if we sold them all you could get is around $17,000. But you don't want to sell them all. You want to keep your stallions and some young mares, to keep the ranch growing. So you could only get about $9,000 or less. You have to hire a few more men to make a drive. Men that you could trust, and a couple more to keep up with the ranch with Zack supervision."

"That won't be enough, I owe $11,000. The extra men and a chuck wagon and supplies would have to be paid out of what we get for the herd. I want to leave us enough stock to start over and build it up again."

"I'll go out with Gabe and check the north and east side of the ranch. We might find more, enough I don't know. Any amount I get for the stock will be lots closer to the amount you need. I think you let me know, and by next week we should be on the trail. It shouldn't take more than four weeks to Kansas City and back. That will leave us one and a half months to figure out what our next step will be. Maybe the bank will extend your loan if you pay $7,000 or $8,000 on it."

"Maybe they will now that the ranch is on the mend and looking up and that's over half we owe."

"Don't tell anyone what we're planning. We don't know whom we can trust yet. It's going to be tough to get men that don't have any connections to Mr. Johnson but if you let me and Gabe hire them I think we can do good. Gabe is a good judge of men. I don't know how he does it, but he does?"

"Gabriel how do you manage that?" Emily said.

"Ma, remember that's how pa was. Cause of that he made friends real fast or not at all."

"I don't know it's just that I have a feeling inside. I have that bad feeling about Mr. Johnson and Ben."

"You know John had said the same thing. Maybe that's why I've come to trust you two so fast. You two hire the men and head for Kansas City. Zack what's wrong with you?"

"Me supervising, I don't know. What if they won't take order from a poor black man?"

"You know more about this ranch than anyone. If they won't do anything that you tell them to do then Emily will fire them and hire new men. Just look at your new clothes. You don't look poor."

"They are nice aren't they?"

Jason and I laughed as we rode out north to look for more horses. We found about fifty more. On the way back Jason asked me.

"I wonder when Emily's and John's baby will be born."

"To me it looks like about the time the loans due or about Christmas."

"How would you know?"

"Just a little inside information."

"I don't know about you. To have such knowledge at your age."

"I'm older than I look. Let's just leave it at that."

"Alright, you know I've been working harder than I have in six months. I'm tired but it feels good. This could become a way of life. I'm not that old to settle down and marry."

"Emily is about your age, I think."

"She wouldn't look at me twice. She just found out about John a week ago. Anyway Lilly Ann wouldn't take too kindly to another man trying to take her father's place. John was a right handsome man and look at me, a tall lanky man."

"You've gained some weight since you been eating Emily's cooking. Lilly Ann cares about you I can tell. Why don't we wait and see? You know you don't have to leave when the ranch is on steady ground. You said you didn't have any family left."

"That's true. Look, over their Gabe, what's that?"

3

As we looked around we were among some tall hills that looked down into a very green valley. Most of the hills were covered with trees and vegetation. The one in front of us had no resemblance of the others around us. It was barren of any type of growth and the formations didn't look like rock or stone that I had ever seen.

"Gabe, have you ever seen anything like this?"

"Can't say I have. What do you think?"

"Hand me that pair of wire cutters. I didn't bring a pick or shovel. I need to break some off."

"Here I brought a pick."

"How do you do that?"

I looked up to heaven and said.

"I just have a knack, I guess.

Jason filled a leather bag with the rock, that I just happen to have on me also.

"Gabe, don't tell anyone about this not even Emily. I don't want to get her hopes up. I think I know what it is, but I want to get an experts opinion on it. Let's get back to the house. Tomorrow we go to town and hire five men. That should be a plenty.

That's three to go with us and two for the ranch."

"I won't say anything. I can cook on the drive, but we need one more. That will give you four to help you with the horses."

"That sounds good. Six men and you cook. Now let's get back and eat some of that good home cooking."

That night nothing was said about what we had found. The conversation turned to what was going to happen in the next three weeks.

"Zack, when we leave for Kansas City I want you to put the men that I hire tomorrow to work on fixing more of the fences around the house here and the corral and get everything painted and the house finished being painted. Keep a sharp eye on them if they ride off for no reason let Emily know. Don't tell them anything they don't need to know. I've looked around this ranch and John and you have the making of a fine horse ranch in the future if we can get that loan paid off and keep the buzzards away. Lilly when we get back I want to teach you some things about the ranch so one day you will know what to do. Right now you need to go to school and learn all you can."

"You mean I can learn more about the ranch. I know some. Zack has shown me. But I don't go to school. Ma's been teaching me. The kids make fun of me and ma."

Emily said. "You know how kids are. They repeat what their parents say and you heard what Ben said. That is the opinion of most in this town. It is getting worst, as I get larger. What they say hurts but it will not run me off this ranch. Some of these church going people were our friends."

"I just wander who started the rumor that it wasn't John's baby. Could it be the one that acts so nice to you? I'm going to talk to the teacher and the preacher tomorrow. Try to get Lilly going to school and you back to church. No matter what happens tomorrow I'm taking everyone to church Sunday. Now I'm going to ride the fence with Gabe all night. Just to make sure none of the fence gets cut again. It seems Gabe doesn't need any sleep. That's another thing I don't know how he does."

"Jason, you notice to much. It's already dark, we better get going."

We headed down the fence line. The night went by slow. Nothing was happening and I could tell that Jason was getting sleepy. He kept dosing off and I would let him sleep. Then a noise would wake him up and he would tell me to keep my eyes open. I would let him think, it was I asleep but he knew better. He was trying so hard to make this all turn out right. Then about two in the morning I heard a noise that was more than a deer or a rabbit.

"Jason, there is some different sounds."

"What direction did it come from?"

"Up ahead, I think. There it is again."

"Be as quiet as we can and be ready for anything. I wish you would use a gun. Let me handle it, I don't want you getting hurt I need your help."

We moved forward, and then in about a hundred yards we saw four men on our side of the fence. They had already cut the fence. They headed east onto Emily's land.

"Are we going to go after them?"

"No, they're after the horses. Let's wait here. They have to come back this way. We have to stop them when they come back. They'll get as many as they can and they won't stop they'll drive them to where they can sell them. They don't want to take a chance of Emily getting them to market and paying off that loan."

We waited two hours and moved about a half mile away from the cut in the fence before we heard them coming. They were coming fast for it was light in the eastern sky and they couldn't take a chance of being seen on Emily's land. Jason said out loud over the roar of the horses.

"Let's head toward the horses and I'll shoot my rifle and turn them away from the cut in the fence. Then we'll deal with the men."

We lit out toward the oncoming horses. Jason had his rifle out firing in the air over the heads of the horses. As they came toward us I could see they were starting to turn some to the right of us some to the left. The men behind them started firing at us, not over our heads, but right at us. That's when Jason started shooting at them head on. One of the men fell off his horse and didn't move. That's when I felt a bullet hit me right in the chest and I was on the ground. I saw the horses start to turn but it was to late they ran right over me. As I got up I saw another man fall to the ground. Then I saw Jason look at me dumbfounded. The horses were turned and the last two men were thru the cut in the fence and out of sight. Jason came over to me and looked at me. I looked down and I had a bullet hole thru my shirt and chest and I looked like I'd been hit by a herd of horse, which I had. I didn't know what to say.

"Guess I was lucky, those two on the ground weren't as lucky."

"We better get them two across their horses and fix the fence again then get back to the ranch. We need to take these two to the marshal and let him know what happened and then hire six men. I know what I saw Gabe, and you shouldn't be alive. I don't know who you really are but I'm glad you're on our side."

"I can't say anything about my mission, but it's to your and the girls benefit to keep me around. I'm on your side."

"Let's get going."

Jason didn't say a word. I stopped by a creek, before we got to the ranch, to clean up. I turned back toward Jason and the hole in my shirt was gone and the bullet hole in my chest was gone and all the scrapes and cuts disappeared from my body.

"Jason, please don't say anything to anybody. They won't believe you and I am here to help."

We came into the yard and Emily and Lilly came out of the house and Zack came from the barn.

"You had trouble."

"Yes, they and two others tried to take about a hundred head."

"We stopped them and Jason fixed the fence."

"We need to take these two to the marshal and then hire the hands to take the horses to Kansas City."

"Come on in first and eat some breakfast. It's on the table."

We sat there eating and Emily said.

"What's wrong Jason?"

"I just don't like killing, had enough of that during the war and I thought Gabe was hurt bad. But he was alright."

"What happened?"

"Oh, I fell off my horse, and I think from where Jason was, he thought the horses ran over me, but they just missed me."

"You sure you're alright."

"Yes, I'm fine. It's Jason, he looks like he's looking at a ghost."

"I'm sorry, it's just I can't believe they missed you. I'll be all right. Gabe, we better get to town."

We rode off toward town with the two horses and dead men in tow. "You're good now."

"Sure, I got my head back on business now. Just let me do the talking. "That I will do."

We came up the street and got off in front of the marshal's office. He saw us and came out.

"What happened, Jason? That is your name isn't it?"

"Yes sir, it is. These two and two others were on Mrs. Truman's ranch last night. They had cut the fence and were trying to make off with about a hundred head of our horses. We stopped them. The other two got away thru the cut in the fence to Mr. Johnson's ranch. If you'll notice the brand it is the Johnson's brand."

Just then Mr. Johnson walked up.

"What happened Tom?"

"These two brought your two dead men on your horses they said they were trying to steal Emily's horses last night. Two men got away."

"Did you see who they were Jason?"

"No, I didn't, day was just breaking but it was still too dark."

"Tom, it must be those four I ran off yesterday. I caught them trying to get away with some of my cattle. I guess they thought it would be easier pickin' over at Emily's."

"Well, looks like they were wrong."

Sam walked off down the street to his office.

"Marshal, this isn't the first time the fence was cut and horses missing. I don't know if you know or not but John died at the end of the war. I was his best friend and I promised him that I would see that Emily would keep the ranch. Someone has been stealing her horses and I'm going to find out who is doing it. I'll leave these two with you. Come on Gabe we have business elsewhere."

We walked into the saloon and went up to the bar and Jason ordered one beer.

"I don't know if you drink or not."

"I'll take some sassafras."

The bartender said. "I ordered two bottles last time the liquor salesmen was in and I thought I never would sell them. Here you go mister."

"You know anyone that needs a job for a month or two."

"How many you looking for?"

"Six, and it pays forty a month."

"Boy's these two gents are hiring six men."

One came up, "Hello Jason, Gabe remember me?"

"Sure Jason, it's Jay, that directed us to town when we first got here. He was with Ben."

"Sure, how you doing?"

"I sure could use a job."

"What happen to the one you had?"

"Ben saw me giving direction to you that day and he fired me. I never liked the way they do business anyway."

"Just maybe you can be of more help to us than you know. Anybody else you know that feels like you do?"

"Jeff, Tim, Bob, James and Jan come over here. They have all been fired from Sam's ranch in the past three months. None for stealing, just doing or saying something Ben didn't like. Boys this here is Jason and Gabe. They need some men I guess to work on Mrs. Truman's ranch. Am I right Jason?"

"Yes you are, we're driving a herd to Kansas City. May take a month and a half. You'll get paid for two."

Bob said. "I don't know if I want to work for that kind of woman."

"Look boys I don't know who told you what, but I know John came home right before the end of the war and stayed one night and came back. He told me, I was his best friend. Before he died I promised him I would make sure his family and ranch is all right. The baby she is carrying is John's. Lilly and Zack saw him leave the next morning."

"We been told it was Zack's."

"Who told you that?"

"It was Ben, he said Sam told him. Said Emily confided in him."

"See here men do you believe me and Gabe here or the one's that fired you."

Tim said. "What you say makes more sense. I always thought she was a good woman. I never thought that she would do that with John off to war. They were always good people."

"If all of you believe me and think the way that Tim thinks come out to the ranch in the morning and we'll start rounding up the horses. It won't be easy we leave Monday morning. Gabe is going to cook and wait 'till you taste his cooking."

We left and went to the stable.

"You still have money. I'm sure Emily will pay you back when we sell the horses. If you even need it."

"I have money left."

We bought a wagon with a cover on top. Then we went to the general store and had Mr. Jimson put together an order for the trail and the ranch.

"Gabe, come with me while Mr. Jimson is filling our order. We're going to see the preacher."

We walked right into the church and there in the front was the preacher.

"Sir, may I talk to you for a minute?"

"Yes sir, you may."

"My name is Jason Benning and this is Gabe Owens. We are new in town. We work for Mrs. Truman. I've just heard some troublesome things about Emily. I would like to speak to your congregation after your sermon Sunday. I want to straighten things out. I can't believe you told her not to come to church anymore."

"I've heard the rumors. I did not believe them, and I never told her not to come. She's always welcome here, this is God's house. Who am I to forbid anyone from coming to worship in his or her own way?"

"Mr. Johnson told her you said for her not to come back."

"Mr. Benning, you may speak and tell Emily and Lilly they are welcome."

Gabe said, "How about Zack. This is God's house and he is one of God's children."

"Yes he is. Tell Zack to come to. This excites me, it's looks to be a rip-roaring Sunday. It will do them good to be taken off their high horse for once. It sure will wake them up. You sit everyone and yes, Zack in the front roll. We'll see how Mr. Johnson likes them apples. I here tell he started the rumor."

"Thank you, we'll see you Sunday."

We went and picked up our new wagon and two horses. Then we loaded the supplies and headed out of town for the ranch. Jay was standing in the front yard when we pulled up.

"What are you doing here? I said in the morning."

"I know, but I didn't have any more money for the hotel. I said to myself Jay you might as well go on out there."

"You'll have to sleep in the hay loft."

"That do me fine, I hear tell that Mrs. Truman is a fine cook."

Emily stepped out on the porch.

"I sure am son. It's on the table waiting for you."

As we sat around the table we started talking.

"Emily, we are all going to church Sunday. You too Zack."

"Me, you sure Mr. Jason."

"Yes sir, the preacher said you too."

Emily said, "I don't know Jason, Mr. Johnson said that Mr. Simms said for me not to bother to come back."

"He told me today he had wondered why you had stopped coming. He never said that. I found out that Mr. Johnson is the one that is telling everyone that your baby belongs to Zack."

Zack said, "What!" At the same time that Emily said "What!"

I could see Jay was a little uncomfortable and so was Jason but it had to be said.

"How could he do that?"

"Miss Emily, I'm sorry, I never."

"I know Zack. It's not you it's that Mr. Johnson no wonder all the women in town wouldn't speak to me. They thought me unfaithful to John, and poor Lilly Ann."

"I told you ma, that man was no good. I remember what pa said. He didn't like him at all."

I said, "I think he is trying to keep you away from everyone and out on this ranch and steal you blind. Then you would have to come to him and sell this ranch."

Jason said. "I think you're right Gabe. That's just what I think. We're not going to let that happen. Tomorrow we start rounding up horses and take them to Kansas City."

In the morning the other five men showed up and we got started. On one piece of the ranch there was a canyon. We collected rock and cut down some trees and made a temporary gate across the open side of the canyon. It took less time to construct and that is one thing we didn't have much of. As we found horses we would put them in here until we left. There was plenty of grass and back a ways there was a waterfall with a small lake at the bottom with a creek flowing out of the canyon from the lake. It was a nice place to have a picnic someday. Most of the herd was already branded, but as we brought them in we would check a second time. We had the branding irons with us now all the time. We worked until dark and we had a hundred head in the canyon. Tomorrow was Saturday, we had to gather the rest then 'cause the next day was Sunday and Jason had plans. Monday we were leaving.

Jason called the seven of us together.

"Men, I don't trust the people on the next ranch so after dinner tonight I need someone to stay out here with the herd with Gabe. He doesn't carry a gun and he doesn't require much sleep. Don't ask me why of either, ask him."

Jay said, "I don't care why. I like Gabe, I'll stay with him."

I said, "Thanks Jason for that vote of confidents. You too Jay, I might just sleep like an Angel knowing you are on the job."

Everyone laughed, as we rode back to the ranch. Emily was on the porch as we rode up.

"Men, I know you have been working hard, and I thank you, but you need to wash up at the well before you set at my table. Cleanliness is next to Godliness. There's a great big dinner waiting for you."

The men were off their horses and at the well, except me, I didn't need to eat, mostly I pretended to eat. Then Bob said.

"Ma'am, how about our clothes, can't get them to clean."

"Just the hands and face, and wipe off your feet before entering my home. And take off your hats and spurs. I'm not going to have my chairs scratched up."

"Yes ma'am."

As each man came in he took off his hat and spurs and their eyes bugged out when they saw the feast before them. They sat and started to reach for the food.

"No, boys, in this home we pray before we eat. I don't want to be mean but those are my rules. Now bow your heads and I'll pray. Thank you Lord for all the food we are about to eat and for Jason and Gabe you sent to me in my time of need. Thank you for these fine hard-working men. Finally for my late husband John whom without him I wouldn't have this baby that I am carrying. I better let you go now or these men are going to starve. Amen! Now everyone help yourself and I hope you enjoy it."

Jeff asked, "No disrespect ma'am, but do you really believe the words you said."

"Yes I do, I prayed every night since my husband left that morning just before the war ended. Look, I didn't know how I was going to save this ranch. Then Jason and Gabriel showed up and started fixing things up and put a stop to the stealing of our horses. Then you all came to us for a drive to Kansas City. It is short of my prayers but it is a good start. We still have two and a half months for my prayers to be fully answered, but it's a start."

James said, "I don't know about the others but I wish you were coming with us. I ain't ate this good since I left home. My mother was a fine cook."

"I wish I could but I can't. But thanks for the compliment."

Jay said, "Come on Gabriel we have horses to look after. We need to leave before I pop."

"Alright Jay, Emily is the only one that calls me Gabriel. Don't forget I'm going to be cooking for you on the trail. I know which plants are good and which will give you a bellyache."

"Alright Gabe, I'll remember that. Got to have my belly. Couldn't enjoy Emily's cooking without it." Everyone said so long, "Gabriel." Then they laughed. As we got on our horses we could still hear them.

We rode along the fence line where the cuts were, but they were still secure. We headed further north to the end of the Truman ranch. Jay asked:

"Gabe, should we go on to the east side of the ranch?"

"I don't think so, the two cuts in the fence were over this way. Jason thinks that the horses were taken and sold over the last four years. Zack, told John about it when he was here when the baby came about. But he had to get back to the fight. He told Zack he would deal with it when the war was over. He thought it would be soon."

"I know it's not proof but when I worked for Mr. Johnson, Ben would tell some of us to stay away from this part of the ranch. Now I think I know why."

I looked up to the sky and thought,

"Peter, can you help me see what has been going on around here?"

Peter's said to my mind, "I'm sorry Gabriel, I can only help in small ways. It's for you to help Jason and Emily find out that. By the way that deal with the horses stampeding over you and that bullet that went thru you was a large deal. So don't depend on that again. Jason's shouldn't have seen that. So be careful."

"What you lookin' at Gabe?"

"Just the moon and the clouds flowing by it."

"Jason said you didn't need much sleep so if you don't mind I'm going' to roll up and get some shut eye. Wake me if there's any trouble. I'm buildin' a fire so you won't run over me in the dark. Goodnight."

The next morning Jay was up when Jason and the men rode up.

"How'd it go last night?"

"Not a peep except a coyote once in a while. Maybe they gave up."

"I wouldn't count on that too much. Men spread out and head east and check every draw and every canyon for horses. Bring all you find to this canyon. We'll brand all we find without brands. Then we'll take out the stallions and about seventy mares and all the colts under two years old. That should keep this ranch going. Get to it we only have today. Tomorrow is church and Monday we leave."

There were horses up draws in ravines down canyons. Some of the horses were along the river and by two small lakes. Jason had said that John had picked a good piece of land, with plenty of water and grass. Not a large ranch but big enough to make a good living and raise a family, if left alone. By the end of the day we counted about three hundred head. Taking out the stallions and seventy mares and colts that left us with about two hundred head to take on the drive. We headed to the ranch with Bob and Jeff to come back tonight after supper. They agreed to take four hours shifts, and one come running if any major trouble. As we were riding in Jason said for everyone to hear.

"You know Gabe, depending on the price, I still think we'll come up short. We need some kind of miracle. Any of you have anything in your mind that may help."

Tim said, "How about selling to Johnson? I heard when I worked there that he wanted to buy this ranch."

"He does, but Emily wants to keep it. That would be the last resort. See John wanted it for generations to come."

James said, "I don't know much but I know when my belly is empty and I just love the way Emily cooks. I'm not wasting any more time. We have to wash up plenty good."

He took off with the others behind him.

Jason and me stayed behind and took our time.

"Gabe, after supper we can get the chuck wagon ready. I didn't want to say anything in front of the others. That sample of ore that we got I'm going to put it in the wagon. I don't know who to trust so don't say anything. I think Jay is all right. But we have to be sure. What do you think about leaving him and Bob at the ranch to help Zack."

"My feeling is that they are the best of the lot. We want Emily and Lilly to be safe. With us gone I don't know. Mr. Johnson hasn't made a move yet but with a chance of her paying off the bank note, he might."

"That's why I said we didn't have enough to pay it off in front of them, in case one is still working for him. Now let's get back before they wonder where we are."

At supper that night Jason spoke up.

"I don't know how many of you attend church. Tomorrow will be a day not to miss I'm going to let this town have it. The preacher said I could speak. It's going to be a humdinger. Lilly Ann you get ready to go back to school Monday. I talked to the teacher and she said for you to come back. Your pa would want it that way. Do it for him and your ma. One day you will have to take over this ranch. Jay, I'm leaving you and Bob here to take care of the women and the ranch. You listen to Zack he's in charge. Any trouble taking orders from him let me know now. I'm sure if you have suggestions he will listen to you. Everyone helps each other and we'll come out on top. You all can come to church or just do what you want."

Jason and me got the wagon packed up that night for the drive Monday morning. Bob and Jeff had left to watch after the herd. The men drifted off to bed one at a time.

4

The morning came early, as it does out in the country. The mornings were starting to get a little nippy. The dew was laid on top of the grass. Good thing we were leaving tomorrow cause in a month this dew would be turning to frost. Jason said that we should make it back by the first of November before the first snowfall. It was nice to be the first up and take in the beauty of the day, before all the noise of the people disturbed the quiet of the beginning of the day. The only sound I could hear was Emily getting breakfast ready for everyone. I knew it was something she enjoyed more than anyone knew. God let me in on her little secret that she kept to herself. Jason was the first to come out of the barn and come over to the water well and bath his face in the cold water. He said:

"If this doesn't wake a person up nothing will."

I said, "Here comes Zack and Jay, must had smelled the eggs and bacon a cooking."

"And that coffee smells delicious. I think I smell pancakes. How she knows those are my favorite."

"Mr. Jason, I think those are every cowhands favorite." Zack said. About that time the rest of the hands came out of the barn. Bob said.

"When you all get back I hope we can start on a bunkhouse with regular bunks. I'm getting tired of sleeping on that hay bed."

"You know Bob with me and Gabe gone the two of you can fight over our bunks."

"That's a thought."

Emily came out on the porch and looked at us and said.

"What a fine looking bunch you make to go to church. Now come in here and eat so you can get ready. It won't stay hot for long."

I stood back as usual and watched as they pushed each other trying to be the first to get to the table. I knew that Emily wouldn't let them eat before she said the prayer. Sure enough when I came in everyone was around the table with Emily at one end and Jason at the other end. Bob said,

"Hurry Gabe, it's going to get cold and you know how I love Miss Emily's cooking."

I sat down and took Jason and Lilly's hands and said.

"We all can see Bob, I think you've gained five pounds since you came to work here."

Everyone laughed. Emily cleared her throat and you could hear a pin drop. She said the prayer and we ate. Then Bob said.

"Jason you know I'm going to take care of this little lady while you're gone. I wouldn't let anybody hurt her the way she cooks. I think I'll work here forever."

We laughed and even Emily let out a little laugh, and then said.

"Now, finish up and get ready for town, we'll make a parade down main-street to the church. I feel so proud of all of you and what you've done in a short time. So now get going."

Everyone was decked out in his or her Sunday finest. Even the poorest cowhand always had a good pair of clothes in their bedroll for special occasions. This was one of them. Jason was on the seat with Emily and Jason was driving. Me, Zack and Lilly were in the back of the wagon. The other six were on their horses behind the wagon. Jason pulled up to the hitching rail in front of the church and tied up the team. I saw him look toward Ben and Sam as he helped Emily down from the wagon. I could hear some of the comments from the women around us.

"I dare her show up to church in that condition with her poor daughter and all those men."

She took Jason and my arm and held her head up high as we went in the church and sat on the front roll, all ten of us. We sang and then the preacher said his sermon. He ended with saying; "I have giving Mr. Benning permission to speak to you. Before he speaks I just want to say, that I have been guilty of not going out to see Mrs. Truman in her time of need. I assure you that will now change. Mr. Benning if you please."

As Jason went up to the podium, I looked up to heaven and said a little prayer to myself. Then I heard Jason start his sermon as it could be called.

"Gabe and I have only been here a couple of weeks. I only know a few of you, but I've heard some vile things about this good woman that has lost her husband in the fight to keep this country together. Most of you if not all of you knew John and the kind of man he was. He didn't want to leave his family like some of you. He had thought that the good christian people of this town would help his wife and daughter. But that turned out not to be the case and when she turned up with child, she was ridiculed and her daughter even quit going to school cause the other children teased her. I do not blame them for they were only repeating what they had heard from their mothers and fathers. I knew John as most of you did. We fought together for four years. We are good men. We didn't like the killing. He said that he was worried about Emily and Lilly Ann. He had not seen them in all that time. He left and came back here for one night. That is when she became with child. I know this may not be the place to talk about these things but maybe God will forgive me. I've also heard that one man is the cause of these rumors and you would know who that would be better than me. I was with John when he died and he made me promise to come and try to help his family. I wandered around for months not knowing what to do until I met Gabe. Then I knew what I had to do. He has that effect on people. That's it, but Lilly Ann is going back to school tomorrow. So if you would let your children know to treat her as one of them again, I'm sure Emily would appreciate it very much. Thank you reverend."

"Thank you Mr. Benning. I know this is not usually done but—

He started applauding with everyone following his led as our bunch, with Emily and Jason in the led, left the church. We all got in the wagon or mounted up and we headed toward the ranch. As I looked up to the sky to thank God, I saw everyone looking at Sam and Ben and turn their backs on them and walked away.

That afternoon two wagon load of women with the preacher and Mr. Jimson driving them showed up at the front of the ranch house. We were getting ready to leave tomorrow. Doing last minute things that needed to be done. Emily came out on the front porch. The preacher spoke up.

"These women would like to ask for your forgiveness. They wouldn't blame you if you didn't."

"There's no forgiveness needed. If you would like to get down and come in I'll make some tea." One of the ladies said as they were getting down.

"We have some goods right here along with some other things. Mrs. Jimson put some small baby things."

As they disappeared into the house Mr. Simms, the preacher came over.

"You know Mr. Benning I don't know where that speech came from but you could had made a fine preacher. Why after you left the church the women came to me and set up this little get together. I truly believe that they are sorry."

"I'm glad for she may be needing some help. Don't tell anyone but me and some of the boys are leaving with a herd of horses tomorrow. I'm leaving two men here to help Zack, so if you and a few lady would check up on her, you know with the baby coming. We should be back in a month and a half. I would appreciate it."

"I think I can take care of that. The women feel so guilty. I think your speech put a little fear in them. If they will get to heaven or not."

He laughed a little laugh. Gabe said.

"You might remind them that He sees everything that goes on." He looked up to the sky.

"Jason, if I may, I feel I know you and Gabe for so long. You were right, Gabe does make us feel different."

The women from town left and later Emily call us for supper. The talk around the table turned to leaving in the morning.

"In the morning we leave. Emily before we leave is there anything that you need us to do."

"I can't think of anything. Just be careful. Two weeks ago I had no one except Lilly Ann and Zack to help around here. Now you and Gabe came and now you are taking our herd of horses to Kansas City and I have two more men to help around the ranch while you are gone. What more could I ask for, except John coming back to me."

"Mother!"

"I know Lilly Ann. I'm sorry men. Don't worry I'll be up to fix your breakfast and see you off before Lilly Ann gets off to school."

"Oh, ma."

Gabe said, "I better get out and relieve James. I'm on duty with the horses tonight. We don't want to lose any tonight."

The night went by without a hitch and the four men showed up in the morning. Jan said.

"Jason wants you to go in and eat, if you feel like it, and you and him can catch up to the chuck wagon."

As I rode away, I saw the men round up the horses and head them north. I got back to eat a little for show and Jason said his good-byes. Lilly Ann came up to me to tell me.

"I'll miss you Gabe. I can talk to you like I use to talk with pa, when I was little."

"It won't be too long, but I'll miss you to Short Tail. Good bye."

She looked at me so funny as we pulled on down the trail.

"What you call her that for?"

"I have no idea. It just popped in my head out of nowhere."

The men had no trouble with the herd of horses, but me, I was having a hack of a time with the team pulling the wagon. Jason rode up beside me.

"What seems to be the matter, Gabe?"

"They have their own head. They won't go where I want."

"You're trying too hard. Just let the reins out loose in your hands and let the lead horse guide them. Only pull back when you want to stop, then to the right or to the left when you want to go those ways.

Let them do most of the work. You'll get the hang of it in no time. You better get ahead of us, I know the men will want to eat at noon and at the end of the day."

"Thanks for the help, I can see what you mean. I'll get going, I know they'll miss Emily's cooking."

The men were grumbling about having to wait a little for their dinner. Before long their bellies were full and when they came in for the night, supper was waiting and all was forgotten. At night two men had to ride the herd. Each night the men would take turns, Jason and me included. The first day was hard on everybody. My fiscal body sure wasn't use to it. Peter must be letting me see what humans go through when on earth. I don't know why but that is the only reason I could think of that my body is so sore. I guess I had forgotten over all these years of being up there. The next morning having to get up so early to start breakfast, it was so hard to move. After this I better get my wings. That's when a bolt of lightning hit not five feet from me. No noise at all. I looked up and said.

"I'm sorry, Peter. I'm just so sore. Forgive me."

It took two days for all complains about being sore and tired to pass. We had passed thru some fall rains. That made it rough going for the wagon. It would get stuck in a mud hole. Jason just hooked some more horses to the team and the wagon would be on its way. After the rain it would clear up and then at night it would be colder. The second week was better weather wise. One night Jason talked to the men around the campfire.

"With the war over and winter coming on I been expecting someone to take a try at our horses. I would like to know how each of you is with your side arm and your rifle. James, how are you with your weapons?"

"I'm not a gunfighter but I can hit what I aim at. Same with a rifle."
"Jeff."
"About the same.
"Tim."
"Same here."
"Me too, Jan said."

"Well, I'm pretty good with both. Starting tomorrow the one in the led will be on the lookout for any strangers or any kind of trouble. If any, get my attention and I'll bring everyone a running. Let me handle the leader and you watch the others, if there's that many. We can't let anything happen to these horses. Emily and Lilly are counting on us. I haven't seen anyone following us, but they will probably hit us just a day or two out of Kansas City. Why do all the work when they can let us do the work and they think they can get all the profit."

I was standing and letting Jason handle things. I just wanted to be here to reassure him if he needed it from time to time. He had come a long way from the first time we met each other. We were more than half way there.

"Gabe, we should be there sometime next week. It hasn't been too bad has it."

"Oh no not at all, just this seat is giving my behind a beating. And don't laugh. It's not funny. I didn't take this job to take a beating, just to help Emily and Lilly and you too. You know!"

"What were you going to say?"

"Nothing, just when I met you, you looked like a lost soul and now you are so in charge."

"You know Gabe, I haven't been able to put my finger on it but I think you're right. I thank you."

"Believe me you had it in you all the time. It was just the war had beaten it down out of sight. But now you met someone you care about and you will do anything to protect her and Lilly and her baby."

"That's the second time you have mention me and Emily. I don't know."

"That is the only part that you are hesitant about."

"I don't know why I'm talking to you about this. I've never talked to anyone about my feelings. But I think I would be disloyal to John if I let my feelings for Emily be known."

"I can't tell you how, but I know John would want her and his children to be happy for all their life. He'll see all of you one day and he'll thank you for their happiness. Now we have to get these horses sold and get the money back to Joplin soon as possible."

The men quit complaining about my cooking. They knew they were going to have to eat it all the way back to the ranch. I told them all the better Emily's would be when they got to her table and just dream about then. None got a bellyache so I don't know what all the fuss was about. Tim came up to the wagon.

"Gabe, do you have anything to make an apple pie. I've got a hankeren for some sweets."

"You know I might be able to oblige you on that one. I'll see what I can come up with."

"Thanks, Gabe."

That night we had apple pie and no one complained one tiny bit. They finished the pie and then I brought out the other one. The smiles were all around the campfire. Even the nightriders took a piece each with them. That night another rainstorm hit and a bitter cold behind it. The next morning the nightrider came in and hurried everyone up.

"We have to get the herd moving, it's below freezing."

"Let's get moving, no breakfast this morning. I'll have some coffee and biscuits later when it warms up."

I got the team hooked up and moving in a flash and Jason and all the men were on their mounts and moving. After the sun was a ways up in the sky the day felt better. We were two days out when a man came up to Jason who was jawing with me.

"Boss, there's, it looks to be ten rider, coming toward us a ways out."

Jason took off toward the front of the herd. Me, now in command of the wagon team, got them going into a gallop. The men headed up to the front of the herd. As I came into view of the point I could see the riders coming from the north. Jason pulled out a small telescope and extended it to its full length. He said.

"I see Ben Warren in the lead. This may be their move let me do the talking. Keep an eye on the others and keep your hand on your guns.

Spread-out, don't let them get behind us to stampede the horses. Gabe you stay down."

Jason watched them as they approached us. I could see and felt the tension in the air. All these men were young except Jason and he was the only one that had been in face-to-face battle. You could see his 6 ft. 2in. slim frame at attention waiting for the command to attack. But that command was up to the men coming toward us. They could leave us alone or take the brunt of the fury I now saw in Jason's face. A fury that stated: why some people couldn't leave good people alone to do their business. I had a feeling that hell was going to break out on earth any minute.

5

"Hello Jason, what you boys doing out here with all these nice-looking horses."

"That's our business. And none of yours, Ben."

"Is that any way to talk to a neighbor that's just out to help another neighbor?"

"We can do without your help at all. We're doing fine."

"You know Mr. Johnson sent us looking for you and your youngsters just to see if we can take over for you since you are just out of the war."

"Like I said we're doing fine without your help and you remember what I did and what I said to you last time you got in my way."

"I do, but this time I'm not alone."

"That doesn't matter you will be the first one dead and then the one on your right and the one on your left. My men can take care of the rest of your men. If you doubt it just pull that gun and have a try. These horses are leaving with us not you. I'll let your boss know where you're buried when we get back to Joplin."

I could see that Jason was cool as a cucumber but Ben had all of a sudden broken out in a sweat.

"Ben, you said he was a coward and would give up these horses with no fight."

"Be quiet fool."

"I may be a fool but I'll be alive tomorrow."

Him and two others turned their horses and rode off down the trail to Kansas City.

"Well, what's it going to be Ben, boys don't shoot the others in less they pull on us. You ready."

Two others turned and lifted the battlefield. Ben pulled his gun but that was all. He was dead on the ground before he got a shot off. Jason was sitting there looking at the others with smoke coming out of the barrel of his gun.

"You boys were right smart. Now we can bury him or you can cause even a bad man should be under the ground not on top. If I were you I wouldn't go back to Joplin or you'll be dealing with us again."

"We'll bury him you have places to get to. I don't know about the others but I'm heading further west and get a nice quiet job on a good man's ranch. So long."

Our men turn to get the horses moving again as Ben's men got off to bury him. We had the herd heading north again. I could see the relief in all the men's faces. All Jason said was.

"Men, we'll be in town tomorrow. Tim, if you would lend Gabe your horse and drive the wagon tomorrow morning after breakfast, me and Gabe will head to town and try to make a deal for the herd. Just head north and if you see a big town pull up and set until we get back."

I said, "I'll make some extra food in the morning so you won't starve to death."

They laughed as the tension subsided. Then Jason came over and said to me.

"You know I hated to do that, but I gave him every chance to back out and he wouldn't take it."

"The Bible says "Thou should not commit murder" but sometimes killing becomes necessary, that wasn't murder by no means. By talking you gave the others a chance to change their minds. You saved maybe ten or more lives today. God will thank you for that later. I'm sure of it. You showed these young men that the gun is not always the way."

"I tell you Mr. Simms was wrong you should have been a preacher not me. I thank you for that it makes me feel a little better. Be sure that we bring that bag of ore samples. I want to get that tested."

The next morning after the men ate and got the herd moving Jason and me took off for Kansas City. Without the horses we were making much better time. By that evening we were coming down the main street of town.

"This is a lot different than Joplin. I haven't seen this many people since I was back east during the war. You still got some money."

"Sure, I knew we'd need some."

"Let's eat and get a room. I know you don't sleep much, but I do. Tomorrow we'll look for someone to buy the horses and someone else to check the ore. That might cost some money as well."

"It's alright right now, but I never know when it might run out. What you going to do when we get back? I mean about Sam."

"I don't have the answer to that yet. If he finds out about Ben, he may hire more than one gunfighter. I heard about a new six-shooter. We had a few in the war but not many. I'll look for one in the morning after we take care of our other business. I don't like what I may have to do but to protect the ranch it may come to that. If Sam hires more than one man I may need more than a single shot. There were times in the war that I wish I had more fire power. You can count on me not to use it unless I have to."

"I have come to realize that by now. I can see that the war was something you didn't like."

"I'm hungry, let's find a diner. There's one over there."

The place was crowded with people. This was not like the little town where we had come. Standing there looking for an empty table a man came up to us and said: "Right this way, we have a table up the stairs on the second floor. This use to be a hotel but the boss made it all a restaurant more profit this way. Will this suit your taste?"

"This will do us. We can overlook what is happening on the floor below. Has your boss been around here long?"

"She sure has, she was one of the first to settle here."

"I would like to meet your boss if that is possible."

"She's kind of busy now but I'll ask."

He took our order, which for me it wasn't much, but Jason it was a lot.

"You trying to make up for those five month after the war that the eating was sparse?"

"Emily's cooking put some weight back on. I'm sure that this food won't be as good as hers. Don't worry I'll pay you back someday."

"Don't worry about that. I'm just glad to know that you like Emily's cooking."

"Tomorrow I want to go to the general store and get one of those new-fangled colts, that I heard about. Load once and shoots six times, if you don't mind. And take this sample to an engineer to see what it is."

Our food came and as we were eating a tall slim woman came over.

"May I help you? Gene said that you wanted to speak to me."

"Yes ma'am, I know you're busy but if you have some time I would like to ask you some questions. If you would have a seat."

"Yes, I have a little time. It would be nice to get off my feet for a while. You two don't look harmful. Some just want to try to get me to go out with them. Now what's on your mind?"

"We just arrived in town and Gene said you were one of the first to come here and you must see just about everyone that comes to town. We have a herd of horses a few miles outside of town. I thought you might know someone that would be interested in buying the entire herd. There're around two hundred head in all. By the way my name is Jason and this is Gabe."

"Like the Angel Gabriel, I knew there was something different about you. I know people and I like you two. I normally don't do this but see that man over there he owns a big horse ranch north of town. He sells horses to the army and he's always looking for a good deal. Don't tell him that I told you but he'll pay more than he lets on at first. Don't let him bluff you. It's like playing a hand of cards. If you're done I'll take you over and introduce you. People call me Jen."

"Gabe, pay the wonderful lady for the meal."

"No, come on the meal is on me."

Gabe said: "Thank you young lady we sure do appreciate that."

"I'm no young lady."

"Where I come from you are."

"You are an angel, now I'll take you over there."

"Mr. Thomas, I hate to disturb you but these two gentlemen told me that they have a herd of horses outside town. I know you are always looking for a good deal. This is Jason and his partner Gabe. If you would excuse me I better get back to work."

"Thanks Jen."

"Sit down gentleman."

"We hate to disturb you while you're eating."

"Nonsense, as Jen said I'm always looking for a good deal. Now please sit down and tell me about your horses and how many you have."

"They're good stock, they're not ours. We represent the owner Mrs. Truman. There are about two hundred head. They should be stopping outside of town any time now."

"Is she kin to a John Truman down Joplin way?"

"Yes sir, he died at the end of the war and I promised him I would come and help her keep the ranch. Gabe is a friend also."

"I had dealing with him before the war. I hadn't heard from him. Now I know why. I'm sorry to hear about John, he seems to be a good man."

"The best that I had known."

"I tell you what, my office is down the street a ways. You come by in the morning and I'll take a ride with you out to the herd and look them over. I'll try to give her a good deal."

Gabe spoke up; "I have a note from Mrs. Truman giving us authority to sell the horses and a blank bill of sell to be made out when cash changes hands."

"That's fine I'll look at it tomorrow. Come by about 9'o'clock, it has my name on the building."

"Thank you so much we'll see you in the morning."

We left and went to get a room at the hotel. Gabe paid for one night and we turned in. After what had happened on the trail I was a little worried about the men and horses.

"Gabe lets go get a beer at the saloon."

"I don't drink and you know that."

"I know but you can keep me company and you have the money. You can have one of those new drinks you ask for before. They have back east. Just one."

"Alright!"

We went in and ordered and they did have my drink, sassafras. We were standing there talking when a cowboy came over.

"I saw you and wanted to tell you before you saw me. I was one of the men with Mr. Warren yesterday. I'm sorry; I didn't know he was going to try to take your horses. I'm from here and been looking for work. He said he was going to help a neighbor into town with his horses and he was offering twenty dollars for one day's work. He said he was going to help you bring them to Mr. Thomas. So I wanted you to know I was the first one to leave. My mother didn't raise a thief. Bye now."

"Thank you son. I know your mother would be proud. And thanks for the information."

"Gabe, now I don't know about Mr. Thomas."

"We'll find out tomorrow."

I heard Jason tossing and turning all night. I knew what was wrong. But we would find out soon cause I could see the rays of the sun starting to brighten the skies in the east. Looking at that sky I knew God had made the world right as only he could. Jason rose. I could tell he was in a bad mood.

"Let's get over and see Mr. Thomas."

"Now Jason, I know you're upset but give him a chance to explain before you do anything that will get us in trouble. Emily doesn't need that."

"You're right I am mad. You're also right that we don't need to get in any trouble. I'll take it slow and easy."

We stopped and ate and I asked Jen if she knew anyone in town that knew anything about rocks or hills.

"There's a man that is always coming in and says he found a strange formation out west of here in the hills. I think he's strange as the formations he finds. I think he has an office at the west end of town. I think his name is Gene Bailey."

"Thanks again Jen. The food is great."

We left and walked in to Mr. Thomas's office at about 9 o'clock he was looking thru his file. He turned as he heard the door open.

"I'm glad to see you. After you left me last night I got to thinking. It bothered me all night. I'm looking for a file from about six months ago. I know it's here somewhere. Here it is, I just can't remember every transaction I do. When you mention John, his brand came to me. See the same brand. A Mr. Ben Warren, see a bill of sale from a Mrs. Emily Truman. The brand and name didn't hit me until last night after we talked. He said he bought them from her and he wanted to make a little profit."

"I'm glad you have that. Now I know you're not involved. Ben tried to take our horses two days ago and sell them to you again. A cowboy told us last night. He left when he found out what he had in mind. Mrs. Truman didn't know the horses were stolen until we came and found the fence cut. Can I ask how many horses he has sells you?"

Gabe spoke up. "Here Mr. Thomas here's the letter from Emily and notarized by Bill Gates in Joplin."

"I'm glad you have this now that I found out those horses were stolen. Here, you can see there were five sells over three years. Let's see, a total of five hundred and eighty head. Where is Mr. Warren? We need to tell the Marshall so he can look for him."

"No need, he's dead and buried out south of here. He didn't say any other names that may be connected with him."

"I'll have to think on that. I'll think while we ride out to the herd. If they are like the ones he sold me I'll be very interested."

As we were riding out of town, kind of to the east and south of town Jason said, "I just hope nothing else happened while we were gone."

We rode on for about thirty minutes and there on top of a ridge was the chuck wagon. As we topped the ridge there in a grassy valley was the herd of horse. Mr. Thomas said.

"From here they look a magnificent herd. Let's go down and take a look."

That's when Tim came out of the back of the wagon.

"Hello boss, just getting some shut eye before you came. We came in late afternoon yesterday. The rest of the boys should be down with the horses."

"Any trouble after we left."

"No, you must have scared anybody else off. Word must have got around by now."

"I sure hope so. Tim this is Mr. Thomas, we're going down to look at the horses. He might buy them. Hold on a while longer and Gabe will bring back your horse."

"Right boss, take your time. It's comfortable in back."

I saw Mr. Thomas laugh. "Typical cowboy, I have a bunch on my ranch like that. Work hard but when they have a chance to rest they sure take it."

As Mr. Thomas rode thru the herd, Jason and me just sit there and watched. The boys rode around watching him. Jeff rode over to us.

"You know that man looks like he knows his stuff. He's looking them over really good. Look at him getting off and looking at their hoofs and in their mouths and feeling their bellies and legs."

"He sure does know his business. I guess he has to look them over since he sells to the army."

Mr. Thomas came riding up the grade to where we were waiting. He stopped and gave us a look, very serious, and then he smiled a smile from ear to ear.

"I like the look on people's faces when I do that. Those are some of the finest horses, except for mine of course that I've seen in a long while. Mrs. Truman must have some find stallions. If we can make a deal I may call on her for more from time to time. Now let me get down to business. The wars been over for a while and the army has cut back a lot. But I'll tell you, I normally don't do this, they are going to be increasing their orders because of the Indians out west. There are some small uprisings as the settlers move west. That's in the future. Right now I can offer you three hundred and fifty dollars a head and some future business."

"You know she lost John in the war and she is going to have his child and she has a fourteen-year-old daughter at home. I'll say four fifty. They are fine horses. You need to come see her stallions. I saw you looking at the mare's bellies, so you know quite of few of them are with fouls. That's worth a little extra."

He laughed, "You saw that, did you. All right, I'm a sucker for a sad story and I did buy her stolen horses a while back. I'll give you the four fifty and future business. You tell her I'll be down to look at those stallions one day and I may bring some for her to buy."

Jason shook his hand and smiled.

"That's a deal." Then Mr. Thomas shook my hand and said.

"I have a good feeling about you two that I haven't had in a awful long time. It sure feels good. Now if I can borrow your men to take the horses to my ranch. I'll meet you in town this afternoon. We can go to the bank and get the money."

"Sure thing, men follow Mr. Thomas to his ranch then get to town and get a bath and do what you want. Just don't get in trouble. You'll get your pay as soon as Mr. Thomas pays us. We will meet you at the diner later."

Jason and me went back to the wagon and Tim got on his horse and headed after the horses going toward Mr. Thomas's ranch.

"Gabe, let's head to the general store and get food for the trip home and see if they have that six-shooter."

"You know Jason, that's ninety thousand dollars. That's enough to keep the ranch going until she can build the herd again."

"I guess I can be moving on when we get back."

"Look you don't know that Ben was the only one behind the stealing of her horses and she is going to have a baby. She will still need you to run the ranch and we still need to find what those rocks are. You can be foreman. She can afford to pay you now and keep these hands on to really fix up the ranch. I know you care for her."

"You mind your own business. You know too much. Now we need to get to town."

"Alright but I see the way she looks at you."

"Shut up now alright."

I did just what I wanted. I gave him something to think about. I know he feels a loyalty to John and that made him unsure about his feeling for Emily. I felt a pat on my back. I looked around and no one was there. Then I heard Peter in my head. "You're doing fine Gabriel keep it up." Then nothing. I pulled up on the side of the general store. We went inside and ordered all the food we would need on the return trip. Then Jason said,

"Do you have the new Colt 45 I've heard about?"

"I sure do, they haven't been out to long for the public. They're over here."

The storekeeper opened the glass case and handed Jason one. He looked at it like a child looks at a case full of toys. He spun the cylinder and looked down the barrel at the sites.

"How much?"

"They're not cheap, they're twenty-dollars."

"I don't know. What you think Gabe?"

"You know we don't know what we'll run up against when we get back. And Emily can pay you now. You can pay her out of that. With your help you two can defeat evil around her part of the country. You just can't sit back and let evil take over good. God backed the Jews against the evil that was in the world at that time."

"Mister, I'll take it and a new holster also plenty of shells. I'll pay you for everything out of the horse sells, Gabe. I'll tell Emily I paid you and I owe her for the gun. I still owe you for these clothes you bought back down the trail."

"Nonsense you gave me a ride. I would still be walking."

I paid and we headed to the restaurant. The men came in and we put two tables together and ordered our meal. Jen came over to take our orders.

"Hello boys, did you sell your herd?"

"We sure did. I don't know how to thank you?"

"I'll be happy if you just eat a lot. From the look of these cowhands they need a lot to fill them up."

"You heard the lady order and eat a lot."

"Will do boss. We'll have to eat Gabe's cooking all the way back."

Gabe said, "None of you died did you."

"Not for the lack of you trying." Jeff said.

Jan said, "It's wasn't like Miss Emily's cooking."

Jen stood there laughing and wrote down our orders.

"Who's this Miss Emily?"

"She's the one we work for back in Joplin. A very good lady and a better cook." James said.

"I hope my cooking can live up to hers."

I said, "Boys this little lady's cooking is right up against Emily's, I can testify to that we've eaten here two times."

Tim said, "You know boss, Mr. Thomas's ranch is downright beautiful. It has a winding road leading up to the house and fences painted white with horses in different pastures. I hope that Miss Emily's ranch will be like that one day."

We ate and said goodbye to Jen. I left her a big tip. Out in the street Jason said.

"Can you loan the boys fifty-dollars to go to the saloon. We need to get to Mr. Thomas's office."

We headed to Mr. Thomas's office. He was their waiting for us as we walked in.

"I saw you eating in Jen's so I went to the bank and got the cash. If you would make out that bill of sell to me here's the ninety thousand dollars. You better be careful with that much cash now days. Since the wars over there are lots of desperate men around."

"We have six men with us but we'll be careful. Thank you for everything and Mrs. Truman will cry with joy when we get back."

"Tell her I will drop by one day I want to see her ranch."

"I'll tell her. The ranch is a little ran down right now but this will go a long way. So long."

Jason had the money in his saddlebags and when we got out in the street Jason asked.

"Gabe, you have that bag of rocks."

"In the wagon."

We got the bag out of the wagon and headed to the end of the street. The sign said he would be back at two o'clock. It was one thirty now so we waited.

"You think he'll know what those rocks are? They look useless to me. But what do I know."

"From what Jen said he sounds like a pretty smart man. I hope he does."

We saw a man coming up the street from out of town. He was tall and thin wearing glasses and carrying a pick and shovel his clothes were all dirty and his boots were all muddy. It hadn't rained in a week or more. The days were cool so I guessed that there were some places that hadn't dried up. His shirt was plaid with brown patches and his pants were green. I said to Jason.

"Now I know what Jen meant by he is strange. Look at the way he's dressed."

"You should be talking remember the way you were dressed when I first met you."

"All right, God forgive me. I know he will be smart about what he knows."

He walked right up to the office and unlocked it and went in. It was like he hadn't seen us. We looked at each other and went inside. He was looking around the office. He finally found a map and put it across his desk. He started making marks on it and low moans under his breath.

"Mr. Baily, I'm Jason Benning and this is Gabe Owens."

He looked up and looked at us like it was the first time he saw us.

"I'm busy, what do you want?"

"You find what you were looking for."

"No, but I'll find it one day. Now what can I do for you. I'm really busy."

"Gabe, show Mr. Baily the bag of rocks. We thought you might know what these rocks are."

I poured the rocks out on the counter. His glass-covered eyes turned away from us and followed the rocks onto the counter. He picked one of the rocks up and looked at it closely then he got a magnifying glass and looked at it even closer.

"Where did you get this? It couldn't be, I've been looking for this for two years and you just walk in and don't know what you have."

"You interested now."

"I'm sorry, it's just been so frustrating. I've been looking for this ore for so long."

Jason asked, "What is it? They seem to be different."

He picked up another piece and looked at it. Then he picked up another piece.

"We found them at different places in the hills on the ranch we work on."

He grabbed the map from his desk. It was covered with red, blue and black markings.

"Where were they found? Here's the map."

"Before we show you, we needed to know how much you charge to tell us about these pieces."

"Don't you understand? I won't charge you anything to tell you about this. I'll go with you and determine how big the find is and if it's big I'll help you get in touch with mining people. They will set us up to mine the ore. Or they can do it their self and pay you a royalty. They thought that most of the ore was gone years ago. I'll charge you five hundred dollars."

"But you haven't told us what it is."

"I'm sorry, but I'm so elated. This big piece is lead, that's what I've been looking for today. This middle one is iron and the small piece is zinc. It never comes in large amounts."

Gabe and me leaned over the desk and looked closely. We saw Joplin on the map.

"See here Mr. Bailey, right here is Joplin and the ranch is about five miles to the east of there. It's in the northeastern part of the ranch. The hill I thought was strange cause nothing would grow on it."

"I don't want to get you excited but it sounds like a big find. When can we leave? Another thing a man came in about six months ago with a similar ore. He didn't tell me his name. He said the property wasn't his yet but he was working on obtaining it. He said by Christmas or before it would be his."

"What did he look like?"

"I can't remember to much but he was about your height and he had a scar on his cheek. If that helps."

"It does, he did work at the ranch next to Mrs. Truman's. She's the one we work for. We were up here selling her horses. She's had trouble with horse thieves. Now I know why. They were trying to run her out of business to get this ore. The man that came in here is dead. He tried to steal from the wrong men. We have a wagon and men to get and we'll be ready."

"I'll have to get all my instruments packed and my clothes and suitcase are right here. About an hour should do it. I'm so excited. How long will it take to get there?"

"Without the horses, should only take a week or so. Like I said Emily doesn't know about this. It will be up to her to do it or not. I want you to understand that."

"I just want to see it." He said as he was packing.

"We'll be back to pick you up. You don't need food and you can ride in the wagon with Gabe here."

We left to get the men from the saloon and as we walk thru the swinging doors a chair came flying over our heads and broke up against the wall. It was our boys against five other cowhands. Gabe looked out the door.

"Jason the sheriff is coming down the street. We have to get them to stop."

He pulled out his new pistol and fired one shot in the air. The whole place was as if it had stopped in motion.

"You hear me stop it right now. We are leaving. My men get outside. Gabe get them on their horses."

Just as the sheriff came thru the door the men were starting to leave with Gabe. Jeff said.

"Jason, they asked who we work for and we told them Mrs. Truman. They said they heard about her all right. How she goes to bed with anyone. And I hit him up against the bar."

The sheriff took over and said.

"Bill where did you hear that and what you doing repeating it?"

"I heard it from Ben, he's from down that way."

Jason said, "Not any more he's dead. Sheriff, Ben tried to take the horses away from us before we got to town. The men he brought with him, some of them are among them. They didn't know he was going to try to steal them. They left him and he tried by himself. He lost."

"That's the truth. It was a fair fight." One of them said.

"Alright, that's settled. How about the damage in here? Joe, how about it, what's the cost?"

"I'd say twenty should get it."

"You boy's paid Joe ten and you ten. That sounds fair."

Both parties said yes and Jason paid and told the Sheriff we were leaving town and said thanks.

As we went down to pick up Mr. Bailey the men were telling Jason how sorry they were. But they just couldn't let someone talk about Emily like that. Jason said.

"It's all right boys. If I'd heard him I would have hit him myself. Let's forget about it."

They all laughed as we rode up to the office of Mr. Bailey. He came out and Jason said. "This is Mr. Bailey, he's going home with us. Treat him like one of us. He may help Emily out of her trouble. Now you ride by and I'll pay you for the work you've done."

As they rode by and got paid Mr. Bailey got up on the wagon seat and put his things in back of the wagon. He said.

"Since I'm one of the boys just call me Gene. That's what my mother named me."

All the men rode by and shook his hand and call him Gene and then we all headed out of town. Jason handed me the saddlebags with the money and told me to put it under the seat close to my feet.

"Gabe here's five-hundred dollars. This is what Emily owes you. She would want me to pay you."

We got out of town a ways and two cowboys rode up.

"We wanted you to know that we were sorry for what happen. I never liked Ben any ways. If you fought like that I know there wasn't any truth to that rumor. I just had too much to drink. Ben said, Mrs. Truman herself told his boss that story."

Our men said it was all forgotten.

Jason said; "You two have a job, I might could use you two, right Gene. We'll pay you the same as the others forty a month and the best food this side of Jen's. Just asked the others."

"I think there's a real good chance of that and some more to boot. I know this one. How you doing Bo? I'm sorry I didn't have enough work to keep you on. Jason, he was a fast learner and worked hard when we had to."

"Good to see you Mr. Bailey. I know you didn't have much work, but I did enjoy what work I did do for you. It would be good to work with you again cause we have been looking for work. Mr. Thomas was all full up. He's the only big ranch around here and the others are just worked by the owners and their son's."

"What's your friend's name? I'm' Jason and that's Gabe and you know Gene on the seat. You can get to know the other men on the way."

"I'm Bo Jenkins and this is Tab Oats. It's sure nice of you. I know now we'll find Mrs. Truman to be a real fine lady."

"You need to go get your things?"

Tab said, "No need everything is right here."

"Gabe, let's move along a little faster. Bo, you and Jeff drop back and look out for trouble coming from behind. Tab, you come with me to scout out south."

Tab asked, "What we looking for?"

"We had some trouble back home. Someone doesn't want Emily, that's Mrs. Truman, keeping her ranch. You know the trouble we had before we got to Kansas City. So I'm just making sure we get back in one piece. You any good with that gun."

"Some, I need some practice but Bo is really good."

"Might come in handy. Now let's get back and help set up camp. It's almost dark."

Jason and Tab rode in and I already had food a cooking. Not much to do without horses except eat and get to know each other better.

Jason said, "Be sure you have your coats handy in the morning. That sky looked kind of dark before sundown. We might get some weather."

Bo said, "That reminds me of the time I was working over in Colorado. Me and this other fellow were out looking for cattle in the snow, it was deep, our horses were having trouble with the deep snow when we saw a hat laying on top of a hill of snow. We got down and picked up the hat and there was a head. He looked up at us and said boys you better get your shovels I'm a top one of your cows."

Everyone laughed as they drifted off to their bedrolls.

"Gabe, come over here. I don't fully trust those two yet. I know you don't sleep much so keep a watch on the saddlebags with the money. I may not sleep much. I'm worried about what's going on in Joplin."

"I'll keep an eye on the saddlebags and those two. I'll have breakfast ready early so we can get going. I'll try to move the team along faster."

6

As Jason had said it was downright cold in the morning. It must had been forty degrees when I put on the pot of coffee and started fixing breakfast. Jason was the first one up. He got a hot cup of coffee.

"Anything happen last night."

"No, not any movement out of either one or Gene. He slept in the wagon."

"You get a chance to check on the money just to make sure."

"I did, it was all there. I covered it up with a burlap sack."

Jason went around getting everyone up.

"Get up boys and get some of that hot breakfast and coffee in you. The sooner we get back the sooner we can build a warm bunkhouse before winter comes. Get up. It's not getting any warmer in your rolls."

As the light of the new day, for there was no sun to be seen, came upon us there was not much talking. We were moving along fast as we could with the wagon just to try to keep warm. By noon when we ate it had warmed up a little but the wind was still blowing hard with no let up. Gene stayed in the back of the wagon looking at his maps. I thought that a little heat from down below would feel good right now. That's when a voice spoke to me in my head.

"Gabriel that can be arranged if you want."

"No sir, I was just thinking to myself."

"You better think better thoughts."

"Yes sir."

Gene said, "Who you talking to Gabe?"

"Just an old friend up there."

It was dark and gloomy for two days then on the morning of the third day we woke up to the sun coming out bright. It had warmed up during the night. It was now late October. Jason said,

"We should be there about November first. Gene you think you can work if we get some snow."

"You get me there and I'll forget about everything except my passion ore and rocks of all kind. You think it would be all right if Bo worked with me in here. He knows maps. It would be a help to get the lay of the land before we get there."

"I don't know your kind of maps, just battle maps in the war."

"They are similar just different goals. I'll show you when we have the hills in front of us. I like a man that is willing to learn."

"Bo, Gene wants you to check out the maps with him. He'll show you where we are going and what you'll be doing. If what we think doesn't happen you'll still have a job with the horse part of the ranch."

"Thank you, Jason."

At dinner after dark, for we were moving twelve to fourteen hours a day, Jason said.

"James, in the morning I want you to head to the ranch and see if they are all right. I've been worried. It's been so quiet out here. Just be very careful, you see any new people on the ranch don't trust them. You talk with Emily, Jay or Zack. But talk to Emily for sure. You find out what's going on and get back here, so we can make plans. Be careful getting there to."

"I will, I'll leave after breakfast."

After James left in the morning we were on the trail again. It had warmed up so we weren't wearing our coats anymore. Bo was spending most of his time with Gene studying the maps. Late in the afternoon, we saw three men coming toward us.

"Gabe, stop the wagon. Bo come out here we might need your gun. Everyone get in front of the wagon. Let me do the talking and watch their gun hand and eyes. Don't shoot unless they pull their guns."

The men rode up and stopped out a ways off and watched us for a while and then rode in.

"Sorry we stopped out a way's. Didn't know if you were friendly or not."

"Right smart of you. We can be if you deserve it. What you up to out this far from town."

"Our boss sent us out this way looking for some of her men that took some horses to Kansas City."

"Who's your boss lady? Don't know many fellows' that would work for a woman."

"The ranch is a few miles outside of Joplin. It's a horse ranch."

"I asked her name and the others on the ranch."

"Miss Turner, and there is John and –boys pull your guns."

As Jason pulled his gun, Bo already had his out. Three lay on the ground dead or dying. Jason walked over to the one still alive.

"Who really sent you out here and what did they tell you to do?"

"I didn't remember the names. They told me but I didn't remember."

"Who sent you?"

"Said you weren't fast with a gun. Guess they were wrong."

"Who was wrong?"

He turned over and died. I got the shovel and started digging. We put them in their gravies right where they died. It was a nice spot with a bunch of trees over them and a creek below. The two times that I had seen Jason kill someone he was always sad afterwards. We kept moving and we didn't stop until way after dark. Jason was quiet until I said.

"James should be back anytime now. Shouldn't we be there day after tomorrow?"

"Should be, I just wish James would get back before we get there."

"Gene, how you making out with those maps?"

"Bo's been lots of help but it's that bag of ore that you brought me that keeps me spell bound. I just can't believe that in a few days I'll be able to see a whole mountain of the ore."

"We're going to have to be careful if James don't get back soon. There might be some more trouble."

I said, "Maybe Sam will give up trying once he finds out Ben's dead."

"I wouldn't count on that Gabe. His kind, won't give up 'til they're dead or in prison. He'll hire more than one if he has to, to get what he wants. Bad men think like that. We just have to out think and out maneuver him as quickly as we can. I hope Gene, you have a chance to see that mountain before the snow flies."

"I do to, I'll pray on that every night. I'll take my chances to get to see the layout of the mountain but I don't want to see Mrs. Truman or her daughter hurt over it."

"Well sometimes good men have to fight bad men to keep what belongs to them. That's the way it's been throughout time and it sure don't seem to be changing anytime soon."

"Here's supper you going to talk all night or eat."

"Why you know we love your cooking."

"Then fill a plate and choke it down morning will be here in no time and you can do it again."

The next morning we hit the trail for Joplin. The weather had turned milder now that we were further south. Gene came up to the front of the wagon and sit beside me with his map in his hand.

"Gabe, you saw the mountain. Can you show me on this map where it is or close to it?"

I handed him the reins and took the map from him. He pointed where the ranch was and the direction we were from it. I could see formations of all different types and where they started and ended. There was the road that went to Joplin from the ranch and north of that was where the ore was.

"Right about here Gene. The ranch house should be to the south a little ways."

Gene said, "Well I'll be look here."

"Give me the reins before you run us into the gully."

He continued, "This line here coming from up north peters out down this way. No one would have every looked down this far. It's not on any of the maps that I have. With this discovery I can make all new maps of this area and sell them to other geologists. Before I do that we'll get the mountain all mapped out. It's on private land so they will have to get permission from Mrs. Truman to even look and study it."

Jason rode up and asked.

"What you two up to with that map?"

"I was just showing him the ranch and about where we found the ore. He said it's not on any map he has."

"It must be because it's on private land. Most of my maps only show public land and end where private land begins unless the maker of the map had permission of the land owner to put it on the map."

"If James don't get back this afternoon I'm going to take Tab and head to the ranch. I'm worried about Emily and Lilly Ann."

"Here I'm wondering about the ore and there are more important things in life."

"Gene, that's alright I know this is your passion in life. That's why we came to you. We'll deal with any trouble there might be and you concern yourself with that ore. That will be very important to Emily in the future."

Gabe said, "James is probably just eating some of Emily's good home cooking before he heads back. Give him until tonight and then if he doesn't show you can see what's going on at night without being noticed."

"You sure are learning fast. Gene I'll want to learn more about the ore and how it's formed when we get back and we know Emily and Lilly Ann are alright."

"That's right we'll have time during the winter months for you to learn and by spring you'll know plenty."

"Right now I'm going to head a ways south and keep an eye out for James."

Jason and Tab rode south and we continued on toward the ranch. Jeff was on our back trail and Tim and Jan were around the wagon just in case of trouble. Jason and Tab came in camp just before sundown.

"Any sign of James out there?"

"No, I think we'll eat and head to the ranch. I know something's wrong. James should have been back yesterday."

Just as night fell and Jason was about to leave we heard a horse coming in from the south. It was James and he was coming in fast. He pulled up and jumped off his horse before it stopped.

"Jason, there's trouble at the ranch. There are six men at the ranch. They didn't see me, that's why I took so long, I waited 'til night and went down to the house. The women are all right far as I could tell. Three men are outside with rifles and the other three are around the barn. Zack, Jay and Bob are tried up on the bunks in the barn."

"Anyone else around?"

"No, but I never seen these six before but they look like gun hands."

"James, if you're good to go back eat fast and we'll head out. Tab and me was fixing to head that way. Bo you come with us we might need your gun hand. Jan you stay with Gabe and Gene. Jeff we'll need you to. Gabe, get a good night rest and when you get near the ranch hold up and send Jan to us. Hide as much as you can and Jan don't let anyone come near and protect Gene he's the key to all our futures and the future of the whole area."

"I'm ready to go. We have to be careful; they're watching the out-laying areas as well. It's like they're watching and waiting for us to come back."

I saw Jason calm as could be but at the same time in a hurry to be there. As they left my power to see them head to the ranch kicked in. In the morning we ate and I said.

"Jan, let's get the team hooked up and get going as fast as we can go. Jason and the men are at the ranch. If we hurry we can make it by night fall."

"Gabe, how do you know they are at the ranch?" Gene said.

"Just my power of logic. They rode all night and they can move faster than this wagon does. Now let's get going." ----------

It was still dark when Jason and the men rode up on the hill that overlooks the ranch house and the barn. One man was on lookout around the house and another at the barn. The other four must be asleep or out on horseback keeping an eye on the trails but I doubt that for this type of men tend to be lazy. We had to make sure where everyone was before daylight. I sent James and Jeff to search the surrounding area and Bo and me were going toward the house and barn.

"Bo, we'll go to the back of the barn there should be a rope hanging from the hay loft."

The man guarding the barn was in front sitting down smoking a cigarette. We worked our way to the back of the barn avoiding the man at the house. That wasn't much trouble for there was no moon out. It was just about pitch black but I had already learned my way around the place. Bo was right on my tail. When we reached the back of the barn there was the rope hanging down. I motioned to Bo to climb up to the hayloft and I was right behind him. From the loft I could see a lantern lit in our room. I pointed and Bo saw Bob and Jay and there was Zack all tied up on the bunks and another man outside the room with a rifle in the crook of his arm sitting in a chair. He looked half asleep or asleep it was hard to tell from up here. I found a hay hook and threw it toward the front of the barn above the door. The man jumped up from his chair and went to the barn door and looked out.

"Did you hear that?"

"Hear what? You must be hearing things go back and keep an eye on those men. You know the boss won't like it if they get away and warns Jason and the others on the trail."

"Alright, I'm glad when daylight comes. I hate these nights with no moon it makes me jumpy as all get out."

I whispered to Bo what to do when I threw another hay hook. He climbed down the ladder and was back in the shadow of the stall when the hay hook hit the top of the ladder. The man jumped up again and rushed over to the ladder and started to climb up when Bo hit him on the head as hard as he could with the butt of his pistol. The man clumped down into the hay in the stall. I climbed down and found some rope and an old rag. We tied him up tight and gagged him. His pistol and rifle were now ours as we made our way slowly to the room with our men. I put my finger to my mouth to let the men know to be quiet. Jay saw me and tried to poke Bob. As we reached them I whispered.

"Be quiet we have one tied up but there is another one outside the barn."

I got Jay untied and he and Bo undid Bob and Zack.

"I am sure glad to see you Jason. They came to----

"Tell me later they're still five more out there somewhere."

I threw the hay hook as hard as I could at the barn door. Bo and Jay were on each side of the door. The man outside opened the barn door a little.

"Tom, you trying to scare me? Where are you?"

As he opened the door further Jay hit him hard and laid him out cold.

"Zack, bring the lantern so we can see better. They're one more up at the house. We don't know where the other three are. Get this one gagged and tied up over in the stall with his buddy."

Bob said; "They came two days ago and we tried to fight them but they got the drop on us and Emily said to give up. She didn't want to see us hurt."

Jay passed Bob a rifle and Zack a pistol. Everyone was armed now as we went out of the barn two out the back and the other two out the front. Jay and me were heading toward the front porch where the man guarding the house was. The other three spread out looking for the other three. As we reached the porch me from one side and Jay from the other I heard a sound behind me and I turned and saw a man coming at me with a knife raised starting to strike me out of the brush. I had just enough time to step to the side and he missed me as I caught his wrist and pushed him back. He came at me again and this time I hit him in the face and the knife went flying out of his hand into the brush. As I hit him again the noise had brought the man on the porch to my side of the porch. As I hit him again and again I could see Jay come up behind him and hit his head hard with the butt of his gun. The man was out cold at the bottom of the steps. Jay stepped up and cocked his gun and put it in the face of the man I had been fighting and he gave up. I went to the barn and got some more rope.

"Jay, tie them up tight they're two more out there. We can't let them get away to warn their boss. I'm going to see about Emily. Be careful it's getting daylight."

As I went on the porch and opened the door a gun was pointing in my face. I reacted fast and ducked my head down and drove into the man's stomach as hard as I could and his gun went flying and hit the floor hard as I drove him back into the room. We were both rolling on the floor as I saw Emily and Lilly Ann come out of the bedroom in their nightclothes. Lilly Ann rushed over and picked the man's gun up and shot it off toward the man on the floor. I was up on my feet and draw my gun and pointed it at the man and pulled him up and pushed him out of the door onto the porch where Jay had rush up.

"Here's another one Jay. Get him tied up."

As I turned back toward the women Lilly Ann dropped the gun and her and Emily came to me and were in my arms. They were both crying. This was the first time I had touched them and it was a good feeling. I now knew I loved them and wanted to take care of them all my life. I had to find a way to tell them for I had never been good at words when it came to my feelings.

"Now, it's all right we have five of them tied up and everyone's fine. The others are looking for the one left that James saw yesterday."

Emily stopped crying long enough to say.

"I'm so glad you're alright. I don't know what Lilly Ann and I would do without you."

Then she was sobbing again. Their grip on my waist was tight as Jay came in from the porch. He looked away and then said.

"Jason here comes the men they have the last one in tow. And here comes Gabe and two other men one on horseback."

"How'd they get here so fast? You two go get dressed and settle down it's all over now. Gabe's here we'll get these men to the sheriff and pay off your note at the bank."

The tears stopped as Emily heard me.

"You mean you got enough to pay all the note."

"Yes, and more. Now go get dressed and I'll tell you all about it."

"I'll fix some breakfast for everybody. I feel great now."

They left my arms and went to the bedroom as Gabe came in with Gene and Tab behind him.

"You got it all under control I see."

He was looking toward Emily and Lilly Ann.

"They were just frightened that's all."

"Sure they were. I don't think they would have hugged me that tight."

"Gabe be quiet and how did you get here this fast."

Gene spoke up. "I tell you Jason it was like we were moving on air faster than a train."

Tab said; "My horse and the team aren't even tired. I've never seen the likes."

"Jason you know how it is when I get my mind set on something."

"I'm beginning to understand you, I think."

Emily came out of the bedroom with Lilly Ann they were both all dressed up.

She took to the kitchen and got the stove going.

"Gabe would you fetch some more wood from out back these men wouldn't let us go get more but they wanted to eat. Now Lilly Ann get the table set for everyone and all you men the rules haven't changed you all get washed up and Jason you explain how you got the money to pay the ranch off. Jay would you go to the hen house and get all the eggs you can lay your hands on."

"Yes ma'am, anything for your home cooked breakfast."

"Jason, you tell me who these three new men are and how we're going to pay them."

"Hopefully, Emily this here is Gene from Kansas City. I didn't want to get your hopes up but Gabe and me found these rocks and we took them with us to get checked out. That's what Gene does finds rocks that may be worth money. He came back with us to look at where we found the rocks."

"You mean that bare mountain that not much will grow on. John always meant to find out what that was. He said that it wasn't normal."

Gene said, "Well now I'm here to see about what it is. I'm hungry, so I'll eat your fine looking breakfast and then if someone will show Bo and me the way I can get to work while you all take care of business in town."

We all set around the table and Emily said the prayers and we ate our first good meal in a while.

"Emily, we got ninety-thousand dollars for the horses. Seems like Ben had been selling your stolen horses to Mr. Thomas. Ben had a bill of sell from you to sell them. It was forged and Mr. Thomas felt bad so he gave you top dollar for your horses. He said John had talked to him once but I guess cause of the war never went back."

"We can tell the sheriff and he can arrest Ben and Sam."

"Ben's dead by my gun shot. He died before he could tell us if Sam put him up to it."

"Who else would have?"

"I know but we don't have proof. Sam's smart not to let anyone know what he's doing but a small number of people but we'll find out soon I hope."

"That's a fine meal Mrs. Truman. Now Jason who can show us that mountain." Gene said.

"Zack would you show them the way and Jay would you go with them and watch out for any trouble. James you and the boys get some much-needed rest I think Gabe and me can handle these six."

Zack said, "I know where you mean, Mr. John was always saying how that piece of land was useless."

"Now Jay you might have to tell Gene when it's times to eat he tends to get carried away with his work and Bo here is a good man with a gun if you have trouble."

"We're ready to go Jason, and Gene you can call me Emily and this is Lilly Ann. I think we might have a long friendship if you find something good out there. In four weeks I'll have a great thanksgiving dinner. I want everyone to be here."

"Gabe, let's get them six in the wagon and let's get to town."

I saw Jay and the others head out to the north and we headed to town in the wagon. On the way to town Lilly Ann spoke up.

"Gabe, when Jason and you left for Kansas City why did you call me short tail? It's been on my mind all this time."

"I've been wondering that myself. It just popped in my head and I said it. I just don't know! I wish I did know I would tell you."

"That's alright, I kind of liked it. It reminded me of someone in my pass."

"I hope it was a good memory."

"It was."

We rode up the dusty street of Joplin. Everyone's heads were turning but for a different reason than before. They were watching where we were taken the six tied-up men we had in back of the wagon. We had taken the canvas off and unloaded what was left of the food from the drive to make room for the six men. We stopped in front of the marshal's office. I had seen a man run inside as we pulled up. Tom was out front.

"What do we have here? Looks like you hog tied you some bad ones."

"Sure did Tom. Emily can tell you about it and sign a complaint. They held the people at the ranch captive for three days 'til we got back this morning. They seemed to have got all tied up in their work."

"Emily, you and Lilly Ann come in and get out of this fall heat. We'll get these six new accommodations. They won't like them very much but it will have to do for now until the trial."

Emily said as she went inside.

"Maybe you can find out who put them up to this?"

"I hope I can. But they look like hired men. I don't know any of them. I'll look at the posters and see if they're wanted. These kind normally don't talk."

Gabe and me got them down. One hit the ground hard on his face. Gabe said.

"Now did that hurt, I'll have to be more careful. Forgive me but I don't like how you treated these women and Emily is with child. It's not very manly."

We finally got them all in jail and Emily told Tom what had happened then we headed down the street to the bank.

"We'll get the note paid and put the rest in the bank if that's alright. I spent a little in Kansas City on food and the men to have a drink. I also owe you for this new gun. I paid Gabe for all he spent up to now."

"I'm glad you paid him and it's nonsense, you did all this for us you don't owe me for anything."

"If you agree, I promised the boys a new bunk house and that they would start to get paid."

"Of course, now where's the money."

"Right under your feet."

As we pulled up to the bank there was a man leaning on the hitching post. Jason helped Emily down and Lilly Ann and Gabe got out of the back of the wagon.

The man said, "I see you brought some of my men in. I don't think you ought to be going in this bank. I don't think that would be very health."

"Gabe, take the women inside this won't take long."

They went in the bank.

"Mister you better step aside if you know what's good for you."

7

"I see that bitch still has that black baby in her. I bet you're glad when she throws it out. My boss told me all about it. I've been on your trail for days."

The vile thing he said shook me and I saw that Jason could have killed him at that moment but he had to keep his head straight. He wanted to throw Jason off but Jason finally shook it off.

"Who's your boss?" I'd like to know so I can send your body to him in person."

Jason could tell that shook him and he could tell that Jason wasn't shaken at all. That's when Jason saw his eyes shut just a split second and Jason knew he was going to pull his gun. The man's hand was on the grip of his gun and coming out of his holster just a split second before Jason's gun was out of his. I could see the fear in his eyes when he realized Jason's gun was level and Jason's thumb had already pulled the hammer back and Jason's finger was pulling the trigger as the man's gun was coming up. It was too late for him and he knew it as Jason's slug was out the barrel of his gun as the man's was just coming up level. He fired a second after Jason's slug hit him square in the chest and his bullet went into the dirt right beside Jason's boot. The marshal came out of his office and run over with more people from around the street.

"What happened Jason?"

"He tried to keep us from paying off the note on Emily's ranch. He looks like he failed. I just wish he had said who his boss was."

The people that had gathered around started talking to the marshal.

"That's what happened Tom. I saw the whole thing that man drew first but Jason was faster."

"That's all I need. Two of you take his body to the undertaker."

As I grabbed my saddlebags from under the wagon seat I said.

"Is that all Tom I need to get these saddlebags into the bank. Emily and Gabe are waiting for me. He said the six you have locked up were his men."

"Sure, go take care of her business. Good to have you back and I'll try to get some information out of them."

I threw the saddlebags over my shoulders and walked into the bank. Emily, Lilly Ann and Gabe were looking out the window at me coming up the steps of the bank. When I walked in Emily said.

"I'm glad you're alright. I was worried."

We walked to the teller. Emily said.

"I would like to speak to Mr. Jordan please, it's about my loan."

"Just a minute I'll see if he's busy."

He went to the office and knocked on the door. I heard a voice say come in and the man went in the office and came out in a minute.

"He'll be right with you."

After about five minutes Mr. Jordan came out and greeted us.

"Emily, good to see you come on in my office. I have your loan papers on my desk. The gentlemen and Lilly can wait out here."

"No, they'll be coming in with me. I don't think you've met my ranch foreman Mr. Benning and his assistance Mr. Owens. They take care of my ranch business. And Lilly Ann needs to know what's going on."

We shook hands and Mr. Jordon led the way into his office. He shut the door and pointed to the chairs in front of his desk.

"Please, have a seat."

We sat down and then he sat and started looking through the papers. In about five minutes he looked up from the papers.

"I see that your loan is due on the twenty-fourth of December of this year. Why that's next month. How time flies. The whole amount is due then. There will be no extension this time. What may I help you with today?"

"That's fine I won't need an extension because I won't owe anything."

"What do you mean by that?"

"We're here to pay my loan in full. Exactly how much is it?"

"It would be $9,845.30. But you don't have to pay it today."

"No, I'll pay it all."

Jason handed Emily his saddlebags and she opened them up and her eyes opened up wide. She looked up toward the ceiling and said.

"Thank you O Lord. This is heaven sent."

Emily counted out the $9,846 and handed it to Mr. Jordan. This time his eyes bugged out as he took it and started counting it.

"I need a receipt and my loan papers with your signature and write paid in full and the date, please if you don't mind. I think you owe me seventy cents."

He finished counting the money and signed the papers and handed her the receipt and signed papers and seventy cents. She tucked it away in her pocket book.

"Is that all I can do for you today?"

"No, I need to open an account for the ranch and for Lilly Ann and me."

Jason spoke up. "Emily can we keep out $2,000. I promised the men a new bunkhouse. If you don't mind."

She handed me the saddlebags and I counted out the money and handed it to her.

"Put this away in your bag and we'll go to the general store after this."

I piled the rest of the money on top of Mr. Jordon's desk.

"You better get to counting. There should be around $73,000 there."

"Mr. Jordan please put down that Jason and Gabe can get money out to buy things for the ranch and pay the men."

"Yes ma'am, this will take a while. If you want you can go and do your business at the general store and come back later and get the deposit books."

"No thanks, we have the time. You know how you gave me so much grief over this I want to make sure this is done right."

"I was just doing my job."

"I understand. Lilly Ann look at the time, you're late for school. Gabriel would you make sure she gets there all right. You know with all the bad men that have been in town lately. We'll be here or the general store."

We left and Mr. Jordan kept counting by the time I came back Emily and Jason was walking to the store.

"Jason, here's the money you and Gabriel know what you need. I'm going to see the doc."

"Are you alright? Did those men do something to you?"

"Don't worry, they didn't touch me. You know it's getting near my time and I just want him to check me."

Emily came in the general store, as we were finishing up. Jason paid Mr. Jimson and he handed Emily the remaining money. We started loading the wagon.

Emily said. "Gabriel don't you want something. All you did for me I owe you."

"I thank you but I don't need much. My boss takes care of my needs."

I look up to the sky.

"I know what you mean. That's the way I felt when John was at war and I know John is up there helping the good Lord take care of us somehow that I wouldn't understand."

"How did it go with the doc? Are you alright?"

"Sure I am. Thank you for caring. He said it should be any time around Christmas."

Lilly Ann came down the street.

"Young lady I thought Gabriel left you at school?"

"Ma, he did. When I went inside the preacher was there and I talked to him about pa and how I miss him. We had a good talk. Ma there's no school today it's Saturday."

We all laughed and got in the wagon and headed to the ranch.

When we rode up to the house the men were out in front.

"We got all the rest we can except James. He's still out like a log."

"Speaking of which, see that stand of trees over there. I think those will do for the new bunkhouse. Now get the axes and get to work cutting them down. Winters not going to hold off forever."

Emily said, "Don't worry boys I'll have dinner ready in no time."

Bob said, "That's what I like to hear. Let's get to work. We have all the timber we need we can make it big for more of us when this ranch grows."

Jason said, "Make it big enough for a kitchen. We need to hire a cook this is too much for Emily."

"But we love Emily cooking but we understand."

"I'll cook for awhile and then after the baby I'll cook more."

By noon they had half the timber cut for the bunkhouse. Emily called for dinner. We washed up as usual and wiped our feet then set down to eat.

Emily said, "I wonder where Zack and the men are? It's not like Zack and Jay to miss a meal."

"They'll be along, you don't know Gene when he gets to studying those rocks he loses track of time. They'll be coming soon. Why when we first went to him he passed us and didn't even see us. He woke out of his trance when we put the rocks in front of him. Then he couldn't ask enough questions. He was packed in less than an hour to head out with us."

We heard horses coming up and four men came in after Emily went to the door and made sure they wash up and cleaned their boots. Gene had to take his off cause they were all muddy. They set down and Emily said the prayer then we all dug in.

I said, "Where y'all been?"

Jay said, "We nearly had to pull Gene out of that pond at the bottom of the hill. He sure gets carried away with his work."

"Jay, I just have a passion for my work. When I find what I found out there I just couldn't help myself. Gabe, where did you put my suitcases? I'm going to need them, they have my instruments and some chemicals in them to test the samples I brought back."

"What did you find?" Emily said.

"I won't know for sure until I do my test. They will tell me how rich the deposit is. For sure whoever's behind your troubles around here wasn't after your horses. They most likely are after the land for the minerals in that hill. I spotted what looked like another hill off to the northeast a ways. I hope it's on your land. Right now I'll concentrate on this one it looks to be the most likely to be the richest."

"Could it be that rich." Jason said.

"For now I don't want to get your hopes up too much. You understand."

"I do, the horses are what John wanted this ranch to be. If you don't find it worth mining then the horses will make us a good living now that the war is over and Lilly Ann and I have all of you to help us."

"Jason where can I set up my lab. I don't need much room."

"Emily, how about that little porch on back of the house. It's enclosed with screen wire."

"That's fine if that will do. We don't use it for much except in the spring when the garden is being harvest."

"That should be fine as long as it's enclosed you know to keep out the dirt for the samples."

"Now boys you got your bellies full we have more tree to fell and get that bunkhouse built. Gene will you need a permanent place for your things. We can add another small room to it and you can sleep there also."

"I'll know when I test this ore. If it turns out good I may go back to Kansas City and close my office there and move here. I should know in a couple of days."

"Let's get to work and Bo you help Gene with his work. If you need tools they're in the barn. We'll be nearby if you need anything. Now let's leave the women to their work. I'm going to help you out yonder."

Everyone pitched in even Zack and Jason lived up to his word. Zack brought the men water and whatever else they needed and Jason and me would tie ropes to the logs, after all the branches were stripped away, and hitch the horses up and dragged the logs to the spot where the bunkhouse was to be. We worked for two days and had all the logs pulled to where the bunkhouse would be. We found tools in John's toolbox so we could make a fine floor. James and Tim seemed to know about all the tools so they started on the floor. Gene came up to us.

"Jason, I need to go back out and get a few more samples. I forgot to get any zinc sample. It shouldn't be much but I should do it all at once. I can tell you right now I will need to go to Kansas City and get my other equipment and close my office. I'll do that next week. I should take some men with me."

"You know where it is, we need Zack here. You take Bo. Jay come over here will you."

"Yes Jason, what you need?"

"Go with Gene and Bo. Take your gun and rifle. If any trouble fire two shots and we'll come running. Whoever wants this ranch will want it more now that Gene's here. They may be watching and know what he's doing."

Jay said. "Bo let's go saddle up and get going before supper."

"Yup, I sure wouldn't want to miss that."

They left and Jason came back to work with us. I saw Lilly Ann head to the barn. This might be a good time to talk to Emily alone. I needed to give Emily a push to start to think about Jason as more than a good friend.

"Jason, I'll be back. I need to talk to Emily for a while."

"I think we can manage without you for just awhile." He laughed.

I went on up to the house, wiped my feet, and went inside. I was having as hard of a time as Jason of what to say to this woman that had just found out about her husband being dead less than two months ago. It had to be done.

"Gabriel, is there anything wrong?"

"No, I just need to talk to you if you have a minute."

"I do, I won't start supper for another hour. What is it?"

"I am having a hard time knowing what to say to you."

"I feel you are a true friend and friends should be able to say what's on their minds."

"I'm glad you said that for there is another man that came here with me that was very lonely. He lost all his family in the war and his best friend died in that war."

"You mean Jason was John's friend."

"Yes, you understand he hasn't said much to me about what I'm going to say, just little hints. Don't ask me how I know but I do. My boss gave me the power to know and that's all I'm aloud to say. Jason was lonely with no family and it was not by chance that he and I met and came here. He has a deep-down feeling for you and Lilly Ann but he is letting his friendship with John get in the way of letting you know how he feels. I don't know if you feel the same. I have a feeling inside of me that John would want you two to be as happy as he was with you."

"Gabriel you just knocked me off my feet. I just don't see how he could have any feeling for me in my condition. I just thought he was doing all this for his friendship with John."

"That was true when we got here but I think it changed after he got to know you and Lilly Ann. Take time to watch how he looks at you and her. I can see he is proud when he is next to you on the wagon. And he's defended your honor three time and once in Kansas City when you weren't around to see it. Believe me the feeling is there and it's called love."

"I have noticed that and I know now I do have feeling for him but like him I have been letting John stand in the way of my true feelings."

"If you are so inclined give him a little encouragement and see what happens. Never let him know that I talked to you for he is a proud man. I think he is a man that will stay and fight hard for you and your children and this land."

"But how will he take to raising another man's baby."

"Give him a chance and find out. I know from talking to him that John was truly his best friend that he had ever known. I better get back now. By the way that baby is sure growing and it becomes you very much."

"Thank you for that. You have given me a lot to ponder on. I better get to fixing supper."

"I'll see you at supper and I'll be around for a while for you and short tail but then I'll have to go on to another job for my boss."

I left her then and went back to work. Jason came up to me.

"Where you been for so long?"

"I thought that you said you could get along without me." And I laughed.

That's when two shots rang out through the air.

"Men let's ride hard. They are in trouble."

We got our horses saddled and headed out. By then ten more shots came our way. They were louder now, as we neared the mountain of rock. As we got even closer I saw Jay pointing to the north up the mountain.

"Jeff, you and Tim circle to the west and try to get to the rear of them. Bob you and James circle to the east. Shoot to kill I'm sick of this. Jan, you and me head up the middle. Gabe and Zack you two stay here. I don't want to see you hurt. Now let's go. If you get one alive find out who sent them."

I could see only five of them up high shooting down on our men. I watched as our men moved around and up the mountain. When they started firing Jan and Jason took off for our men that were pinned down behind some boulders at the bottom. As Jason and Jan rode in they had their rifles out firing at the intruders. Jason yelled to Gene to stay down. When they saw that six men were coming at them from all three sides they took off. The firing was over for their side. Jason yelled,

"Chase them down boys don't let any fence stop you. Let them know we mean business."

As they rode up Jason waved for Zack and me to come on in. As we rode in I asked.

"Is anyone hurt?"

"No just mad as hell that they got the drop on us."

"Jan, I didn't see them either. I think they were lying in wait for anyone that came up this way."

Here come our men. They rode up and Bob said.

"We chased them like you said boss we even jumped the fence. We got two and then there were eight more that were heading our way. They saw us and started firing at us. We turned and headed home. Didn't have time to stop and pick up the ones we shot. Don't know if they were alive or dead but they hit the ground hard."

"Gene, you have all you need?"

"Yes, but I tell you I never been shot at for looking for any type of ore."

"Gene, now you know don't ever come out here without some men. Now let's get to supper I'm sure Emily heard the shots. She'll be worried."

When we rode in and there was Emily and Lilly Ann in the back of the house near the garden shading their eyes against the western sun. They both ran up to Jason, one on each side of his horse. They held on to his legs.

"We heard shooting and we came out and nobody was here. Then there were more shots. What happened? Are you all right?"

"Yes every ones fine. They were trying to stop Gene from getting more rock samples. The men got two of them but were chased off Sam's ranch by eight of his men. Emily you shouldn't be running like that. Now you two go back in we'll clean up and be in."

"Yes Jason, suppers on the table."

We came in and started to sit down and Emily pulled out the chair at the head of the table and said,

"Stop, Jason from now on you sit here. This is where the man of the house would sit. All that you have done you should have that honor. Men wouldn't you agree."

Everyone agreed and I saw Jason turn a little red knowing what that meant. Then she went to the other end of the table and sat where she always sat and we sat and she said to Jason.

"If you don't mine Jason, would you say the prayers tonight for us."

"I'm not up on my prayers much but I'll try, here goes. Thank you Lord for this food that you have provided this family. We are grateful that no one has been hurt with all the trouble we've had. Thank you for bringing Gabe and me to this ranch to help my best friends family.

I hope you give us the strength to continue this fight. Let Emily's baby be healthy. Amen."

Everyone said amen and dug into the food. Nobody paid any attention to what had just happened but I did. I saw the look in Emily's eyes when she looked at Jason now. When their eyes met there was a connection between them. Then James said.

"Jason you said you weren't up on your prayers. That was a humdinger if I ever heard one. Don't you agree Emily?"

"It sure was. I knew he had it in him all the time."

Supper was over and the men started for the barn Jason and me stayed on the porch with Emily and Lilly Ann. Jason said,

"Tim, you and James through with the floors in the bunkhouse yet."

"We'll finish up in the morning."

"When that's done get started on the bunks. We should have the roof on tomorrow. We'll all be waiting to sleep under the new roof."

"Yes sir, we'll finish up fast. See you in the morning.

Jason and Emily sat down on the front porch swing. Lilly Ann said,

"Ma, look at you two. That swing fits you perfect." I said,

"Come on in the house short tail I need to talk to you. Let your ma and Jason talk awhile."

We went inside.

"Look Lilly I would like to know what you think of Jason."

"He's great, no one could take the place of pa but he would come pretty close. I want to know why you keep calling me short tail. My pa use to call me that when I was little and my hair was short and wasn't long enough for a pony tail and ma tied it in a short pony tail."

"Lilly Ann I really don't know it just came to me one day when I saw you. Now what do you think if your ma and Jason got together."

"You mean get married?"

"Sh, Sh, Sh, don't let them hear you. Yes get married one day. Don't say anything to either one of them, all right."

"I won't but that would be great I like Jason a lot."

"Now keep it under your hat. Now go get some sleep."

Lilly Ann went to her room.

"Peter, I know I shouldn't listen but I need to find out how I'm doing. Please understand."

A voice came in my head.

"You're doing fine Gabriel. We understand go ahead this is a righteous undertaking."

I could see them from the dark room I was in. Jason was leaning forward with his elbows on his knees and his hat in his hands slowly turning it. She had a shawl over her shoulders, for it had turned chilly in the evening and downright cold at night. This is when she spoke.

"You know Jason, Gabriel and you have been so much help since the short time you're been here. I don't have to worry about the note on the ranch. That's a great weight off me. But we still have trouble and I don't know what can be done."

"That's been on my mind. I came here for John and to help you keep the ranch. I have gotten to know you and Lilly Ann, she's a fine young lady, and she'll be a lot of help when the baby comes. I'm getting a little off track. I think you know how I felt about John but he's gone and I don't know if it's wrong but I have these feelings deep inside that I didn't know I could have anymore. These feelings are for you."

"I don't think your feelings for me are wrong. I've been holding back also because of John but like you said he's gone. Deep down inside I will always love him but I'm living and I know he would want Lilly Ann and me to be as happy as we can. I just thought you couldn't have any feelings for me because of the baby."

"No, if you don't mind me saying, I think that is what brings out the beauty in you."

"Jason, you're embarrassing me."

"I feel a lot better now that I have said my peace. I better get now but don't worry we'll find out who's causing all the trouble someday soon. Goodnight."

The next morning we ate and the men got to work on the bunkhouse. Jason had sent two men out to check on the fence line and the horses.

The walls and roof were going up and the floor was almost finished. Jason was whistling a tune that was familiar but I could not place. I said, "You sure are happy this morning. Should I know about something?"

"No, I just seem to have a new lookout on life."

"Emily sure looked happy and lit up this morning at breakfast. Could it be for the same reason?"

"Could be; right now we need to go to town and buy a stove and other things for the bunkhouse. We might get to sleep in it in a few days as soon as Tim and James get done with the bunks. I'll ask Emily if she wants to go and if we need to hire a cook yet."

This is when Gene came up.

"I think I need to leave tomorrow before the weather gets even colder. I'll get all my things."

"Come on up to the house I want Emily to hear this. I'll send Jay and Bo with you. They're the best shots around here. You come to Gabe."

We went to the house and Jason knocked on the door. Emily let us in.

"Gene is leaving tomorrow for Kansas City. I think he has something to tell us."

"I am leaving but just to get the rest of my things and maybe send telegrams to some of my acquaintance, with your permission, to tell them about your find, to get them out here to help me get mining operation set up."

"You mean there is something to all this? You have my permission but we have a telegraph here."

"I know but with all the trouble we wouldn't want it to fall in the wrong hands because I tell you right now it will be a rich fine. Jason before we can mine we need to stop this trouble. Men won't go to work if they think there's a chance of getting killed."

"I know we need to find out who's behind the trouble. I'll tell Jay and Bo to leave with you in the morning. I'll give you some money to buy some packhorses for your things it will be faster than a wagon. Emily, do you want to go to town. We need to buy a heating stove and a cooking stove and supplies for the new bunkhouse. The boys will be glad to get warm at night and get a good night's sleep."

"I better stay here and get dinner ready. The men work hard and they deserve a good meal."

"I think we need to hire a cook for the bunkhouse. I know you don't mine but it's getting near thanksgiving. It's just too much for you right now."

"You maybe right, I have been feeling a little tired lately. Go ahead. Tell the men I'll fix thanksgiving dinner for them with the help of the new cook."

Jason told Bo and Jay to get ready to leave for Kansas City tomorrow with Gene.

"Try to get back as fast as you can. The cold and snow won't be far behind you. Here's two hundred dollars for expenses. Don't tell anyone about our business. We never know who we can trust."

Jason and me took the wagon to town. We looked around the general store until Mr. Jimson was done with the others in the store.

"Hello Jason, Gabe sorry it took so long but you know women. They can look forever. What can I do for you?"

"Why we need a cook stove and a heating stove for the new bunkhouse. It don't have to be too fancy. It's just us cowboys."

"Over this way, I think this will do you, these two are my most common ones. Keep you warm at night and keep your belly full during the day. You'll need stove pipe for both."

"We also need pots and pans and food stuff. You wouldn't know a man that is a cook. I'm looking to hire one. It's getting to much for Emily in her condition."

"You and Gabe can load those two stoves and I'll get the pipe and things you need. I know a woman that cooks at the new small diner at the other end of town. She might know someone. Is Emily alright?"

"She is but we have fourteen mouths to feed on the ranch now and it's too much and she's been tired lately."

We got the stoves loaded and the other things. Jason paid for everything and we headed to the diner. As we walked in I could see that this was an up-and-coming business. A young woman came over.

"Can I help you?"

"Gabe, what you have?"

"Just a cup of coffee."

"Me too. Could I talk to the cook?"

"She's pretty busy this time of day but if you want you can go over and talk to her while she's cooking."

"Thank you."

Jason walked over and talked to her and came back in five minutes or so.

"What'd she have to say?"

"She knows a man to the south of town that lives in a shack. He uses to work for her dad before Mr. Johnson bought her dad out and ran everyone off. She was mad it was more like her dads cattle keep disappearing until he had to sell. That was three years ago. Gabe this has been going on for some time. Emily was lucky to had lasted as long as she did."

"If buying up land was against the law we would have him."

"He's bound to slip up one day and we'll have him cold. Now let's get down the road to hire a cook."

This time I paid the girl and we went outside. There was a man in our wagon looking under the tarp covering the stove. There were two more men beside the wagon laughing.

8

"Can I help you, you seem to be in the wrong wagon and I don't see another one around. I think that's the one we came up in. Don't you Gabe."

"It looks like the same one we rode up in. It must be ours."

The man in the wagon said, "This is our wagon. I think we drove it in from the ranch."

"Well, Gabe these must be our fine horses cause you three couldn't bring both in. And look Gabe they belong to Sam's ranch."

The two on the ground quit laughing and the one on the wagon got down.

"You calling me a liar mister."

"No, I just don't see how we could be riding Sam's horses when we work for the Circle T. That must be our wagon."

"You must be new in town or you would know that Mr. Johnson owns everything around these parts."

"I see he owns you but not our ranch and he won't. You can go tell him that Jason Benning will be here a long time to make sure he doesn't. If he doesn't like that he can come see me. Now if you will excuse us we have business elsewhere."

"I'll tell him what you said and you haven't seen any trouble yet until you make him mad."

"You tell him I don't care how mad he gets and how many gun hands he hires it won't be enough. One day I might have to come after him. Gabe let's get down the road."

We went south out of town and Gabe said.

"You trying to make him mad?"

"I sure am. I want him to show his hand as soon as possible. I really can't wait to get this over so we can live in peace."

"Does that mean you're not leaving?"

"I've been thinking on that. Right now I know I can stay on as Emily's foreman and maybe later we can get together."

"Knuckle head can't you see she loves you and I know you love her."

"You know too much. I know she likes me but love I don't know. Here's the place."

We got down and Jason knocked on the door. A man came to the door and said.

"Who are you? What do you want? I'm not looking for any trouble."

"I'm Jason and this is Gabe we work for the Truman Ranch. I'm the foreman and we were told that you use to be the cook for a ranch near. I wasn't told what your name is."

"I was the cook for the Foley Ranch back about four years ago 'til that Johnson came and started to steal Mr. Foley's cattle then bought him out when he couldn't pay his note. I told Mr. Foley but he said that Sam was so friendly that I was only a cook and didn't know. Then Johnson fired me when he took over."

"That does sound familiar, doesn't it Gabe I wonder if there's a connection. Was Mr. Jordan the head of the bank then?"

"Sure was, I get what you mean I never thought of that. I see it now. You boys come in I like the way you think."

We walked in and it was a shabby shack that didn't have a woman's touch anywhere in sight. He was about forty-five with a baldhead and from the look of the bottles he drinks too much.

"We came to hire a good cook to cook for the men on the ranch. There are about nine or ten men working on the ranch."

Gabe said. "What's your name? "Why are there so many bottles around here?"

"My name is Evan Stone and the bottles are from my drinking because Johnson gave me a bad name and I couldn't get any kind of work except sweeping out the saloon at night. They would give me a bottle for half my pay. With a good job I wouldn't need to drink."

"Maybe he could be more help than just cooking."

"What do you mean?"

"Like telling us some more that you know about other dealing that Mr. Jordan had and how Sam maybe connected to him."

"Look, Evan if you can show up at the ranch sober a week from now and no drinking at the ranch. You will have to get up early every morning and sometimes help Mrs. Truman cook at the house. We'll pay you forty dollars a month and you can get out of this shack and live in our new bunkhouse with a new stove. Oh, and tell us all you may know about the takeover of ranches around here."

"For that much I'll tell you all I know and that's a plenty. I would like to see that man get his up comings."

We shook hands and I said one more time.

"Show up sober. You know where the ranch is."

"I will and I know where it is Gabe. I'm glad to see that she got out from under his spell."

We left and headed home. We were about a half a mile from the ranch house when a shot rang out and knocked Jason off the seat of the wagon into the back with the stoves. Then another shot and another and I took the reins and got the horses moving fast. I turned into the ranch gate and made it up to the house. Everyone came running out and Emily came out of the house.

"What's the matter Gabriel? Where's Jason?"

"He's in the back. He's been shot I don't know how badly. Men get your horses it happen about half a mile from here toward town. See if you can find any tracks. It was a rifle shot so it could be some ways. We had a little run in with three men in town that worked for Mr. Johnson."

I could see Emily and Lilly Ann were both crying. I jumped down and got Jason up and carried him inside the house.

"Put him in Lilly Ann's room. I'll take care of him."

I put him down on the bed and Emily came in with a pan of water and some cloths.

"Look it creased his head and his left shoulder. It's not bad. I'll clean both wounds and let him rest. He should wake up in a little while."

The tears had dried up and turned to madness as she came out of the room.

"You said they worked for Sam? I'm tired of these little hit and miss attacks."

"Yes, but we don't know if it was them. Now Emily listen we hired a cook and he said he knows some things that have been going on around here. Jason thinks he might have a link to what has been happening. Let's give him a chance. He's alright for now."

"Alright, we'll see what he says when he wakes up.

It was an hour before the men came back. Emily and me were on the front porch.

"How did it go?"

"Some tracks but they went up into the rocky hills and they ended. There were some rifle shells but they could be from anybody's."

"Thank you men I know you tried. Come on up in an hour supper will be ready. Jason will be all right it's just two creases. He should be up by tomorrow."

We came to supper but after the prayer it was quiet around the table.

Emily said, "Cheer up men, Jason will be alright and things will get back to normal."

Jay said, "Ma'am, with the trouble today I'm worried about tomorrow. Bo and me are good with a gun but it is a big responsibility to get Gene to Kansas City and back. We know how much you will count on us."

"I know it will be alright. You will do fine or Jason wouldn't had picked you two."

Zack said, "Any way when you get back you will be sleeping in that new warm bunkhouse. No more cold barn."

Everyone laughed, and then we heard a noise and out of the room walked Jason.

"Jay, what Emily said is right I picked you two cause I know you can get the job done. I know any of you at this table could do it. Now make room for me I'm hungry."

Emily said, "Your chair is waiting for you at the head of the table."

Then the mood around the table changed and the food disappeared."

Emily had a smile on her face and I could see a small tear of joy roll down her cheek.

I said, "You know those bad men don't have a chance with the team we have around this table. We all have different things we are good at. The good Lord put us all here to help Emily and Lilly Ann in their time of need."

Emily said. "Gabriel that's nice and I think it's true and I know what your job is. You keep us focused on the important things in life the good Lord, family and good friends. You men have become our family."

Gene said, "I'm even feeling a part of this and by the time we get back from Kansas City it will be assured that you all can work here as long as you want."

"I think Jason I need to get you back to bed."

"If you don't mind I would like to sit on the porch awhile with you and Lilly. I do enjoy that."

"Gabe, if you and Jay would help Jason to the porch. I'll be there in a while."

"That was a great meal ma'am. Boys let's get to the barn and get some sleep tomorrow we have a bunkhouse to finish." Zack said.

We left Jason on the porch and as we left for the barn I saw Lilly Ann come out of the house and sit beside Jason. He put his arm around her and she put her head on his shoulder, the right one. Just before I entered the barn I saw Emily come out and sit beside Jason. I didn't need to listen tonight because I knew they were becoming a family. I don't think they are going to need my help too much longer. A voice came in my head. It was Peter.

Angel Without Wings

"You stay there and help them through their trouble and you stay and see the babies be born. They will name the boy John. We'll pull you out when the time is right."

"Yes sir and you said babies are they going to have a girl also?"

"Yes, do not tell them. Human's don't have that knowledge yet but they will in years to come."

"Who you talking to Gabe?"

"Just my great boss upstairs."

"We know you don't sleep much but we do so quiet down."

"Yes, Bob."

I heard a noise and looked up and it was Jason coming in the barn and going to his bunk.

The next morning things got moving after breakfast. Two men went out to check on the horses and as always to check if the fence had been cut. Now that the loan had been paid there was no reason for them to be stealing horses but Jason wanted to make sure. Jason was out there directing the men, even with his arm in a sling and a bandage around his head. The men had brought a chair from the house for him to sit but he was on his feet walking around making sure everything was done. Gene, Bo and Jay were leaving for Kansas City and Jason hoped that they would return before the snow flew.

"Jay here's some money. Send some telegrams to the sheriffs around the state. I wrote the name Sam Johnson and a Mr. Jordan and I wrote a message to send. Stay 'til you receive several answers. Bring them with you don't send them here. They might fall in the wrong hands."

They were off at a good pace.

I walked over to Jason.

"You have a nice time on the porch last night? I thought Emily would keep you in the house last night."

"I told her it wasn't right for me to stay in the house that she has had enough trouble with rumors. She understood and yes we had a great time on the porch just getting to know each other better. Lilly Ann is something else; she knows so much about this ranch. I just couldn't believe it.

"She had four long years to learn from Zack and I just bet John showed her a lot, years before he left for the war since he didn't have a boy to take over yet."

"What you mean yet?"

"Have you already forgotten about the baby?"

"You're right, it could be a boy. I wonder what she will name it if it is a boy?"

"John would be a great name and you could help her with that decision when the time is right. She might think that you wouldn't like it if she did."

"Gabe what would I do without you around to keep reminding me of the important things in life. This trouble is like a bug landing on your arm you swat it and go on with life."

I took Emily to town to see the doc. Tab came along in case of trouble. Jason didn't come because his head bandage was gone but his arm was still in a sling. He didn't want people in town to see him like that word might get back too Johnson and he might make a big move to take over the ranch. After the doc told her she should get more rest. I told her.

"Emily you have no business making covers for the mattress and pillows we'll buy them."

"I do feel a little tired. Maybe you're right."

We went in the general store and Emily looked around then Mr. Jimson came up.

"I saw you coming out of doc's. Is everything all right with the baby? When is it due, Jen will want to know?"

"Yes, thank you for asking. The baby is due for Christmas. We built a new bunkhouse for the men and I was going to make covers for the mattress and pillows but doc said I should get more rest so Gabriel thought we could buy them to put straw in."

"Yes, I bet just making meals for the men wares you out. Over here I have what you want but look here we have them already made and pillows too."

"We have a cook for the men in the bunkhouse coming at the end of the week. That will help me a lot in this last month and a half."

I felt them and they felt great a lot better than straw.

"Look Emily how soft just ask Tab how the men would like these and the price isn't much more."

"Tab, come here. What you think of these to sleep on?"

He felt them and pushed down on them then said.

"I never felt anything so soft the men would sleep like babies."

"Well, they deserve the comfort, they work hard. We'll take fourteen if you have that many and pillows to."

"I do, in the back. Gabe if you and Tab- it is Tab isn't it."

"Yes sir, I'm new at the ranch."

"You two can help me get them out of the back to the wagon."

We started taking them out to the wagon. When we got the last of them in and covered up and Emily paid Mr. Jimson we left the store. We got to the wagon and the three men that we had encountered yesterday were at the wagon. Their hands were under the cover feeling the new mattress.

"Where are you taking these new-fangled things? I sure wish I had something nice to sleep on."

"You can, there are some in there." Tab said.

"What if I want these right now?"

"You can't have them and I'm here to see that you don't. I think you've had enough fun. We're leaving now."

"Boy where is that other man we talk to yesterday did he have any trouble."

"Who you calling boy? I don't need any help with the likes of your kind."

Emily said, "Come on Tab don't pay any mind to those three."

"Tab is it. You better listen to your knocked up mama, Tab."

I saw Tab take a swing at the man closes to him and knock him under the wagon. The next man came at him and Tab knocked him under the horse's feet.

I said, "Stand back Emily."

The horses ran right over the second man and he yelled over all the commotion. The wheel hit the first man in the head and knocked him back down in the dirt. The horses didn't go far. The loud mouth looked at what had happened and drew his gun. Tab's gun was out and a shot rang out. It was Tab's gun. The man dropped his gun and was holding his wrist.

"You broke my wrist."

"You're lucky that I didn't kill you. I ever hear you talk to my good boss lady like that again and I will kill you. You can count on that. You better pick up your friends before they get ran over again."

"You alright Mrs. Truman?"

"Thank you Tab, I am."

The marshal came running over out of his office.

"What happen here?"

Mr. Jimson said, "These three tried to take Emily's goods out of the wagon and they keep egging Tab on and calling Emily dirty words. Tab finally tore into them and that one drew on him and Tab shot him."

"Okay you three I had enough from you you're going to jail. I don't care if you work for Mr. Johnson or not. He can come and talk to the judge."

"Emily, are you alright? You want me to get the doc?"

"No, I'm fine. Let's get home. I just wish we could do something about Sam. I know it's him giving us all the trouble."

We came up in the front of the house.

"Tab would you help Emily in the house. I'll take these things to the bunkhouse."

"Yes, Gabe."

"I'm alright Tab just help me down."

"You sure. I'll be happy to."

"No, you go with Gabe. I'll be fine."

We drove the wagon to the bunkhouse.

"Boys wait until you see what we have here come unload the wagon."

They came over and Tab got in the back and handed the things to them. I heard them say, "Soft, how soft they are."

"Emily was nice enough to buy these for you so you all can sleep like babies at night and work hard during the day. So thank her at supper."

Jason said, "Tab what happen to you?"

"Three men were trying to get the things out of the wagon and calling Emily names. So I hit one and then two."

"Jason, they were the same three that we had trouble with at the diner. The loud mouth drew on Tab and Tab shot him in the wrist. The marshal put them in jail. You should see Tab he's near as fast as you are. The man pulled first and didn't get a shot off. They're pretty well out of commission for a while. One got ran over by the horses and the wagon wheel hit the other in the head. The marshal did say they work for Johnson."

"Tab, why didn't you tell us how fast you are?"

"Well, I grow up pretty much alone so I learn to shoot young and I don't brag cause I never know who I can trust. But today I knew that I wanted to be part of this ranch. I don't know how but I just do. That I can trust anyone here and Emily is a very good woman and I like Lily Ann."

"She's a little young yet, don't you think. She's only fourteen."

"I know sir. But she said that she's nearly fifteen and I'm only seventeen."

"Well I'll be. I'm feeling old, Gabe."

"Not too old to act like a father."

"Your right. Tab you can talk and become friends. Maybe that friendship will grow into something more as you two get older."

"I believe so, Jason. Right now it's good to have a best friend you can talk to. I better get back to work."

"Gabe, I am about mad enough to go over to Sam's ranch and confront him. I'm getting tired of this."

"Don't you think you better wait for Gene and the men to get back and find out what information they have? And Evan will be out in two days. He may know something more. Don't forget about your arm. It may throw you off having it hurt like that."

"You're right, I'll wait longer. I better go see about Emily. You keep the men working. It's too mild the cold might hit us hard one night."

I walked over to the bunkhouse and went inside. Both stoves had been installed with the stovepipe out of the roof. The bunks were built and the mattress and pillows were on. But we forgot covering and blankets for the cold.

"Tab, let's ride into town. We'll take the horses we forgot blankets. That's about all we'll need to sleep in there tonight. I don't want to bother Emily. She's had enough to handle today. Bob you cut a stack of wood for the two stoves. We might get to sleep on those soft beds tonight."

"Yes sir, for that soft bed I'd cut wood for a week."

"Here you go Gabe, the horses are ready."

We hit the road for town and rode up to the general store. We went in.

"I know Gabe you forgot bedding and blankets. I remembered after you left. Here you are I have them over there put away for you. That a be twelve dollars."

"Thank you, we may get to sleep in a warm place tonight that old barn is drafty."

We got the things packed on the horses and headed back to the ranch. We heard shots coming from behind the house.

"Look Gabe, take these packages, I'm heading behind them and get them in a cross fire."

I saw him as he went up behind the hill and then to the top. Then he dismounted and crouched down and moved forward. His rifle was in his hands and he started firing. He fired ten shots before the men knew what was going on. Three were down and five others turned and started firing at Tab. That left them open to the side of the ranch. Our men started moving up the hillside toward Tab and the bad men. They were caught and they knew it. There were two more down and that left three standing with their hands in the air. I rode in and our men checked the dead and gathered up all the guns and led them down in front of the ranch house where Jason, Emily, Lilly Ann and me were standing. Tab was coming in with all eight horses with three dead men draped across their saddles. He stopped and picked up the other two dead men and came into the yard.

"Where you two come from?"

"We went to town we forgot the blankets and things for the bunks. I thought Emily and Lilly Ann would do a better job of making the bunks than these boys. I thought we could sleep in a nice dry, warm place tonight. We came riding up and heard shooting and Tab saw them up there and went around to the back of them."

"Well, Tab you saved our bacon again today."

"Gabe, would you and Tab make one more trip to town and take these live ones to the marshal and the dead ones to the undertakers. You go to Jeff."

Emily said, "Men, Lilly Ann and me are going to make your bunks and I have three apple pies in the oven for you tonight."

"Bob, did you get the wood cut?"

"Gabe, I was kind of busy getting shot at. I'll do it now Jan you can help me. We can have that place nice and warm by tonight."

We took the eight men to town. Tom just shook his head when he saw us coming down the street with a line of horses.

"What happen this time?"

"They attacked the ranch. Please take notice of the brands on the horses. I tell you Tom, Jason and the boys are about ready to reach their limit. We are tired of being attacked. Ben, Sam's foreman tried to gun down Jason and steal the horses. He's buried out there somewhere on the prairie."

"I'll go out to Sam's tomorrow with the dead men and have a talk with him."

"You want some of our boys to come with you."

"No, it's my job. Having your men with me might spark a gunfight. This is getting to bad. It has to stop."

Once again we headed to the ranch and this time for good at least for today. We were just in time for supper. Emily had the pies and they were gone in a split second.

Jason said, "Boys tonight you get to pick your new bunk. I don't want to see any fighting, maybe a little pushing to get a better spot."

Emily said, "Oh Jason, they're all the same. Men you know me I don't want to have to tell you to bring your bedding to me for washing. I may need help so the last man to bring me his pass a week will help me. This is Wednesday by next Wednesday morning I want to see the porch full so they will be dry by nightfall. Jason maybe you can hire a woman in town to come out every Wednesday to help me and Lilly Ann until the baby comes and a month or two after."

"You got it. I'll do that tomorrow. Gabe and me are going to see if Evan is ready to get to cooking for the men."

All the ahs went through the air as I said that.

The men went to the new warm bunkhouse to get settled in. The fight of this afternoon had been all forgotten. Jason had stayed at the house on the porch with Emily and Lilly Ann. This was now a routine every night. I think everyone of the men expected them to get married one day. I could see that they were becoming closer. It wasn't about getting my wings anymore. I really wanted to help these three people that had become my good friends. There was a giant bell that rung out loud in the bunkhouse. I looked around but not anyone moved. It was only me that could hear it. I think I'm doing something right. There that loud bell went off again.

In the morning I looked around and everyone was up and around.

"Did any of you hear a loud bell last night."

"I didn't hear or see nothing except the girls I counted in my sleep."

"You must be going crazy Gabe, where would a bell come from way out here."

"Why don't you put some cotton in your ears tonight. Maybe it won't wake us."

Everyone laughed and went to breakfast. I sat there wondering what had taken place last night. I was still wondering when I sat down to eat. I looked Jason's way and he was sitting there without his arm in a sling. Jason spoke up.

"Men when you go out today make sure you're carrying your sidearm and have your rifle with you. We don't want any of you hurt."

"Jason, I forgot to tell you, Tom said he was going to talk to Sam today. He didn't want any of us to go he thought it might spark a fight."

"He was about right."

"Emily, Gabe and me are going to get Evan and try to hire you some help. One of you boys stay close to the house at all times in case Emily needs help. You know it's getting nearer her time."

"Jason, I'm not due for six weeks."

"I've heard of woman being early."

We headed to town. When we came down the street we saw that there wasn't many people. We stopped in at Tom's office but he was out. We rode to the diner to talk to the girl that told us about Evan. We went in. She came up to us.

"We'll have some coffee and do you know any woman that may need some extra work one day a week. On Wednesday morning every week to help Emily Truman do the washing. She's going to have a baby in six weeks. We have fourteen men out at the ranch. Their bedding needs washing. She won't put up with dirty beds.

9

"I do know someone, me. I'm Jane and we don't open until noon. I don't have to be here until eleven- thirty. I'll be happy for some extra pay. How much is she paying?"

"Ten dollars a week. But she needs someone she can count on cause her daughter Lilly Ann is in school. It may last after the baby comes and so next Wednesday morning she'll expect you early. Do you know where the ranch is?"

"I think so. It's to the east of town about two miles."

"That's it, her name's Emily Truman is on the post near the road. We better get going."

We left and went south out of town. It was a ways off.

I spoke up. "You know Jason, when I met you on that lonely road you was just like that road, lonely. Now you are out going and talking to people."

"Gabe, I went through a lot during the war with the killing and seeing my friends get killed. Then I went back home and my family was gone and the carpetbaggers had come in and taken over my parent's farm. I was so down and I think if I had money I would have started drinking like Evan. Now I think I can see a purpose in life and I know you and Emily are a big part of it."

We were within half a mile from Evan's shack when we heard shots being fired towards where we were heading. Jason stepped up the pace of the horses and as we neared the shack we got off and went to walking.

We were overlooking the shack and there were three men firing at Evan's place and he was firing back at them.

"Gabe, sneak around and see if you can get their horses and bring them over here. I'll give you five minutes and I'll start firing and moving down in Evan's direction."

I headed to the back of where they were. There was lots of brush and some trees to cover me from their view. I spotted the horses and made sure there wasn't anyone with them. I slipped the reins off the branches of all three horses. I now could hear firing from Jason's direction toward where I was. I hurried through the trees and could still hear shots coming in my direction. Jason was reloading as I came up and tied the horses. Jason said.

"Stay low and I'm going around to the back of Evan place. I think I hit one. I don't know how badly. Bring all the horses behind me and tie them close to his shack."

As we kept moving Jason would fire six or seven rounds and move on and fire more. I tied the horses and Jason went behind the shack. He took two boxes of shells with him and headed to the south. He kept firing every time he moved to another spot. The men had stopped shooting at the shack and were firing where Jason had been. Then I didn't hear anymore firing from the way that Jason went. Then in a while all shooting had stopped. I went in the shack. There on the floor was Evan. He was holding his side. I went to him.

"Let me see how bad it is."

I took away his hand from his side and there was blood covering his shirt. I raised this shirt a shallow crease along his side from his belly to his back. I looked for some water and clean rags. I found some rags and was bathing his side when Jason came in.

"One got away I got the other two on their horses. They have wounds but they won't bleed to death they can wait 'til Evan can ride. The other one is on foot."

I said, "What happen Evan?"

"It was kind of my fault. Last night I went to the saloon. I was going to have some last drinks and I drank too much and talked too much. How I got a good paying job with the Truman Ranch and was cooking for all the men. I said I liked to cook and this was my last time to drink for a while. You know, I was bragging. I'm sorry. I think I'm going on the wagon. This has sobered me up for good. I'm glad you showed up a day early or you might had only found my bones cause I was out of shells."

"We came a day early cause the bunkhouse is finished and we slept in there last night. So I wanted you to start today. If you can make it Emily can take care of that wound. But you come without any bottles. The kitchen and your room are separate from the men's room cause you have to get up early. If you can get mounded and make it to the ranch you'll be all right."

"I can ride it's not as bad as I thought but the hurts smarts some."

We made it to the marshal's. Tom still wasn't in so I left a note and locked the two men up and we headed to the ranch.

"Gabe, after what we've been through I don't care if those two bleed to death."

"If they do they'll have some explaining to do to St. Peter."

"Evan, hold on a little longer we're nearly to the ranch."

"It stopped hurting so bad I'll be fine. You show me that hum-dinger of a kitchen and I'll be good. When Johnson fired me it just took the life out of me. I just hope you can get something on him."

"We'll talk later, I'll let Emily take care of you."

We got Evan on the front porch and Emily came out.

"What happened to Evan?"

"You know him? He got shot at his old place by some more men from Sam's ranch."

"Yes, I know him. He used to cook on the Foley Ranch until Sam bought it out and fired everyone. Let me take a look at that."

She went inside and came out with a pan of water and some clean cloths and opened his shirt and was bathing it with her easy touch.

"I'm sorry that I didn't tell you I knew Emily but there were some rumors about me that I think Johnson started and I just made it worse by drinking. No one cares about me cause I was drunk most of the time."

Emily said, "I know about rumors. But I don't need a drunk man feeding my men."

"Please Emily I know I can stop if I have a great job like this. I promise you if I don't you can fire me. I just need a chance. I heard the rumors about you and I knew that you wouldn't ever do that to John. I'm sure am sorry. I heard he died in the war."

"He did but we go on and now we are in a war for this ranch."

"Gabriel would you help him into the house."

Evan said, "Jason said I have my own room by the kitchen. Can I rest in there?"

"You sure can."

"Yes, ma'am."

"Gabriel, please take him to the bunkhouse."

I helped Evan to his new home.

"You know Gabe I knew that woman when she was a young lady and then married John. You know I think she's prettier now than then."

We went in the bunkhouse and Evan's eyes lit up. I let go of him and he seemed to have forgotten about his wounds. He looked at everything. It was like he was in another world that only he could enter.

"Gabe, I've never seen the like. Just like a fancy diner."

Then he went in his room and nearly fell down.

"Try the bed. In fact you better get in bed. Take off those dirty clothes before Emily comes out to doctor you. She'll have a fit. Yes even the long johns. I'll lend you some of mine. Don't get in bed until you take a bath. I'll be right back. And Emily doesn't like a dirty kitchen either."

I brought the tub in and I filled it with water.

"Now Evan get in and here's some soap. The bed clothes are new."

He got in and started washing.

"Don't forget your hair and beard."

"You have a razor I'll shave it off."

"Here goes and don't get that dressing wet just clean around it."

He got out and looked better without that beard. He got into his clean long johns and got in bed.

"Your clean clothes are here and I'll have Lilly Ann wash your clothes when she gets home from school. Now tell me some things that you might know about Johnson and Jordan at the bank."

"They came to town about the same time. You never see them together even at the bank. Someone else always helps Johnson and at the diner or saloon they never sit together. I've had time to watch them. I know Johnson has a so-called loan at the bank but I've never seen him pay a red cent on it. I'm pretty sure he steals cattle and Emily's horses. That is where he gets the money to buy out the ranches he's stealing from. He's built a pretty good empire of other people's stock and land."

"You don't have any solid proof though?"

"I'll try to think of more after this whiskey gets out of my system. I can think clearer."

"You get some rest now."

"I truly mean it Gabe, thank you for a chance."

The next morning we were awakened by the smell of coffee, eggs and bacon and even pancakes. Jason came in and looked at Evan. He was cooking up a storm. The door opened and it was Emily. Everyone except Jason and me ran for cover. They didn't have their pants on yet we did.

"I smelled cooking from down this way. Evan why are you out of bed? You need to heal."

"Yes ma'am I'm healing right now. This kitchen is my medicine. I've missed it for so long. I hoped that you hadn't started yet."

"Stop let me check that wound. It looks all right. When you're done you get back in bed. And you look better clean and no beard. Jason you and Gabe come up to the house to eat. Men I need someone to cook for."

Later in the morning a rider came up to the ranch. It was Doug the deputy.

"Jason, I saw your note in the office and thought you might know something about the marshal getting shot."

"What! I left those men in jail I thought Tom would be back soon. They shot up Evan out at his old place. He wasn't hurt too bad so we brought him on out here. How bad is Tom? I know he was going out to talk to Sam Johnson sometime."

"Pretty bad he's at the doc's unconscious. Somehow he managed to stay on his horse or climb back on and it came in last night."

"I'll be in as soon as I can. You might ride out Johnson's way and see if you can spot some blood on the trail so you'll know where he was when it happened."

He took off back to town and Jason told Emily that him and me were going to town.

We went to the doc's office but Tom was still unconscious so we went to talk to Doug.

"I went out Johnson's way and found some dry blood on a rock and the ground. Looks like he leaned on the rock after putting his hand to the wound. Doc said he was hit twice once in the head, that just creased him, that's why he's unconscious. The other wound is in his side it went clean through but doc said both wounds were from the back. He should be all right. I guess we just have to wait and see if Tom can tell us anymore."

"Why don't we take a ride out to Johnson's ranch? Did you get anything out of the men in jail? They're six of his men in there now. That should be a clue."

"They didn't say anything while doc treated them yesterday. I don't know about going out there without Tom telling me to."

"What if Tom was dead? You would have to do something. I'll get some of my men and we'll back you up."

"I better wait."

"All right, but I'm not waiting for long. We'll be at the ranch. If Tom comes too, you send someone for us."

"Sorry, Jason I'll send someone."

"That's what Tom told me and look where he is now."

We returned to the ranch and everyone wanted to know what had happened. We told them what we knew and no one was happy especially Emily.

"How much has to happen before they do something? I just don't understand what's going on."

"Emily, we're not waiting. James you worked over at Johnson's. Didn't you?"

"Yes sir, you don't think I'm with them?'

"No, I just want to know if tonight you could get us close enough to the ranch house where we could see the house and the road without being seen."

Emily said, "Jason you can't you may get hurt."

"I've already been hurt. Next time it might be you or Lilly Ann or one of the men that may be killed. I don't want to wait and find out. We're just going to see who, if anybody, comes and goes at night. Gene and Jay will be back soon and maybe they will have some information. But we can't wait and find out."

"You know best, but you be careful."

We left a little after dark and an hour later we were up on a hill overlooking the road and the ranch house. Lanterns were on inside the house and two near the front porch. It worried Jason a little because the moon was out bright so we had to leave the horses back in the trees and we had to stay low to the ground. They both had their rifles with them and their pistols. Men came up from the barn and went inside and back out and rode to the northwest. Others left the bunkhouse and went down the road to town. It looked like a very usual night. A rider came up the hill we were on and turned to the south before reaching us and he rode down to the small pond and got off his horse and let his horse water and the man sat down in the grass and was looking at the stars. I wonder if any of the hands didn't know what had been happening. Then about an hour after we got there a buggy came up the road. The cowhand that was sitting in the grass got on his horse and went to meet the buggy. They talked for a while then the buggy followed the cowhand up the road to the house. Jason got out his telescope that he had used in the war. He watched for a while as two figures got out and went in the house. The cowhand waited by the buggy. Jason said,

"Well, I'll be."

"What is it?"

"It's Mr. Jordan from the bank and it looks like a saloon girl."

James said, "Can I see Jason?"

Jason handed him the telescope and he look for a while as they went up to the house.

"That's Billie from the saloon. When I worked for Johnson her and me were cozy for a time. That's right, she broke it off after Ben fired me."

"Maybe she keeps an eye open to see if his men are talking to anyone that they shouldn't be."

"You know, that makes sense. A couple of nights before I was fired I was talking to Evan, when he swept the floors at the saloon and he used to work for the Foley spread over east of here."

"I think we've seen enough for tonight."

Then the door open and the two came out and Jordan was carrying a briefcase that he hadn't been carrying when he went in. The cowhand follow them back down the road then headed back to the bunkhouse.

"Let's go, we'll talk when we get out of here."

James led us back out to the main road and we high tailed it back to our ranch. Emily and Lilly Ann were on the porch watching as we rode in.

"I'll talk to you two later in the bunkhouse."

"If I'm not asleep those bunks are so nice and soft and so warm."

"Don't get to comfy we have work for you to do later tonight."

"What?"

"Just wait I'll be back in an hour. I'll tell Emily what's going on."

"Gabe, you think he's every going to kiss that woman."

"I heard that James."

I whispered. "I don't know. But I hope so."

"Me too I think they are made for each other."

"I'd say it was heaven sent."

Jason came in the bunkhouse and men were playing cards and talking. I was talking to Evan about if the men were complaining about the food. Jason came over.

"No, not really I just don't have that touch a woman has and I'm sure not as pretty to look at." Jason said.

"That's for sure."

The men heard that and everyone laughed.

"All right boys at least I took a bath.'

They laughed again.

"James, come over here."

"Now I want you two to go to town to the saloon."

"What! I just promised you I wouldn't drank."

"I know it will be hard to pour it out somewhere but this is work. Evan you are known to get drunk and talk. I want you to pretend to be drunk and tell James you don't think it will work. Just say it over and over for some time. James, just keep telling him to be quiet. Then tell Evan to go home and sleep it off he has to get up early and feed the men. Evan, you leave and come get to bed. I hope your side is good enough for this."

"I've been so happy I haven't notice if I hurts or not."

"That's good. So you come home and talk so Billie can hear you. Then I hope she'll come over to you James and try to get close to you again. If she does and asks you what Evan was talking about keep saying nothing. Then pretend to be a little drunk and tell her this. That I sent a letter to a mining expert and the reply should be in this week's mail. That's in three days. Then we'll watch Johnson's tomorrow night to see if Jordan and Billie go out to talk to him. If so and the mail is taken from the stage we will have them. I hope. Now get going."

They left and Gabe said.

"You really think it will work."

"I don't know what else to do besides just going into Johnson's ranch shooting and Emily won't have anything to do with that. I think I'll go into the bank and talk to Mr. Jordan tomorrow."

"What are you going to say to him?"

"I don't know yet. I guess it depends on what happens tonight at the saloon."

The next morning I got with Evan and James.

"Evan you make it all right last night. I know how hard it must have been. But I thank you."

"Don't thank me. I thank you. It wasn't as hard as I thought it was going to be to pour those drinks in that spit-tune. I needed to find that out. I know I can make it now."

"James, anything happen?"

"She came and talked to me but she never said anything about what he meant. I'm sorry."

"It was a thought, I'll have to think of something else. Thanks you two. Gabe let's head to town."

We headed to town and stopped by the doc's. Tom was awake and talking.

"Jason, I'm glad to see you. Doug told me you brought some more men in. I sent a telegram to the circuit judge and he is wondering what has happen around here. You are stirring up a hornet's nest. I went out and talked to Sam about all his men attacking Emily's ranch and other things around here."

"Things need to be stirred up around here. There has been a lot of good men that lost their ranches to the same man that are stealing their cattle but we have to prove it to the judge. They shot me too but my men lost their trail in the rocks. I thought it best not to report it 'til my arm was well."

Tom said, "Johnson said that they must had done it without his knowledge. I told him it has been too much happening that it was going to fall back on him if it didn't stop. Then I got shot. When I get out of here I'm going back out there."

"I don't want to see you get killed I have a plan. I'll tell you and no one but us three will know. If it happens the way I have planned we'll have them."

The marshal agreed to stay out of it until we could see if Jason's plan would work.

"That might work. Emily might have to testify in court and some of her men and you Gabe also so they can be put away I'll have to see what the judge says."

"There shouldn't be any problem with that. We better head to the bank and get the ball rolling."

The street was bustling with people now with no clue to what was happening around this town. They didn't know that the trouble was keeping this town from attracting more people. More people would create more business and more people could start up businesses that would create more competition and lower prices for them. We walked in the bank and went up to the teller.

"I want to draw out all of Emily Truman's money out of this bank. I have her permission. Here's her note. Her money will be safer at home than a corrupt bank."

Jason said it so loud so everyone would hear what was happening.

"For this I have to talk to Mr. Jordan would you wait a minute?"

"We'll wait but just a minute."

The teller disappeared into Mr. Jordan's office and Mr. Jordan appeared right away. All the people around us were just staring and trying to hear more.

"What seems to be the matter here Jason?"

"There are rumors around the area about this bank."

"Would you come in my office and we'll address this matter?"

"Gabe, you think we can trust him in there?"

"With all these people around I think we can go in his office. He wouldn't do anything in front of people. He may be like Johnson's men that only shoot people in the back."

"All right we'll talk to you in your office."

As we went in his office I looked back and people were lining up at the teller's window. After five people left the teller knocked on the door.

"Yes, what is it I'm busy."

"I know sir, but I thought you should know look at all the people lined up at my window."

"So what?"

"They're all closing their account and you know what that means if this gets around town. We'll have a rush."

"I'll be back. See what you've done. This is all it would take."

"Take for what?"

He stormed out of the office. We could hear him try to explain to the people in a calm voice. He seemed to know what to say in this situation.

"Gabe, you think he's mad."

"Just a mite it looks to me."

Things seemed to quiet down. But Jason knew people would go out and spread the rumor. Mr. Jordan came back in his office and sat in his large chair behind his big desk. He had to take out his handkerchief and wipe the sweat off his baldhead.

"See what you could have cause by talking like that. Now let's get down to business. What were you talking about?"

"Right, Gabe we heard that you have been loaning out money or should I say giving out money with no paper work to show where the money is going. Then you have had good written note with other people that start getting their cattle or horses stolen after the note is sign. Then this other someone sells the stolen cattle and horses and buys up the ranches for less than they're worth before you can foreclose on the ranches. Then he gives you money for starting this scheme. But you know it's just a rumor. Ask Sam what can happen when rumors get started. He's an expert on that subject. Now we would like to have Emily's money out of this bank."

"You know I make loans out and people pay it back. I don't know where you heard such an accusation like that."

"Does that mean that you don't have enough money to pay us? So Gabe it looks as if the rumors are true."

"I could give you all the money but we would be nearly out of money."

"Well, all that you have to do is go to your partner and get another big bag of money from him. Now if you don't mind we have other business."

He kept wiping his baldhead or the sweat would fall in his face.

"I'm not stopping you from your business."

"Yes you are. We're waiting for the money. Are would you rather me go and send a telegram to the state board of banks and they can come and audit you. I may do that anyway. Are you can use all your money that someone has been paying you over these four years since you came here."

"I'll get the money."

He left and came back with the money. He started counting the money. It was all there. He had a bag to put it in. We walked out of the bank.

"Gabe, you take this to Emily and tell her to hide it for now. We may put it back in the bank later. I'm going to see if Jordan goes to visit Johnson. It might take a while. I think the money will be all right 'til Jordan tells Johnson. Call all the men in close to the house in case they attack the ranch. I hope to be able to warn you."

"This is an enticing prize for them. The deputy should have some men close by if you have time to warn him."

"You get going."

I left Jason in the street near the bank and rode to the ranch with the money. I put my one ability to see other places when I needed to. It was working fine. I got to the ranch. Emily was on the porch.

"Come in the house Emily."

"What do you have in the bag?"

"All your money."

"What? Why?"

"Jason is trying to draw the crooks out of hiding everything. Mr. Jordan seems to be a part of it. This nearly broke the bank and we started a little rumor like Johnson started about you so Jordan has to make a fast move to get some money."

"Where's Jason?"

"He's in town to see what Jordan does. Now you have a hiding place for this?"

"Yes, no one knows about it except me not even Lilly Ann or Zack. John built a small room over here."

She walked to a wall and pushed a piece of wood up on top of the frame of the door to her room and a small door, about four feet high, opened up and we started in with me carrying the money. As we bent down, Emily had a little trouble cause the baby was really showing now, but she made it in. It was a very small room about four feet by four feet. We barely fit with the other things that were in there.

"I don't understand why, but I have trusted you since you came here and I looked in your eyes. They reminded me of John's eyes. I never told anyone that. Since that day I have always felt safe when you and Jason are near me and Lilly Ann has told me the same. John put some things in here that would look valuable to us and no one would look any further. Look here. John didn't trust banks."

She moved some of the things and pulled up a small door in the floor. There was a small opening to put the real valuables in; it was only about one foot by one foot.

We put the money in and closed it up and placed all the things back on top of it and left the room. I took Emily outside and I rang the dinner bell and kept ringing it until the men came up to the porch even Evan from the kitchen in the bunkhouse.

Evan said, "Gabe what's wrong with you it's not dinner time yet. I just put it on the stove."

"I know, men Jason thinks we might have an attack soon but we don't know how soon so he wants you to watch everything close and come a running if you see any movement coming our way. He's going to try to warn us before it happens but we can't count on it. I don't have to tell you to be sure to carry your pistol and have your rifle with you at all times. This might end our troubles for good. If you see anything warn as many men as you can and get here and ring this bell we need to protect Emily and her baby and Lilly Ann. So go about your work for now and be on the watch."

They went about their work after going to the bunkhouse to get armed.

"Gabe, I'm worried about Jason and Lilly Ann. She's at school and she'll be riding on the road home by herself."

"Jason can take care of himself and I'll tell Tab at dinner to go to town with me and we'll get Lilly Ann home alright and we'll take her in tomorrow if need be. You just rest and don't worry. Things will work out. Gene and the men will be back any day now and your ranch will become busy with so many people that they won't come near. They're the kind that will do things behind your back but not in front of witnesses. I'll stay close by until Tab and me go to town. I'll get Zack to stay with you."

"I'm going to lay down for a while. You stay on the porch if you want. I'll feel better."

I stayed on the porch and could see Jason in town watching the bank for Jordan to make a move. Then the men came in for dinner and I went to the bunkhouse. I talked to Tab while we were eating.

"Tab, we need to go to town about three to get Lilly Ann from school. Emily is worried that they might try to take her."

"I'll come in by three and we'll head that way. Tell Emily not to worry. You know when I first came here I didn't know if I would like it but I like working with the horses and the men we all get along with each other. Jason is a great boss. Emily I can't say enough about her. She doesn't really know what she has with that ore that they found. I've seen it happen in other town if it is done right it will be clean and help this town after that devastating war. Gene is a good man and will keep the operation on the right path."

"I better go to the barn and get my horse saddled and take up to the house. Zack can I talk to you."

"Sure thing Gabe."

"With all the goings on around here we haven't got to talk like we used to when we first came. How you getting along?"

"It wasn't long ago when it was just Emily, Lilly Ann and me around here. But we were just barely hanging on to this ranch and now we have all these men and things are getting fixed up and this new bunkhouse. I'm helping Evan with the kitchen work. I liked John but he's gone and I see how Miss Emily and Miss Lilly Ann look at Jason and I see how he looks at them. Gabe, I'm glad they will one day make a good family. I think it is all for the best."

"Zack, would you come up and stay with Emily at three Tab and me are going to get Lilly Ann from school and Emily doesn't want to stay alone."

"Sure will be nice to get to talk to Miss Emily like we use to."

"Zack I know that Emily would like to talk to you anytime."

"I don't know. Now with the baby coming and you know with that horrible rumor."

"You come up to the house about three and stay with her. You can see for yourself that she needs to have you to talk to. She knows that rumor was Johnson's doing. You were right about him."

At three in the afternoon Tab came riding up to the house and Zack came up from the bunkhouse. Tab and me left for town. This part of the country has come to grow on me and it seems that I have been here before. I must leave when this assignment is done for I am not from this world anymore. I will be on to another assignment with or without my wings. This is the first time since my death that I have felt that way. A big bell went off in my head again and then a second time. I looked around then at Tab.

"You hear that Tab."

"Gabe, don't start that again. Someone might think you're crazy. If I didn't know you better I would say you were."

We rode up the street and there by the marshal's office was Jason. We rode over to him.

"What you doing in town Gabe?"

"Emily was worried about you, but she sent us in to take Lilly Ann home. She was afraid they might try to take her. Any move yet."

"Not yet but the bank will close at three. So maybe then he'll make a move. The bank has been busy all day with people coming out with money. He has to be short of money I'm also keeping an eye out for Billie to make a move."

"We better get to the school. Will you be back tonight?"

"If I don't tell Emily not to worry. He might go out to Johnson's ranch tonight late or send Billie. He may even get up early and go out there before the bank opens."

Tab and me waited for Lilly Ann to get out of school. She came out and saw us and hurried over to her horse.

"What's wrong is ma all right. I've been worried about her and the baby."

"She's also worried about you. That's why we're here to escort you home my lady."

"Oh Gabe, but I'm glad you came Tab. We can talk on the way home."

Lilly Ann asked. "How old are you Tab? I'm fourteen almost fifteen come January."

"I'm seventeen and almost eighteen next March."

"That means you are only two years and ten months older than me. That's not much."

"That's the way I had it figured in my head."

We rode up to the front porch and Emily and Zack were talking.

"You have a good talk Zack."

"You bet Gabe, this woman is so kind to an old one-armed man. I tell you."

"Well Zack we only made it that four years because of you and Lilly Ann told me that you didn't trust Sam."

"Jason is still in town keeping a watch on things. He said not to worried if he don't make it home tonight."

Tab spoke up, "Mrs. Truman may I come up here tonight after supper and sit on the porch with Lilly Ann and just talk. You can sit with us. It's nice and cool tonight. I can watch you and you can always count on me in case of trouble."

"Emily, he is really fast with that gun of his. He sure saved us that one day in town."

Emily looked over at Lilly Ann and she was smiling.

"How old are you Tab?"

"I'm seventeen and will be eighteen next March."

"How come you are working on a ranch and not in school?"

Lilly Ann said, "Oh ma, you ask to many questions. We're just sitting and talking."

"No, Lilly Ann I don't mind. Your mother has the right. She just wants the best for you. To answer your question, I was in school until the eleventh grade. Then these outlaws came to the town we lived in Independence near Kansas City. They robbed the bank and my parents were coming out of the general store when the bullets started to fly. My parents were killed right there on the spot. I was alone and I bought a gun and started practicing with it until I was good, really good then I went to Kansas City where I met Bo and Gene. I've never killed a man and I hope I never have to but I will if someone tries to harm any of my friends. And everyone here is my friend. I'm not dumb just ask Gene when he gets back."

"Tab I am sorry for your loss. Lilly Ann and I know about the loss of a love one so yes you may visit with Lilly Ann on the front porch and I will be happy to sit with you."

"Thank you ma."

"That's all right. Tab seems to be a fine young man."

"Thank you Mrs. Truman I'll get cleaned up after supper. I better get back to work now before Jason tans my hide."

We laughed and he went back to work. Jason and me were still taking supper with Emily and Lilly Ann but tonight Jason was still in town. I could see him by the marshal's office. Then Jordan came out of the bank and went to the saloon and came right back out in less than five minutes and went home not far down the street. Jason now moved so he could keep an eye on Jordan's house and the saloon. We ate supper and Tab came up to the house all spruced up and knocked on the door. Emily answered the door.

"Have a seat and Lilly Ann will be out after she is ready."

I was sitting on the steps of the porch when the door opened and Lilly Ann came out with her mother. Tab and I stood up and this wasn't the young girl I knew that wore pants and a shirt that was a little too big for her. This was a young lady wearing a pretty dress with her hair up in a bun not a ponytail. We all sat on the porch and the two young people were talking and Emily and me were down a ways so the young people could talk alone. I could hear some of what they were saying.

She was saying, "They have to sit out here."

Tab said. "She just cares about you and I respect her for that and I know all you two have gone through."

That is when a shot rang out in the dark of the night and then another.

10

I got Emily in the front door before the second shot came. I saw that Tab had pushed Lilly Ann down and stood over her with his gun out.

"Gabe, get her in the house and keep them down."

Lilly Ann crawled to the door and I got her inside. By now the cowhands were out of the bunkhouse with their rifles in hand. They were mounted and out in the dark toward where the shots came from. Then a series of shots could be heard up in the hills beside the house. The men rode in with two bodies hung over their horses.

"This was all that there was so this wasn't what Jason was expecting so we still have to keep our guard up."

"Lay them out over by the barn and cover them up until morning and take them to town."

Tab said, "You know Gabe not anyone's been hit except Jason and I think those men were just mad. I think they're still just trying to scare us. I don't know why. They should know we aren't going anywhere. I better get to the bunkhouse. Tell Emily and Lilly Ann that I had a pleasant night even with what happened."

I could see Jason still watching into the night when I saw Jordan come out of his house and go to the back and come back in his buggy and he stopped in front of the saloon. Billie came out of the saloon and got in the buggy and they headed out of town. Jason mounded up and was a ways back from them. I could see that Jordan went up the road leading to Johnson's house. Jason went up to where we had watched from two nights before. Jordan pulled up to the house and they both got down from the buggy. The door of the house opened and Johnson came out and they were talking there in front of the house. Jason moved and stumbled over one of the tumbleweeds that had blown into his path in the dark. The three looked in Jason's direction and Johnson sent a man to see what it was. The three went in the house. Jason ran toward his horse and stepped in a hole and fell. The door of Emily's house opened and Lilly Ann came out. I lost the image of Jason as Lilly Ann spoke to me.

"Gabe, ma wants to know if you want some lemonade to drink before you head to the bunkhouse?"

"Sure, tell Emily I'll be right in."

I searched my mind but the images had left my head. I was upset for I knew Jason was in trouble. Then a voice came in my head. I recognized the voice. It was Peter.

"Gabriel, you can't say anything to Emily. This part is up to God. He alone will decide the faith of Jason and your faith in him. You can pray to God tonight that always helps. But I repeat do not say anything. If you do you could get more people killed."

I went inside and sat with Emily and Lilly Ann and had my lemonade. It was hard and then I had an idea.

"Emily, I think Jason will need all our prayers tonight. Could we pray now together?"

"That's a great thought. Gabriel, will you say the prayer."

"Emily, I think it should come straight from your heart. That will do the best. Always speak what you feel deep inside."

We held hands and Emily looked up to the sky.

"Dear Lord, I loved my John so much, but you took him from us and I know you had your reason. I know he is helping you in some way but Lord this new man has come into our lives. Jason has found his way deep in my heart and I admit this to you and my daughter that I love him. Wherever he is please protect him from any evil that might come his way. Bring him home to us safe. Thank you Lord, our lives are in your hands. Amen."

Emily hugged Lilly Ann and they both were crying. As I left for the bunkhouse I heard Lilly Ann say.

"Mama, I love him too."

The next morning the men put the dead men on their horses and took them to Doug at the marshal's office. Tab and me rode in with Lilly Ann. We watched as she went in the school then we looked for Jason around town. I saw Jordan go in the bank. I didn't see Billie but it was to early for her to be out I thought but then I saw her come out of the rooming house and go in the bank. I had to know.

"Tab, let's head to the bank. See that woman, I know that she and that banker knows where Jason is. If she leaves town we'll follow her."

"You sure, I don't know how she would know anything."

"She was with Jordan the other night at Johnson's ranch and Jason had been watching those two since then. Now he's disappeared. Let's go."

"I've never seen her except dressed for work. She looks different with that normal dress on."

We went in and watched her storm in Jordan's office. I pray that I can hear them.

"Bill I won't have anything more to do with this. So many men have been killed and all for money. You better tell Sam he better leave that woman to her life. She's had enough pain. You better get out before this blows up in your face or I won't let you come visit me in my room anymore."

"You and I can't get out we're in it to deep. Just hold on awhile longer and we could be rich and go off together where no one knows us."

"Was that cowboy dead last night he hit him pretty hard?"

"No, Sam is going to hold Jason to get what he wants from Emily."

I told Tab, I'm heading back to the ranch. Would you stay in town and watch both of them and see if they leave town and follow them. Be careful and don't get caught they may already have Jason. I'll be back when Lilly Ann gets out of school."

When I got to the ranch Gene, Bo and Jay were back. They were unloading two pack horses into Gene's office.

"Hello Gabe, Emily said that you were in town and Jason was watching someone."

"He was yesterday but this morning he wasn't around. He said not to worry that he might be following someone. I think he can take care of himself. Did you have any trouble Bo on the trail?"

"Should I tell him Jay?"

"Go ahead Bo, but don't tell Emily I'm afraid she'll get to upset."

Bo started, "We were ten miles from Kansas City when three men rode up at night. We thought them to be friendly. Then I make a bad mistake and told them we were getting Gene's laboratory equipment and head back to Joplin. Then it happened. They said that we were the ones they were looking for and started to draw their guns. Mine and Jay's hands had a cup of coffee in them. I yelled to Gene to get down and Jay and my coffee went flying and we drew a split second after they did. We buried them on the spot. I know not to trust anyone from now on like Jason said."

"At least you made it back safe. Gene if you go out to get some samples you take Bo and Jay with you. We are still being attacked. Last night they shot on the porch where Emily and Lilly Ann were and Tab was on the porch talking to Lilly Ann. The men got them and took them to the undertakers this morning. So be careful."

Bo said, "Well I'll be, that boy, I'm out working and he's here courting that pretty young lady. Good for them. He needs someone good in his life. I'll have to tease him a little. All in fun."

Gene said, "Can we go up to the house. I need to talk to Emily about the ore."

"Now that Jason hired a cook she has a lot more time to rest. Let's go."

We walked to the house and Emily came out and sat in the swing.

"I don't think they will shoot at us in the daylight with the men coming and going."

"I don't think so, it's not their way of doing things."

"Emily, I have all my equipment here now. I sent for two of my friends that know more than I do. I told them about the discovery and about the trouble but they said that wouldn't stop them. They should be here by Thanksgiving. I hope you don't mind. We'll get this mine going in a few weeks. We'll have to hire some local men that you can trust."

"That's alright with me but with the trouble I'll worry about you men out there on that mountain. It will be dangerous but I know we can't let them stop us."

"Emily, good men have always ran into trouble when bad people want to take what they have. I can tell you if we do this right you can become a wealth woman. I know from what Jason has told me. I don't think money means that much to you but you can use money for the good of others. I'll get back to my room and get everything set up for when Guy and Eugene get here in a couple of days. I'll get Tab and Bo to help me start digging and see what we find."

I rode out to the pond that was back in the hills not too far from the ranch. It was there that I tried to focus on what had happen to Jason. It started to come to me but not clear. I could see a shack out away from anything. Then it became clearer. There in the corner of room was Jason struggling to get lose from the ropes that bound his hands and feet. No one seemed to be around. I left and headed for town to get Lilly Ann and see what Tab had seen all day. I came into town and there was Tab leaning against the corner of one of the buildings.

"Anything happen?"

"She came out of the bank and went to her room and then came out dressed for work and went to the saloon. Jordan left and went to the diner and ate. It seems that they only do their dirty deeds at night when they can't be seen."

Lilly Ann came out of school and we headed for the ranch.

Lilly Ann said. "Gabe I think something's wrong Jason hasn't been around in two days and I think mother knows something has happened."

"You hear me, don't say anything to Emily but I think that Johnson might have him I don't know. Tab you set with Emily and Lilly Ann tonight more to protect them. I don't think you'll mine that job."

They looked at each other and smiled.

"No, sir I surely won't mind. "

When we got to the ranch I waited for Jay and James to come in for supper. They might know of a shack on the ranch that I had seen. I looked up.

"I'm sorry Peter but I can't wait around and let Jason die or beaten to death. Maybe God can help me in some small way. I'll hope you understand. He is my friend."

They rode in from different directions and washed up to eat.

Jay said, "Look at us James washing up. I sure do miss Emily's cooking."

"Yea, but Evan's cooking isn't like Emily's but it is good."

I said, "I want to talk to you two after supper. I think we are going to have a job to do tonight. It has to do with Jason. Try to think of an old shack somewhere on the Johnson's ranch where no one might be near."

"Alright Gabe we'll be ready. You think he's been taken? Don't You."

"Tonight we'll go and we'll see what happens."

We headed over to Johnson's ranch.

"There are some old line shacks out a ways back in the hills that aren't used much. We can start there. If it were daylight there wouldn't be any problem. We use to have men out late at night just to watch for rustlers. Now I know that they were afraid of the same thing that they were doing."

We wound in and out of some hills and came to a stream. We stopped to water the horses. There was some noise to the west of us. We led the horses toward what we heard. We saw that down in a small valley there was a campfire and three men around it. We watched for a time to see what they were up to when we saw another man ride in out of the night and go up to the fire to warm his hands. Then one of the others rode out. They got their bedrolls off their horses and lay down by the fire. We mounted up and made a wide berth around the fire. We had to keep an eye open for the one that left camp.

James said, "I think there is one of the line shacks over this way. We rode up slow watching for that lone man.

"You two stay here. I'll be right back."

I left my horse away from the shack and worked my way down the small hill. It was dark inside. I couldn't see anything through the window so I went to the door and slowly pushed it. There was a loud creak from the door. I looked fast inside and there was nothing. I left the door alone and hurried back to my horse. I got back and we headed back further into the hills.

"Is there one with a creek or pond around it?"

"How do you know what to look for Gabe?"

"I don't know it just came to me in a dream."

"Mean we're out here following your dreams in the dark. Was it dark in your dream."

"No it wasn't dark. Don't make fun of me bear with me for a while. Now is there one like that."

"Yes, seems like about a mile from here up this way."

Jay led the way slowly. We moved among the cattle as we moved closer to the shack. The cattle stirred and made a little noise but not enough to disturb any cowboy in his bedroll. It was getting late it must had been two in the morning.

"Is it soon?"

"Look I see a light over to the right."

"Let's all go in. There wouldn't be a light if there wasn't anyone in there but it may be a line rider."

We tied the horses and worked our way down the small rise we were on. There was some noise from a small creek on our left. The trees were large around the pond and the branches were hanging over the shack as we could see when we got near. There was a horse tied beside the shack.

I said, "That looks like Jason's. Let's not rush in, it could be some kind of trap."

James went to one window and Jay to the other. I went to the door. I turned the handle and pushed the door. It gave and swung open. There in the middle of the floor was a chair with Jason sitting in it with his hands and feet tied and a gag in his mouth. Jay and James came through the door as I reached Jason. I took the gag out of his mouth and Jay untied his feet and James was at his hands. His face was full of cuts and bruises.

"Glad to see you boys. Let's get out of here they send someone in every hour and they just left about five minutes ago."

"They left your horse out back. Ours are up on the rise."

Jason limped out to his horse and we hurried up the rise to ours and Jay and James led the way.

"You need some help."

"I'm alright, just get me the hell out of here before daylight."

We came up to where the campfire was and moved around it as fast as we could. Then we heard a ruckus behind us, as we started moving faster. We now could see the first light of day and we were still on Johnson's land. We could see a little better now so we stepped up the pace. Then there was rifle fire coming at us as we neared the road leading out of the Johnson's ranch. They didn't stop and then there were bullets flying all around us. Jay and James took out their pistols and started firing back. There were six men on our tail. We were now up to full speed. They kept firing and James and Jay fired back. Then two hit the ground. I felt a bullet fly by my head then one caught me on top of my shoulder. The sun was now coming up and we didn't slow down as we turned on the main road leading to our ranch. Then another one hit the ground hard. They continued to pursue us as we turned into our ranch road. They kept up and kept firing. I was sure that our men could hear the shots being fired by now. As we came around the next corner we saw six of our men coming our way at full speed. I yelled.

"Get them they're still on our tail. We slowed our pace as our men passed us and rounded the turn. We heard firing as if a war had started. Then three men came back. Bob said.

"They're hi-tailing it back to where they belong."

As we rode on up toward the ranch the other three men came up and Jan said.

"We got one more but the others got away."

"Let's get to the house I got some explaining to do. How's Emily? I was worried."

I said, "She's doing good but she was worrying about where you were. I didn't tell her we went looking for you."

The men rode off and Jason yelled.

"Thank you men. I'm glad to be home."

They waved back as they headed to the bunkhouse to have breakfast.

"Jay is Gene back to."

"Yes, we didn't leave him. He wouldn't let us. I'm just glad we made it out of there."

"Me too, how you know where to look?"

"That man right over there. He said he had a dream where you were. I don't know, that's what he said. I better get back to eat and get some sleep. He kept us out all night. When you get time Gene has some telegrams for you."

I said, "Tab would you come up and take Lilly Ann to school."

"Sure thing, Gabe."

"What's that all about?"

"I thought they might take her so we have been taking her and going in when she gets out."

As we neared the house Emily and Lilly Ann were on the front porch shading their eyes from the eastern sun. We got off our horses and Emily said.

"Where have you been? We heard shooting. Are you alright?"

"I was kind of tied up and you did hear shooting and I am all right now that I'm back with you two. Emily and Lilly Ann came down the steps and into Jason's arms. There right in the sunshine with nothing to hide and right out in the open Jason gave Emily a real kiss for the first time and she excepted it and hugged him and then he gave Lilly Ann a great big hug.

"It's good to be home. I bet you have breakfast ready. I can smell it. Gabe let's go eat."

He had his arms around both of them at the same time as they walked up the steps and into the house. They looked very much like a family. I washed up and headed in. As we ate breakfast Emily said.

"What happen to your face we need to clean it up?"

"Johnson's men did this to me. They were trying to make me tell them where the money was and when I sent a telegram to the banking board. They said that they killed Gene and that mountain of iron was going to be theirs. They said they attacked here and killed half the men including you Gabe. I didn't say anything except call them names that you wouldn't want to hear. I knew they were lying when they said they killed you Gabe. I know about that."

We finished eating and Emily took Jason out on the porch when Tab rode up with Lilly Ann's horse.

Jason said, "Tab you be careful we just had a small war out on that road."

"Yes sir, I wouldn't let anything happen to this little lady."

They rode off down the road.

"Emily, what's that all about?"

"She likes him. And he likes her. He's been sitting up on the porch with us at night. They just talk like we do. He was here when they attacked us. He protected her and me. They didn't kill anyone it was them that was killed. There you're all cleaned up. At least your wounds and now you get to the bunkhouse and take a bath and get some sleep. Jane will be out soon to help me with that pile of bed linens that is right over there."

Jane rode up as we went to the bunkhouse.

"I'm Jane, I can tell you must be Emily. What you need done?"

"Come up here and have a cup of coffee and some sweet rolls."

"I think I'm going to like this job."

I heard Emily laugh as we walked in the bunkhouse. It was sure good to hear her laugh again.

When Jason woke up he came into the kitchen where Gene and me were having coffee. Well Gene was mostly having his coffee. Then Zack came over.

"Good to have you back Jason. I haven't seen Emily so unhappy in a long while."

Gene said, "Jason I have four telegrams from different sheriff's and different towns. They all talk about Mr. Johnson and Mr. Jordan. Here they are."

Jason sat there and read all four. He read them two or three times.

"How could two men dupe a whole town for five years?"

"You forget this nation was at war and people wanted someone or something to believe in. They seem nice and protective to a lot of people."

Zack said, "Mr. John knew, Emily said he told her to watch him and then I came about five years ago and I saw something wrong. Even Lilly Ann could see it. I don't think we knew what was wrong just that it was wrong."

"Look here this one says they spent two years taking money away from old people with the ideal that some water in a bottle by drinking it every day would made them young again. They took in over $50,000. This one says they took in over $100,000 by selling land out in the semi-dessert to men that wanted to farm that it had been dry for so long it had to rain. The third one was a fake bank that promised that if they didn't take their money out for five years they would be rich. They left after one year. That took in $150,000. The fourth said that they sold people on the ideal that if they paid them $200 that they would be protected against anything that might happen in their life. They would see to it. This ended up making them $200,000."

I said, "Then they came here and put some part of some of their plots together to work here. They added stealing and got a local girl involved. I know he was trying to marry Emily to get his hands on that ore and be happy and rich. He may have had John followed and murdered in the pretense of war. I don't know how we could prove that."

Jason said, "Now what can we do about it? He has to be stopped."

I said, "We'll take these telegrams and show them to the marshal. Maybe he can arrest them both. If we go on his ranch he will have the right to kill all of us and get away with it. That maybe the last resort we have."

"Then we'll go in tomorrow and see what the marshal can do."

"Gene, you been out there yet."

"While you were asleep Bo and Tab went with me out to dig some more to get some more ore to test. When my friends come we'll dig down more and really get going. I am testing the sample as we speak. You know I'm not afraid of getting dirty. We dug down further than we had before and the samples you brought to me in Kansas City were just off the top. It could be a lot different than those. I guess from the limestone that was down there I think that there is quite a bit more lead than I had thought and less iron."

"Does that make a difference?"

"No, just different kind of mining. We could get some off the surface but not as much as if we went deep in the mountain. I'll know more when I get the test results and when Guy and Eugene get here we'll go even deeper. I have been thinking if we could ride out about a day or two so we could meet Guy and Eugene. Just take Bo and Jay and Tab just to make sure they're safe. I know you have enough here to deal with but Mr. Johnson may have found out about my friends coming."

Jason said, "I'm glad you said something. Thanksgiving is a week away so two days before you take three men and go find them. I think we can handle the trouble here unless Johnson amounts a full out attack on us. I'll head to town tomorrow and show these telegrams to the marshal and see how he's doing. I know he wants to get out there but I think he knows that Doug is too young to handle it by himself."

I said, "Tab went to get Lilly Ann at school. They should be back soon. I'm going up to the house and see how Emily is. She shouldn't be left alone for too long this close to the baby."

Jason said, "I'll come with you Gabe. Gene come eat up at the house and we'll talk more."

"I will it's about time to see what the test results are from the ore."

Jason and me walked up to the house and Emily was on the porch. She was fanning herself.

"What's wrong Emily? I said.

"It's just too hot for this time of year. Here it's just a week away from Thanksgiving and it's still hot."

Jason said, "It is a little warm and that kitchen doesn't help."

I sat down on the porch and Jason went to Emily setting in the swing and kissed her and said as he sat beside her.

"Do you think you should cook Thanksgiving dinner for everyone? It may be too much for you."

"I'll be alright I'll have Lilly Ann to help me, she's out of school that day, and I'm sure Evan will pitch in. He seems to love to cook."

"There comes Lilly Ann and Tab. Gene will be up to eat. You think it's alright for those two to be alone."

I laughed, "Jason you sound like a father."

"I'm sorry Emily it just concerns me a little and I said it out loud. I like Tab and he's a good kid." Emily was smiling.

"It's alright Jason. I think I understand."

Gene came up for supper. Lilly Ann served the meal and let Emily rest. She was really a good daughter and was looking forward to her mother having the baby. I think she can't wait to take care of her little brother and sister. I already had the word from up above what it was going to be but they wouldn't believe me. For some unknown reason I was anxious to see her babies. Gene spoke up as we were eating. He seemed to had been holding in something.

"I just have to tell you. I'm so excited and I need to have it verified by Eugene and Guy you understand but I think you are sitting on a mother lode of lead. It doesn't sound as exciting as gold or silver does but I think in the long run it could bring you as much wealth."

Emily said, "I don't know what to say. When will you get started mining?"

"As soon as it's verified we can start a small operation. As we get deeper we will have to cut some timber for shoring up the walls so it won't cave in. After we get down a ways I'll contact some men that buy raw ore to refine it. It has to be separated from the other minerals. That could bring some more money in. There could be some copper and zinc and small amounts of gold and silver. Sometimes the gold and silver is in such small amounts that it's not worth the trouble of separating it from the copper or zinc. I don't want you to get to excited about that part."

"Will it interfere with the horses? I still love the horses. I used to ride with John and we would look out over the land and see the horses running up the hills and down the valleys. It was so beautiful. Since I knew the baby was coming I hadn't ridden."

Gene said, "Your property is large enough to operate both if it is done right."

I said, "You know Emily I think you should think about making Gene your general manager of the mining operation."

Jason said, "You know Emily I think Gabe has a good point. I know about running a ranch but nothing about a mine."

Emily said, "That sounds reasonable to me. Gene, you are very knowledgeable about the ores and you sound like you wouldn't want to destroy the land. We would have to start small until the money started to come in. The money we got from the sale of the horses was great for us but it sounds small for all you are describing."

"I thank you for the vote of confidence. I had always dreamed about a mine like this. You are right we will start small I know about the money with the war not too far in the pass. The future does look bright for us once Johnson is out of the picture. His ways are going to be the thing of the pass. I will take care of the land as much as possible."

The rest of the evening we sat on the porch and there was a cool breeze in the air. Jason had his arm around Emily and Lilly Ann didn't seem to mind at all. We were away from Jason and Emily so I asked Lilly Ann.

"Lilly would you mind if your mother and Jason got married one day. It looks to be a sure thing, but I think Jason needs a push towards that. I would like them to get married before the baby's arrival."

Lilly Ann said, "You mean it, that is a short time."

"I know, but you have a way with him. I see it he trust your judgment."

"I'll see what I can do."

Gene said, "I'm heading to the bunkhouse and tell Bo, Jay and Tab we'll be heading out toward Kansas City. Good-night."

I said, "Lilly Ann don't you have some dishes to do. Come on I'll help you."

"Oh Gabe." I pointed to the couple that Emily and Jason had become.

"Oh, you know you're right. Mother, Gabe and me are going to do the dishes."

"Fine Lilly Ann you two have fun."

We looked back as we entered the house. They were holding hands and looking in each other's eyes. I don't think either one of them realized it but Jason other hand was on Emily's stomach.

11

The next morning Jason and me took the wagon to town to get supplies and take Lilly Ann to school. We left the wagon in front of the general store and watched as Lilly Ann went into the school. Jason gave Mr. Jimson a list to fill for the ranch and some extras for Thanksgiving then we headed to the marshal's house. Tom's wife, a short and plump woman, told us that he had already returned to work.

Mrs. Whatson said. "I tried to get him to rest another two days. He is determined to get the ones that shot him. You may catch him before he and Doug head that way."

"Thank you Mrs. Whatson."

We rushed to Tom's office. He was loading his shotgun and rifle to the tee.

Jason said, "Tom look at these before we leave. You can get a warrant from the judge."

Tom said, "One thing you're not going. Doug and me will take care of this."

Tom started to read the letters and as he got through with each one he just looked away in amazement.

"I'm headed to the Judge and show him these and get a warrant we can search through all his paper work and the banks also. I'm wiring for the bank examiner today. I won't go out there 'til I hear from the bank examiner and get a warrant."

"Tom, they nearly killed you last time you went out there. You need some help let us come."

"No, it makes me so mad that they have ran over this town and took away so many good men's ranches right under my eyes with the help of Jordan at the bank. I should go arrest him but it would warn Johnson. I don't think Jordan is as dangerous. He can wait."

"Alright, but you know where I am if you need our help. Gene and some of the men are going to meet some of Gene friends that are coming from Kansas City. Gene's the geologist we hired to look at some rock we found. I wouldn't let anyone know about this. It might get back to Johnson and Jordan might leave town."

Jason and me left for the ranch after loading the goods in the wagon. I didn't realize that we spent that much time in town but Tab stopped us.

"Emily was worried about you two and sent me in to see about you and pick up Lilly Ann."

"It's that time already. We had a time with the marshal. I just hope him and Doug can take care of Johnson. Bring Lilly Ann home as fast as you can. I don't know when all hell will break loose. It won't be long I have a feeling."

Tab said, "I'll get her home."

He rode off toward town and we went to the ranch. My work was almost done. I had another month and less than a week to get Emily and Jason hooked up for good and to get the ranch secure for Lilly Ann's generation and beyond. I think I've come along ways but had a lot further to go. I spoke to Jason.

"Remember what I told you a few weeks ago."

"About what? You have an opinion on just about everything."

"Emily and you. I've noticed and Lilly Ann has to, that you two are getting along so well."

"It seems that way. She doesn't refuse my kisses. I don't know how you get me talking about things I would never discuss with anyone. I might as well tell you, somehow you'll know anyway. We talk out on the porch at night. She thinks I'll feel different about her once the baby comes. I don't know why she would think that. I think about John and

I know she does to. Maybe she thinks that John will come between us. I have told her that wouldn't happen but she must still have her doubts."

"I know she loves you she admitted it to God in her dinner prays when you were missing and so did Lilly Ann."

"I don't know what to say. Right after the war I didn't think I would ever think about any woman like this and settle down in one place. Now I can't picture me anywhere else in my lifetime. I would be happy with just the ranch and raising our kids to take over the ranch one day."

The rest of the way home we were quiet. We got to the house and unloaded the wagon. Jason looked at Emily and at me.

Jason said to me. "How could I not always love her? She's in my blood and deep in my heart forever."

Emily said, "What are you two talking about?"

I said, "Nothing, just some men talk."

Jason said, "The marshal is going out to Johnson's with a warrant. He won't let us go with him. I feel a little uneasy about it. I just hope word of it doesn't get back to Johnson. I have a feeling that someone in town is in with them besides Billie."

The men worked Saturday and we got in some cold weather that night and woke up to some frost on the ground. The raids on the horses and the cutting of the fences had stopped. Of course there were more men around now to see to it that it wouldn't happen again. I think now that we had discovered the ore on the ranch there was a larger stake than horses. Johnson had been trying to get the ranch by Emily not being able to pay her note at the bank. We went to church Sunday morning and all of us had to wear our coats and when we got to the church all that the women could talk about was how long until Emily had the baby.

Emily said, "Doc says it should be around Christmas."

Mrs. Whatson said, "That's just around the corner with Thanksgiving this week."

Mrs. Simms said, "I bet you're going to need some baby clothes."

Emily said, "If it's a girl I still have Lilly Ann's."

"What are you going to name it?" Mrs. Jimson asked.

Emily looked at me and said. "If it's a boy we'll name it John Gabriel Truman and a girl will be Susan Gene."

I looked at Jason and he winked at me. We sat and listened to Mr. Simms sermon. Some of the men came with us but most had stayed at the ranch but Zack never missed a Sunday. The marshal was there and after church pulled Gabe and me to the side.

"I'm not going out to Johnson 'til Friday after Thanksgiving. Something is wrong."

"What you mean?"

"I showed the judge the telegrams that you gave me and he wouldn't give me a warrant. He said that all those incidences happened in other states and we had no proof of any wrongdoing. Billie has been at work for a few days. So Doug and I are going to investigate for a few days. I thought I'd keep you informed."

"Thanks Tom, I'm still willing to go if need be."

We got back to the ranch and to Emily's surprise and mine Evan had gone to the house and fixed Sunday dinner for everyone. We had so many men now that we had to bring a table from the bunkhouse.

Emily said, "What's all this Evan?"

"I just wanted to show my thanks for all that Jason and you do for us."

We all sat around the table and Emily said the prayer. We served ourselves and talked as we use to when there was only five of us and then eight and now thirteen. After dinner some drifted off to the bunkhouse for Sunday was the only day they had to do what they wanted. Gene and Jason and me talked about Gene leaving in the morning. I asked.

"Jason, what was that all about naming a boy's middle name for me?"

Emily said, "That was my idea. I don't think without you we wouldn't be together and I would have to sell this ranch to Johnson. No one would have known about him."

Another loud bell went off in my head. There was no sense in asking cause I knew no one heard it but me. Supper was a small affair for Evan had out did himself and we all ate from what was left over. I was going to watch and see when Gene met his friends. If they ran into trouble there wasn't much I could do with my limited power but I could watch. That night I left the three on the porch alone to talk as a family would. That night a vision came to me. I saw me as having the power of helping in small ways when I was not there. I didn't know the small ways I could help but that I was grateful for any help I could receive.

The next morning Gene and the men left toward Kansas City. Jason and me were going to take Lilly Ann to school these next three-day since Tab was with Gene. We left her at school and went to see the marshal.

Jason said, "Is there anything new Tom?"

"Not yet but I sent Doug out to keep an eye on Johnson's ranch to see if he makes a move of any kind. I saw the judge going out of town but I didn't follow him. If he goes out again I will be on his trail cause there was no reason for him not to issue the warrant."

"Sounds like you have it covered so we better get back to the ranch."

The days were getting colder. We had gotten more weather in this morning. It was near freezing now that we were near Thanksgiving. It had been warm for so long that there was talk of us not having a winter but that ended with this last weather. It was over casted all-day Monday and that night it dropped below freezing for the first time. The men were sure glad for the new bunkhouse and the two stoves that kept us nice and cozy. That night I lay in my bed and I could see Gene around a campfire getting ready to turn in. Then it went dark and I was asleep. Sometime during the night I was woken with a start and Peter was on my mind.

"Look Gabriel, something is happening, you can use your new power by thinking about it hard. Only certain things that it will work on and you won't know until you try."

My mind searched the area I could see and there near the campfire were four figures. They must be asleep and the next moment my mind focused on the dark away from the fire. There were three more dark silhouettes. They were hard to make out who they were. Then I saw them draw their guns. I went back to our men and concentrated hard and I could see Bo and then Jay and Tab wake up and draw their guns and look around. That's when I looked back at the other men in the shadows and this made Bo and Jay look their way and three shots rang out toward the dark from three different guns. They hurried over and looked at the dead men and holstered their guns. Gene came running out and looked at each man.

"These are not my friends. My friends wouldn't wear guns that I know of."

Bo said, "I don't know but someone or something woke me or we all may have been dead. Look the hammers are cocked on their guns and ready to fire."

Tab said, "We better keep a lookout. I'll take the first watch."

I was happy with my new power; I put my hands together and said.

"Thank you lord for granting me the power to help my friends. Bless you Peter."

I rolled over and slept all night and woke up the next morning all refreshed. It's not like me to sleep all night it can get to be a habit. Evan had breakfast ready and the men were eating when I joined them.

Jason said, "You know I had a dream that three men tried to kill Gene and the men last night but they woke up in time and shot the three. What you make of that Gabe?"

"I wouldn't know about such things. I just know I slept all night and am hungry."

"What's wrong with you Gabe? I never seen you take more than a couple of bits."

Zack turned to Gabe and said. "You know Gabe I woke up and you were sitting up in your bunk and I swear you were praying. I have nothing against praying but in the middle of the night. Somehow I think you know about Jason's dream."

"I don't know what to tell you Zack. Only that you and Jason think too much. Jason we better get and take Lilly Ann to school."

We went to the house with Lilly Ann's horse and she was out on the porch.

"You ready to go already."

"Yes, mother is still in bed. She woke me up during the night. She didn't feel good so she is still in bed."

"Gabe, would you get one of the men to go with you. I'm going to see about Emily. I may have to take her to the doc's."

"I will, I'm sure it's alright."

So Bob went with us to town and Lilly Ann went in school and I told Bob to head back to the ranch I would be fine. I went to see the doc.

He said, "She has a month until the baby. She had this trouble with Lilly Ann. Just tell Jason to keep her in bed today and have her drink a lot of water and food if she feels like it. She should be all right tomorrow if not send someone for me and I will come out. She should not be riding in a rough old wagon until after the baby comes and some weeks after."

I was riding back to the ranch when I felt like someone was behind me. As I looked around I saw two men on my trail and they had their pistols drawn and started firing at me. I remembered my power so I rode fast and concentrated on them and the bullets were flying all around me as I rode faster. I concentrated harder and the firing stopped. I looked back and I saw their guns go flying off into the underbrush. They pulled up and turned around fast and didn't bother to stop and look for their guns. I rode up to the house and Jason and Emily were sitting on the porch. She was still in her nightclothes and robe.

"Are you all right? I stopped in at docs and he said you were like this with Lilly Ann for you to stay in bed and drink lots of water and only eat if you feel like it."

"Really now, I'm all right. I just had a stomachache. I must have eaten too much at Evan's dinner party yesterday. I think that is all it was but I'll take it easy today and eat less at Thanksgiving. Speaking of that Jason you better go out and get a turkey this morning so we can start to prepare it for Thursday. I tell you I don't know what to think. I have two men worried about me. Now get going."

We went to the east on the ranch just to stay away from Johnson's ranch and I told Jason about what had happen.

Jason said, "They are stepping up their small attacks. They're the only ones getting hurt. How did you get away?"

"They seemed to have dropped their guns in the brush and turned around."

"Gabe, I don't know what to make of you. One day we might find out something about you. Right now we have a turkey to find so be quiet."

We left our horses tied and walked a ways off and there was a little creek. Water was running down stream making a gentle sound that was pleasant to the ears. The leaves were falling all around us and the gentle breeze was making the brown leaves swirl around us for now it was late fall. We had our coats on for it was cold for late fall. We were up a bit on a small hill above the creek. We were there for about an hour when we heard a strange noises. It was a sound that I had not heard that I could recall. It sounded like a small animal that was caught and couldn't get away. Then I saw it. The bird had brown feathers hanging down to the ground and a baldhead with a red gullet hanging about six inches below its mouth. It kept making that sound over and over again. It was now drinking out of the creek and raised its head like he heard something. It was Jason's rifle as he squeezed the trigger and a bullet came out the end of the barrel and hit the bird in the head. We ran down and Jason raised it up in the air by its legs and yelled.

"Gabe, we have Thanksgiving dinner. Let's get back so Evan can start on it."

Jason carried it to our horses and tied it to the saddle horn and we rode back to the ranch.

"Jason, when are you going to ask Emily to marry you? I know she would. She knows that you love her. Have you told her how you feel about her?"

"Gabe, you're my friend but you're so nosey about our business. I've just got up the nerve to kiss her and now you want me to ask her to marry me."

I know you're happy even with all the trouble we're having. I see the brightness in your eyes and the happiness in hers. Lilly Ann thinks the world of you. Why don't you ask her what she thinks about it?"

We rode on and got back to the bunkhouse.

Jason said, "Evan here's Thanksgiving dinner."

"You could have gutted it out there and plucked all the feathers."

"You want me to cook it too?"

"That would be nice." He laughed.

"Gabe, would you go up to the house and stay with Emily just to make sure she's all right. I'm heading out on the range and see how the horses are doing and make sure the men are checking on the fences."

Jason rode out and I started up to the house. I stopped and could see in my mind that Gene had met up with his friends and they were heading back this way. When I got to the house Emily was dressed and was puttering around the house.

"What are you doing? You should be resting like doc said."

"I'm all right. I know how I feel and doc's way in town. I'll call for him when I know I need him."

"Emily, would you marry Jason if he asked you?"

"Gabriel, that's kind of our business. Anyway we have time. He may be waiting until the baby is born. I know you mean well but."

"I do mean well. I just may have to leave and I want to see you two together. I can't say much but my boss may pull me out of here anytime and I care a great deal about you both and Lilly Ann."

"You can't leave we need you like we need each other. You brought us together and we care about you. You can't leave."

"I will have to one day and you won't even remember that I was here."

"What are you saying? We'll always remember you. Yes I would marry him. Are you happy now? I said it, but please don't tell him."

That afternoon Bob and me went in town to bring Lilly Ann home. As we rode in I saw the marshal was riding out of town toward the Johnson ranch and the judge was out in front of him a ways. We went to the school and headed back to the ranch. When we returned Jason was back at the house. We ate dinner and sit inside the house this evening for it was colder than during the day. I guessed that everything was all right with Gene cause I didn't have another wake up calls.

In the morning Emily seemed to be all right so Jason and me went to town with Lilly Ann and we went to talk to the marshal.

I said, "How's it going with the investigating?"

"I followed the judge and he did go to Johnson's ranch. I met Doug out there. I watched for a while and left. Doug stayed and came in at night. I sent him back out this morning."

Jason said, "Gabe was attacked yesterday on his way back to the ranch. He got back safe but we're getting tired of these attacks."

"I know, we'll see by Friday what happens and I'll go out there."

We left the marshal and I told Jason.

"I have a hunch, let's go out and see what Doug is doing?"

"The marshal told us he was watching what happens at Johnson's."

"Let's see how well he's watching and what he's doing?'

I could see a little hill overlooking the house and where Doug was. I told Jason.

"Up this way, we can see over the whole place and Doug. Let's leave the horses down here."

We crawled up to the top of the hill and we could see all the roads leading in and out of the ranch and there was Doug. Jason looked and said.

"Gabe, he's supposed to be watching the ranch and look he's right on the road. Anyone can see him."

"Just watch and see what happens."

We lay there watching for an hour and nothing. Then we could see someone coming. Jason got his telescope out and watched as the rider came closer.

"That's the judge, look he stopped and is talking to Doug. They're laughing and he patted him on the back. What's that all about?"

"Just watch, notice he doesn't have anything with him when he went inside."

We watched and then another rider came up in a buggy. We recognized that buggy. It was Jordan's and Billie was with him. Everybody was in there about two hours.

Jordan came out carrying a bag that he had not taken in and no Billie. Then the judge came out with a bag. Johnson came out and waved at them. A man came out carrying Billie's limp body and Johnson pointed toward our ranch and the man put the body on a horse and headed out. Jordan stopped and opened the bag and handed Doug, we saw it, some money out of the bag. Then the judge did the same thing. We saw money as it was handed to Doug. They were gone.

I told Jason, "Let's go."

"Why?"

"We have to get to the fence line of Johnson's ranch and ours before that man get over there."

"You don't think they would do that?"

We headed to the main road and I tried to see, in my minds power from up above, where the man was. I could see he was heading to our ranch all right but slow. Like there was no reason to hurry. Hopefully waiting for dark. We turned up our road and everyone was eating.

"Boy's we don't have time to explain but get out to the fence line to Johnson's ranch and look for a man leading a horse with a body on it and don't let him get to our side. Shoot to kill."

Jason and me headed that way and the men had mounted up and were right behind us. We spread out all up and down the fence line. We could see each other. Then Jan yelled out.

"Jason up this way. He's coming."

"I changed my mind. Get him alive and we'll take him to Tom in town. Let him cut the fence and then we'll get him."

As he cut the fence and came on our ground the men jumped him before he had a chance to draw. They tied him up and got him back on his horse. Jason said,

"Fix that fence and go back and finish your meal. Gabe and me are taken these two to town. Thank you boys."

Jeff said, "You don't need our help boss?"

"No, but if we don't show up at supper come a running. Tell Emily we're in town."

"Sure thing." Tim said.

We headed to town leading the man that had probably killed Billie that was dead on the other horse. Both horses had Johnson's brand on them. Billie seemed to have been chocked. That's why we didn't hear a gun shot. Jason asked the man.

"What were you going to do with Billie's body?"

"Bury it. What do you usually do with a dead body?

"I wouldn't bury it on someone else land. What's your name?"

"That's my business."

"We'll see what the marshal has to say about it."

"Johnson will get me out. He always does."

"You better shut up or we might have two bodies to bury."

As we came up the street heads turned as we went by and stopped in front of the marshal's office. We took the man in but Tom wasn't there. Jason untied him and locked him up.

"Stay here Gabe I'm taken Billie over to the undertakers."

"Make sure people see the brand on the horse."

I watched as people came around and looked at Billie's body and the horse's brand and the undertaker came out and Jason showed him the brand. He helped Jason carry her body inside. Jason came back and we sat and waited for the marshal.

Jason said, "No one seen Tom since noon. I told anyone that asked and the undertaker what had happened out on our fence line. That we caught the man, that is in jail, cutting our fence and he was leading that horse with Billie's body on it coming from Johnson's Ranch."

Jason left a note for Tom and left it sticking out of the wanted posters. After we got Lilly Ann from school we passed by the bank and Jordan was standing there with the judge looking our way as we headed out of town. Emily was waiting on the porch for us.

"Where you been? I saw you and the men rush by. Gene just got in an hour ago with his friends. He had a strange tell about something that happened out on the trail."

"We went in town and left a present for Tom all wrapped up. Where is Gene?"

"He took Guy and Eugene with Bo and Tab in tow. They took more shovels and picks with them. They didn't want to wait until Friday. They thought no one would work tomorrow. They wanted to dig deep enough to get some new readings. They said they could do test tomorrow. A strange lot they are."

"I'll get with them later. I'll just be in the way out there."

Jeff came up.

"Jeff can you take our horses to the barn."

"Yes, Jason how did it go in town?"

"Tom wasn't in but I got Billie over to the undertaker."

Emily said, "What's this Jason?"

"Come inside I'll tell you."

We four went in out of the cold.

"Emily, I didn't have time to stop. Johnson was having a man bury Billie's body on our land. We stopped him and we took him and Billie to town but Tom wasn't in his office so I left a note explaining everything and took Billie's body to the undertaker's."

"You weren't hurt."

"Ma, does he look hurt?" Lilly Ann said.

"I guess not, I just worry. I already lost your father and I couldn't stand it to lose Jason to."

I looked at Jason and he at me.

"I told you didn't I."

"Gabriel, what's that supposes to mean?"

"Nothing Emily."

"Well then come and eat before it gets cold."

Lilly Ann and me did dishes and Emily and Jason sat on the divan in the front room. It was pass dark when someone knocked on the door. I opened up the door and there was Gene and his two friends.

"Can I talk to Jason and Emily?"

"Come on in."

"I'm sorry Emily we get so excited about this find. I forget myself. Jason, Emily."

He turned toward the two other men that came in.

"This is my friend's Guy and Eugene." Jason and Emily shook their hands.

"We have more test going on in my lab. We dug down about twenty feet. We should be able to tell if it's like the surface or more or less of the same ore. We'll head to the bunkhouse."

Emily said, "Be sure you bring Guy and Eugene to Thanksgiving dinner tomorrow."

"We will be here. I'm sure they will, even we love to eat. We just get evolved talking to each other. We'll talk more after tomorrow. Goodnight."

Jason said. "You know I saw Evan already starting to bake some pies and cakes. The men are going to have a filling day."

Emily turned to me. "Gabriel, has Evan got the turkey plucked."

"Yes, Emily he has."

"Jason tomorrow morning after breakfast would you send Evan up here. Have some of the men help him bring the bake goods up here. This is exciting."

12

The next morning was like a battle that was not far off. Evan had the oven full and the firewood box kept having to be filled to kept the oven hot. Evan had refused to fix breakfast he said.

"Jason, I have just too much going and Emily is waiting for me. The men can eat some beef jerky if they are too hungry but they will get their fill at dinner time I assure you."

"Alright, Evan we'll start taking some of these deserts up to the house. Jay, you and Bob come help me."

Evan turned to me. "Tell Emily I'll be up to the house as soon as these pies come out of the oven. Tim, take the turkey and Jason help Emily put it in the oven. She has no business lifting that heavy bird. You boys keep that firewood box next to the stove filled if you want to eat turkey for dinner."

As we went out the door Jason turned to Evan and said.

"Yes sir, boss." Everyone laughed.

Then Evan yelled out. "That's right today Emily and me are in charge."

I even had my hands full of goodies as Jason knocked on the door with his foot. Lilly Ann let us in and Emily was already in the kitchen with the stovetop going.

"Lilly Ann where can we put these pies and cakes?"

"Over here on the table."

Jason took the turkey from Tim.

"Emily, Evan will be up when the pies are done. He sent the turkey."

"Good, Lilly Ann open the oven for Jason. Jason, just shove the turkey in the oven and close the door. Be careful the oven is really hot.

Jason said, "Yes dear I won't burn myself. Jay you and the others move the furniture around in the front room and go get two tables and help Evan up here with everything he needs."

"Sorry Emily, we are going to take over the front room today. There are so many of us now that we are nearly outside. Are you sure you're not doing to much?"

"Jason, that's fine you can take over the whole house as long as we're together. It's been a lonely home these last four years. I couldn't be better this makes me happy."

I stayed out of the way while the men moved the furniture around and then they went to get the tables and benches from the bunkhouse. Everything was in full swing. Evan was in the kitchen helping Emily and Lilly Ann. The men had the tables finely arranged to Emily's satisfaction. All the rest of the men were in the bunkhouse for there was a freeze last night. Gene and his friends were in his lab working with all the ore they had dug out of the ground. They said that a tunnel was starting to take shape.

I returned to the house and the long table was filling up with all kinds of food. I saw Evan, Lilly Ann and Emily took off their aprons. Then Emily said.

"Jason, it's time, ring the dinner bell."

Jason went out on the porch and as he rang the dinner bell a sound went out to all the men that told them it was time to come together and eat. The men washed up for they knew not to come to eat in Emily's home without being clean. Gene's friends saw that and they washed up. Everyone wiped their boots before entering and once inside they removed their hats and coats and hung them by the front door. The house was nice and warm because of all the cooking and the fireplace was full of logs and a roaring fire was going strong.

Emily said, "Welcome to our home on this special day of Thanksgiving. We all have our own reasons to be thankful. So before we are seated let each one of us tell the Lord why we are thankful. I'll start and then Jason and on around the table."

Emily started with, "Dear Lord we are very grateful for all this food and all these fine men that have gathered here today and especially for Jason and Gabriel for this would not be without them and for my John that is up in heaven helping you in some way. Jason."

"Lord I don't talk to you as much as I should but thank you for bringing me to Emily's ranch to help her and Lilly Ann, whom I have become to love both very much. Thanks for all the men that have helped, and Gene and his friends that have got the mine started. Lilly Ann"

Thank you for Jason and Gabe whom I have become to love like a father and uncle. Just tell my daddy I will always love him until I died. Gabe"

"Thank you Lord for giving me a chance to be with this wonderful woman and her pretty daughter short tail. Please help Emily have a beautiful healthy baby. Amen. Zack."

"Thank you Lord for bringing me here five years ago and for Emily and Lilly Ann and Jason and Gabe and everyone that has accepted me and treated me with respect. Amen"

Each and every person said a prayer about what they were thankful for and then came the last one Bob.

"Thank you oh Lord for all this wonderful food staring us in the face. Amen"

We all had to laugh a little even Emily.

Evan brought out the turkey and sat it in front of Jason and everyone sat down to a great thanksgiving dinner and waited for Jason to carve the turkey. For it was a custom, in a good wholesome family, for the man of the house to carve the turkey and pass it out. Everyone knew that Jason had become the head of this now large family.

The many people that were on this ranch now started talking and eating and there were so many of us that the noise became loud at times. I think the new men now knew what kind of good people they had come to help.

The rest of the day was just being full of talk among friends and the men going back for more pie and cake. The turkey and dressing with mash potatoes were all gone now as the men came for more that night. I knew there were other things on Jason's mind as he sat and talked to Emily and Lilly Ann. It was now four weeks or less until Christmas and I knew that was my dead line for helping get matters around here resolved.

The next morning Gene came over to Jason and me as we sat eating breakfast and sat with his plate. Then came Guy and Eugene to the table.

Gene said, "You know Jason. I know money is tight for Emily but I don't want to take your men away from their duties for the ranch. I think with Bo and Tab's help we could use four or five more men to help with the digging down and cutting timber for support for the shaft of the mine."

"Then your samples were good going deeper down."

Guy spoke up. "The samples were very good as we expected. We only need to make exploratory tunnels in different directions to find the main vein. There are large pockets all through the mountain but there should be a main source and we need to find it."

Then Eugene jumped in the conversation. "We should send off for some specialized equipment that we don't have. It will make the profits come faster."

Jason said, "Gene you are in charge of the mine. I say let's do it if it looks that promising. You three go to town and send off telegrams and get what you need and you hire the men you need and get this thing in full swing."

Gene said, "We also will send some telegrams out to some people that buy ore so we have a place to sell it. That means wagons and horses to deliver the ore or we could look into the railroad they are coming this way now that the war is over. I know I think in the future but later when the profits start rolling in it would make since to have our own processing plant and deliver the finish product."

Jason said, "Gene, I like a man that thinks of the future but come up to the house later and we'll discuss the money part with Emily. Right now you three go to town and get the men you need to get this mine started. Hears fifty dollars to send off the telegrams. Get good men and offer them what you think is a fair wage for mine work."

"I'll start a ledger that will detail all the money spent and the wages for the mine and Emily and you can see what's going on."

"Just make sure that they don't have anything to do with Johnson and his men. Maybe someone that has been fired by him like Jay, Bob and Jan were."

We all headed for town but for different reasons. As we came into Joplin Main street Gene and his men went to the telegraph office. Jason and me rode up in front of the marshal's office. When we walked in Doug was sitting behind the marshal's desk and the jail cell was empty.

Jason said, "Where's the man we brought in the other day for killing Billie?"

"The judge let him go he said there wasn't enough evidence to warrant a trial."

"Where's Tom? He was going out to Johnson's ranch to arrest him for keeping me tied up out at his ranch and beating me."

"The judge told Tom to leave Johnson alone. There was no need. But Tom went out there anyway this morning. I don't know what he planned to do after the judge told him to stay away. I just stayed here to look after the office."

I said. "Jason look here's your note from the other day. I don't think Tom's even been here."

"It looks that way. I know he looks at the wanted posters every day. Doug why did the judge and Jordan give you money the day you were watching the road to Johnson's ranch."

"What money? I don't know about any money. I just watch the road and report to Tom."

"Come on Gabe, no since in staying here. We better look for Tom. We'll be watching you. We know you saw Billie when they carried her body out of the house."

We left the office and took our horses down the street a ways and watched. Sure enough Doug came out and went to the judge's office. Then both came out and went to the bank. Then they all came out of the bank and looked around and went to the livery. As we waited I spotted Mrs. Whatson walk in the marshal's office. I headed that way and left Jason to follow the three men. As I walked in Mrs. Whatson was looking around the office.

"Mrs. Whatson have you seen Tom? We have been looking for him."

"I've been looking all over town for him. He left yesterday after Thanksgiving dinner. I begged him not to go but he said he had proof to put a stop to all that has been going on around here. I haven't seen him since."

"Did he tell you what the proof was?"

"I'm afraid not. But I'm so worried. He doesn't stay away this long."

"Jason and me are going to try to find him. You go home and get some rest."

I left and got back to where Jason was just in time to see the three come out of the stable and head toward Johnson's. As we started to follow we saw Gene come out of the saloon with four new men and head to the ranch. We headed for the rise overlooking Johnson's ranch. They went in and came out in a short time and headed back to town. The cowboy that we had taken and put in jail was standing next to Johnson. Johnson pointed to the north and the man took off in that direction and we followed. We followed for two hours. He finally went in between two huge boulders and disappeared. We stopped and waited to see what would happen next. As we waited I spotted two lookouts on top of the hill overlooking the area where the man disappeared. It was getting late. Jason said.

"I know Emily will be worried but we need to find out if Tom is in there. He now is the key to this."

"It's better if we can end this as soon as possible."

We still waited for two more hours and then the man came out and rode away. But we didn't follow. We stayed put until dark. The two men came down from the boulders just before dark and went into, what Jason thought was a canyon and disappeared. We left our horses where we were and went in between the two boulders and was surprised after about a hundred yards. There had been enough space for a horse to make it through. It came out into a wide-open valley. We could not see much for it was dark now except for a light at the far end of the valley. We could not see anyone as we crossed the open space toward the light. There was a creek that we almost fell into as we neared what was a cabin with smoke coming out of the chimney and Jason spotted two glows in the dark coming from lit cigarettes. The back of the cabin was backed up to a rock wall with the sides and front exposed. The two guards were not fully aware of their surroundings because who could have found this valley. We worked our way around to the side of the cabin that had a window in it. As we peered in the window there was Tom tied to a chair like Jason had been. His head was hanging to the side as if he was unconscious. There was another man inside near the door in a chair leaning against the wall asleep. Jason peeked around the corner of the cabin. Jason whispered.

"Gabe, if you can get their attention by walking out front they might turn their backs to me and I can hit them over the head and knock them out and then get the one inside."

I stepped out from where we were and the men turned toward me and drew their guns. Jason jumped out behind them and came down full force on their heads with the butt of his gun. They crumpled to the ground and Jason turned toward the door as it opened and the man inside started to step out to see what he heard but it was too late as Jason hit him with his shoulder full force. The man flew back into the room and hit his head on the wall across the room. Then Jason was up and punched him in the stomach as he tried to get to his feet. Then Jason hit him again under the chin and he was out. We drugged the two outside in and tied them up with the ropes that Tom was tied up with. Tom was beaten pretty bad and wouldn't wake up. We found a lean-to on the other side of the cabin with the three men's horses under it. We had to tie Tom's hands to the saddle horn and his feet to the stirrups. We mounded and headed for the mouth of the canyon. We went across the creek and then found the crack in the rock and went through. We found our horses and I led them and Jason led Tom's horse all the way to town. We were going to our ranch because we didn't know whom we could trust in town. Jason told me.

"Gabe, I'm headed to our ranch. Take the two horses to town and bring Tom's wife to the ranch on a horse."

I went to behind Tom's house and knocked on the backdoor of the house. Mrs. Whatson came to the door.

"Gabe, what are you doing here so late?"

"We found Tom I don't have much time to explain. Jason took him to our ranch. If you could get in some pants I have a horse out here for you. Emily and you can look after him. He's beat up pretty bad. We didn't want anyone to see we have him. We don't know who we can trust here in town."

"I'll be just a minute and we'll be on our way. I can ride a horse well."

We were out the back door and on the horses and out of town in twenty minutes. It was dark but I knew the way by heart now as we turned up the road leading up to the house. As we stopped in front the house was lit up and Jason came out and we helped Mrs. Whatson inside. She said as she rushed to his side.

"How is he Emily? He looks so bad. Who did this to him?"

Emily said. "I think he'll be fine. It might take a while. This is Lilly Ann's room. You can stay here and help take care of him."

"Jason, why did you bring him here instead of to the doc's? You can trust Doc Wade."

"I know we can but someone might be watching his place. I'm going to send Jay to town early this morning to get the doc. Everyone will think it's about Emily. I'm sure he'll be fine. He must not have told them what he knows and what evidence he has or he would be dead like Billie. I know she wanted to get out of this mess and now she's dead. I know that

Johnson had this done like he did to me. Mrs. Whatson we know Doug is in on some part of this. So don't trust him."

"Doug, Tom has trusted him for years. You can call me Janet. If you don't mind."

Emily said, "Here's some water and rags if you could clean his wounds, Janet. I need to get some rest."

"I'll be glad to Emily. Go get some sleep."

I sent Jay to town early to get the doc and told him to make any kind of noise that he could about Emily needs the doc and to get him out here fast. It was seven in the morning when doc and Jay came in. Doc looked at Tom and turned to Jason.

"Jason you should have brought him to town. Janet you're here to. What's going on? Who did this to him?"

As I explained what had happened doc looked him over. The head wound and his gun hand had been smashed. He was still unconscious.

"For sure he has a concussion that's why he hasn't woke up. His hand is bad real bad. That must have been done at least a day ago. There are two ribs broken and are close to puncturing his lung. He needs to stay here cause if we move him that rib might go into his lung."

Emily said, "They can stay here as long as need be."

"That's fine just let me know when he wakes up. Soon as that happens get some food in him and don't let him move. I know Tom he'll want to go after them right when he wakes up. I better get to town."

Jason said, "Doc, don't tell anyone, not even the judge, Jordan or Doug, that Tom's out here just say that Emily had a little trouble with the baby."

"I won't say a word."

Jason and I went to the bunkhouse and sat with Gene.

"Gene, you better take more men when you go to the mine. There has been an attempt on the marshal. Have the ranch men watch outside while you all are inside working."

"I sent off the telegrams about the mine. The equipment will be here in ten days. They had it right there ready to go. The mine people will send a man out. I don't think they think it is anything but they will when their man sees what we have."

"If we have to we'll buy the wagons and take the ore where it needs to be taken."

"We'll see what happens. That will be down the road a ways yet. In time the money will start to come in and we can see what our options are."

Jay, Jason and me went to town while the women took care of the marshal. There wasn't too much that could be done, without an all-out war, until Tom could tell what he had found out. Jason was just going to irritate them all that we could. War maybe the only way to get rid of the irritation. We walked in Tom's office and there behind Tom's desk was Doug.

Jason said, "You've seen Tom yet."

"I can't seem to locate him. Johnson saw Tom out his way but he seemed to have disappeared into the night. You wouldn't know where he is and his wife is gone also."

I said, "You know Doug it seem funny that you were watching Johnson's ranch and Johnson saw him and you didn't. How could that happen?"

Jason said, "That's right just like when you were watching Johnson's ranch when Billie was murdered. You should have seen that."

"I don't have to justify any thing that I do to the likes of you. The judge made me the new marshal."

Jason turned to him and got in his face.

"Look boy only a federal judge can make you marshal not just a county judge. You better watch yourself or you might find yourself on that gallows with the rest of the murderers in this town. It may already be to late."

We turned our back and walked out. We walked up the steps to the bank. We passed up the teller and walked right in Jordan's office.

"What you mean just barging in here. Now get out or I'll send for the new marshal."

"You just do that Jordan. I just talked to him and I would like to get a crack at him. This isn't just one of your schemes to just take money away from people. This is murder and you are up to your eyeballs in it. Billie was last seen with you and she shows up on our ranch dead. Now Tom is missing. I'm going to prove it and you'll be hung like the rest."

We turned and walked out into the dusty street of Joplin and took our horses and tied them up in front of the courthouse.

Jay said, "Jason you really think you should go in there?"

"Jason I think Jay might be right."

"I'm mad, you just watch me. You stay out here if you want to."

Jay said, "No, I trust you."

We walked right in the judge's office.

"Jason, what you mean coming in here like this? You need an appointment."

"I seem to have one right here on my hip."

"Alright, what is it I'm busy?"

"You know that you don't have the authority to make Doug U.S. marshal when you don't know what happened to Tom. Are do you know what happened to him? Doug said that Johnson saw him and then disappeared. You were seen out at Johnson's ranch when Billie was murdered and then Tom shows up missing. You know your neck will stretch as far as the next mans will."

"I dare you with the accusations. I'll have you arrested and sent to prison."

"You just do that and a real federal marshal will show up and investigate all that has been going on around here. You and Doug shouldn't have listened to Jordan and Johnson. They were already crooks and Tom showed you the proof of that. I want to see you talk your way out of that."

We turned and walked out. Jason said.

"Jay stay in town and watch what these three will do. If you see anything happen unusual get to the ranch."

I said. "Jason you were hard on him. You told him just about everything we know."

"They have to be drawn out of hiding or they will keep on 'til they have Emily's ranch. They will use the money from the lead mine for their evil doings. I can't let that happen. Jay, just keep hidden and don't let them see you. I don't want to have to bury you."

"I would hate to see that to." He laughed.

As we came up in front of the house Emily, Lilly Ann and Tab came out on the porch.

"Jason, go out to the mine. Gene sent me to the house to protect the marshal and these two. There were four men that came up from out of nowhere and started shooting. Gene and his men made it inside and Bo and me got two of them and two got away."

"We're heading out there. Any change in Tom?"

Then I saw Janet come out of the house.

"Jason, Tom woke up for about five minutes but he didn't seem to know what was going on. I tried to talk to him but he went back to sleep. I see now all the trouble you are having out here."

"We'll be back, maybe he'll wake up later for a longer spell. Let's go Gabe."

Jason and me were careful as we came up to the mine. The shooting had stopped and Bob was sitting on a rock up a way's from the now entrance to the mine. I looked around and things seemed to have calmed down. There were two bodies covered up over to one side out away from the mine and there were two men cutting trees to shore up the mine inside and there was a beginning of three small and one large pile of rocks to the east of the mine. We went inside and there was Gene and Eugene looking at a hand drawn map of the inside of the mine. He looked up.

"Jason, Gabe glad to see you. You missed all the excitement but not anyone got hurt on our side." As he was walking a little deeper into the mine he said.

"Come on over here Guy is showing Steve and Mat what to look for and how to extract the lead and other minerals from their surroundings. It is a slow process right now but when we get the new machinery it will come out easier. You had to see that large pile outside that's the lead and the smaller piles are iron and zinc also some small amounts of gold. All of this will have to be assayed to see how much there is to each ton. The man that is coming from the company is an assayer and will give us a good estimate of what we have."

"You know Gene that was two days ago when you sent the telegram. We don't know who might have seen it. I think tomorrow I'll send Jeff and James to meet the wagons with the equipment to make sure they get here."

Bo came over.

"Gabe this is some doings. I can tell what Gene was talking about when I use to help him in Kansas City."

"You probably thought Gene to be a crack-pot." Gabe said.

"Gene I kind of did but I know better now."

"That's alright I'm use to that even my parents never understood what I was doing."

At supper I told Jeff and James to head out to meet the wagons. Tim reported that the men that attacked the mine cut the fence again and he had fixed it. We still had a horse ranch to run. I told Jan to get some supper and go to town and relieve Jay.

"Get him to tell you what has been going on and keep a good watch and follow them if they head out of town. Keep hidden and come back if you see any men heading our way."

Jason and me went to the house to have supper with Emily and Lilly Ann. As we entered the house Emily came to Jason and put her arms around him and put her head on his chest.

"What is it Emily?"

"You've been gone all day and I watch Janet taking care of Tom and see the love she has for him. I just hope he pulls through."

"I'm sorry I've been gone but there is the mine now to watch over and the attacks on the ranch. I worry about you and the baby and that somehow they could come and take you and Lilly Ann at any time. Now we know there are three crooks in town and Johnson on his ranch. They murdered a woman and Tom has some type of proof and he lies unconscious and can't tell us. I try to keep things from you so you won't worry."

"I know you do. Gabe has told me."

We were eating and someone knocked on the front door. It was Gene and he came in and sat with us as we ate.

"Gene you want something?"

"No, ma'am I ate at the bunkhouse."

"Maybe a piece of apple pie and a cup of coffee."

"Yes, that might hit the spot."

Lilly Ann went to the kitchen and brought a big piece of apple pie and a cup of coffee."

"That's so big, I may not get that down."

Lilly Ann said. "Ma still cooks like she's feeding all the cowhands. We need to get rid of it before it goes bad."

"Alright I might get it down." He laughed.

"Jason said, "I can see you like Emily's pie. There must be another reason that pulled you away from your lab."

"To tell you the truth. The lab work is done now. We're just waiting for the man from the company I telegraphed to. But I didn't tell you Jason that the people wanted money for the equipment I ordered and I thought we could take it to them tomorrow. They want it before they get here. I didn't mention it because I know how tight the money is."

Emily said, "How much is it?"

"A little over $6,000. I know that's a lot but it will come back to you when we get in full swing. I think we have that much out of the mine already. Of course we'll have to wait for the assayer."

"Jason you know where it is would you get that and a thousand more for Gene, Guy and Eugene."

"Ma'am you don't need to do that. We have a place to sleep and do our work and eat."

"I didn't expect you and your friends to do this work for free. Did we Jason?"

"No, we didn't."

Emily said, "When the mine is in full gear we want you to stay on and run the mine for us cause we have a horse ranch to run."

Jason came back and handed Gene $7500.

"I do have some ideas that could be implemented someday when the trouble is over and the mine is paying for itself. Well that's for another day. I better get to bed. We're going to get on the road early. So good-night."

"You know the future of Emily and her ranch is in your hands. I didn't know you were going also."

"Well I wasn't but Eugene and Guy can handle it around here. I'm going to take some ore and the assayer can get a firsthand look sooner."

As he left for the bunkhouse Jay came riding up to the house and stepped out of the saddle and came in the house.

"Barr, it's getting down right cold. I filled Jan in on what and who to watch for. The judge went to talk to Doug and they both went to the bank and were behind closed doors but I could see them and they were hot. They were shaking their fingers and sometime their fist at each other. They got so loud at time that the people in the bank would stop and look their way. I just wish I could have heard them that would have been interesting. Then they went back to their own offices. Jan might have to take a ride tonight."

"Tell the men to keep the guns and boots close in case we get a rude awakening tonight."

"Will do, good night Miss Emily."

"Emily, Gabe and me better get some sleep also."

Jason kissed her as he held her tight and said.

"Please don't worry it will all turn out alright. I have a real feeling that John is up there looking out for us. I love you."

"That's the first time I've heard you talk like that. I do have that same feeling down deep inside. I love you to Jason."

We left and went to bed. There was another big bong in my head. Then a voice came to me during the night.

"Gabriel you are doing fine but you have only three more weeks on earth."

"I sure could use some help with the bad men. But the ranch is almost secure and Jason and Emily are becoming very close."

Peter said. "We know that but they need to be married and the bad men gone so the ranch will be secure for future generations of Benning's."

"I know but I'm so close."

"Yes we know. It's the closest you have gotten in any of your assignments over the past 150 years. But it has to be completed. I'll tell you that tomorrow will be a very important day. Just get Jason up to the house early."

"I know it will be done. Is that all you can tell me?"

"Yes."

The night went by like a flash of lighting in the sky and I was up. I saw that Jason was already up and the men were eating. Gene and the men were heading down the road. I hurried and got dressed and Jason and me went to the house. When we knocked and went in the house both of us got a shock.

13

There eating breakfast. Emily went to Jason as I walked to the table and Janet and Tom turned. I could see the pain in Tom's face as he held his side.

I said, "Tom, what are you doing out of bed?"

Janet said. "He woke up this morning hungry and yelling about those sidewinders that bushwhacked him."

Emily looked into Jason's eyes. "I couldn't believe that he was up wanting breakfast." She and Janet were laughing.

"It's so good to have him up."

Lilly Ann told us. "He said some words to descript those men that I never heard."

Tom said, "I'm sorry Lilly but I'm so riled up and I didn't know where I was. Jason, you and Gabe get me to town."

"Dear, I don't think you should go to town doc said you will take time to heal."

"I don't have time. These men have been laughing at me for five years. They have gotten away with stealing and now murder for four years and I won't stand for it anymore."

I said, "Tom I saw the pain in your face when you turned. You should be in bed."

Jason said. "Tom I think I have a solution to this. We can start to round up some of the men that did this to you and doc can check you out at the same time. Let's get to town. Gabe hitch up the wagon and tie our horses behind it and bring it up here."

Janet said, "You think that's a good idea?"

Emily said. "Janet you need to trust these two. I think there is something special about them. Look at what they've done here since they came. Jason, you and Gabe sit and eat. Lilly Ann, please bring them some breakfast."

Gabe said, "None for me I'll get the wagon ready and get it up here."

As I was leaving I heard Tom say as I then turned on my power to hear what they said after I left. I prayed for some more powers to help these good people.

"I'll be careful. They need to see me and know that I'm out to get them at any cost especially Doug. I trusted him for a long time. I thought he was my friend."

"I hate to tell you this but the judge made Doug Marshal. I told him that he couldn't do that. A federal judge is the only judge that can do that. He laughed in my face. We were coming to tell you when we found that you had disappeared and that we already knew Doug had taken money from Johnson."

"I knew that cause I followed the judge and Jordan out to Johnson's ranch and I saw Doug in the middle of the road taken money from them when they came out of Johnsons. That's when someone hit me over the head."

"They had you in a canyon that can only be entered by a crack in the cliffs."

I pulled up in front of the house and Jason and Janet were helping Tom to the back of the wagon and Emily and Lilly Ann put a blanket down in the bottom of the wagon and one to cover him up with a pillow for it was cold this morning. I then told Jason.

"I told everyone to be on alert at the mine and along the fence line and be well armed and have plenty of ammunition."

Jason said, "Let's head to town and round up some bad men."

Janet said, "Jason I trust you. Please go slow and take care of my Tom for me."

"I will Janet."

I looked back, as we headed down the pathway to the main road, and Janet had her head on Emily's shoulder crying. We made our way to the main road to town slowly. Every bump and every hole we could tell Tom was in pain by the expression on his face. He was strong and he kept from yelling but this was just too much for him. I prayed for him to be out of pain until we reached his office. I then looked back and Tom's expression had change to one of pleasure. Tom told us.

"Pull up Jason before we get to town."

"You hurting to bad?" Jason asked as he pulled to a stop.

"No, the pain has gone for now. I know Gabe you don't wear a gun but I need for both of you to raise your right hand."

We both raised our right hands.

"Do you Jason and you Gabe solemnly swear to up hold the laws of the state of Missouri so help you God?"

"We do."

"Now let's get to my office and start to throw those crooks in jail. We'll start with Doug and take that badge off of him and get yours out of the right-hand drawer of my desk."

We came into town and Doug was standing on the porch of the marshal's office when we pulled up. Doug said as we stopped.

"Glad to see you boys come on in the office we found Tom dead out by your ranch."

As Doug went in we got down and told Tom.

"Stay down 'til we come to get you."

As we walked in there were two more men in the office and they both had on deputy badges. Doug came over to us.

"You two are under arrest."

"For what! I would like to know."

"For killing Tom and Billie."

As Doug started to reach for my gun we heard the door open and Tom was there in the doorway. Doug and the two men heads turned towards the door and I grabbed Doug and threw him against the desk and grabbed his gun out of his holster and pointed it at the two men that were starting to draw their guns.

"Drop it boys and put up your hands up toward the sky, now." Jason yelled "or you're dead where you stand."

They dropped the guns in their hands and raised them high in the air. Tom went over to Doug and ripped the badge from his chest. He told Doug.

"You don't deserve to wear this. Now get in that cell all three of you."

Tom sat down on the bunk against the wall. As Doug entered the cell he said to Tom.

"Wait until the judge finds out about this."

Jason and me locked the cell and got the badges out and put them on.

"He's about to find out. You better save room in there for him."

"He's a judge you can't arrest him just like that."

"Tom, are you alright?"

"Go ahead and get the judge and Jordan. I'm better now I'll lay down and rest."

We left and went to the courthouse. As we walked in, the courtroom was filled with people and the judge was behind his bench and was sentencing Mr. Jimson.

"You had no business with merchandise out on the walkway in front of your store. You are sentence to one year in prison and your store will be sold to Mr. Johnson for your fine of $3,000."

He hit the gavel on the top of the bench. Jason spoke as we walked up the aisle.

"Mr. Jimson you can go back to your store it's not being sold to Johnson or anyone else and judge you're under arrest for accessory to murder of Billie and abusing your office in a scheme to help Sam Johnson take over this town."

"Jason lookout."

He pull his gun and turn as two men pulled their guns and Jason's gun went off twice as everyone in the crowd hit the floor and the two men were lying dead on the floor and he turned to the judge and pointed his gun at him.

"Judge let's get to jail. Tom wants to talk to you. Would some of you take those two bodies to the undertakers and tell him to bill Johnson."

There were people all around patting us on the back as they got on their feet.

"Mr. Jimson said, "We'll get them over there and thank you Jason. They started running roughshod over this town two days ago."

The judge walked down the street to the marshal's office with his hands up and his judge's robe on. Jason pushed him in the door.

"Gabe get him locked up then we'll get down to the bank. Tom you may want to talk to the judge. I'll be back."

As Jason walked to the bank I walked out into the street and saw the two dead men being carried to the undertaker. I caught up to Jason as he entered the bank. We walked to the office of Jordan's and Jason threw open the door and we walked in.

"What's the meaning of this Jason and what are you doing with that deputy badge on. Doug's the marshal now that Tom's dead."

"You're under arrests for accessory to murder and scheming with Sam Johnson and the judge and Doug to take over ranches and the town."

Jason drew his gun and Jordan put up his hands and we walked out of the bank down the street. I saw a man come out of the saloon and head out of town toward Johnson's ranch. We walked in to Tom's office.

"Tom here's the last crook in town. We have one more."

I said, "Jason I think he'll be coming to us. I saw a man going out of town."

"Gabe would you go get the doc to come and check Tom before we have any trouble. Hurry and get back. I want to go to the general store and get some ammunition and a couple of rifles."

I came in with the doc and he went to check Tom.

Dr. Wade said. "Tom, what in the hell are you doing here? This is not good. I thought you were dead. I see you have the ones in jail that were telling everyone that they buried you out on the trail by Emily's ranch. They were to go to her ranch after Jason."

"Well doc as you can see I'm not dead just hurt a little."

"Those ribs of yours are alright. You didn't do any damage. Now take it easy. Let Jason handle things around here."

The doc left and Jason went to the general store and came back with food, two buckets of water and saddle-bags draped over his shoulder full of ammunition with rifles tucked under his arm.

"Mr. Jimson was glad to supply us with all we needed for getting him out of that mess." The judge spoke up.

"Tom you know you can't hold me I will have your badge."

"Judge you better shut your mouth 'til a federal judge gets here. I have proof that Johnson killed Billie and you three were there and tried to make it look like Jason did it."

"I didn't think I had time to get some men from the ranch before Johnson and his men came into town so I asked Mr. Jimson to send someone to the ranch to get Jay and Tim in here. We can get a badge on them that will give us three men to fight Johnson. The others I need on the ranch to protect Emily and Lilly Ann and the men at the mine."

Jordan said. "You know Tom we could use another partner. I'm sure that Sam would give you a $100,000 if you let us go and help us get our hands on Emily's ranch and mine."

Tom said, "Judge you better tell him to shut up he's just digging your hole deeper."

The judge said, "Shut up you fool."

We waited for something to happen. I knew that Emily and Janet would be worried but this had to be done if this town was to prosper.

"Gabe would you go out and watch for Johnson and his men and come a running if you see him."

I left and headed out of town leading to Johnson's ranch and found a nice high hill so I could see them coming a good ways off. I could also see into town and the road leading to Emily's ranch. It was a long wait but I saw dust flying in the air toward our ranch. Then as it got closer I could tell it was Jay and Tim. They rode up to the office and took all the horses and the wagon to the back of Tom's office and went in.

I heard Peter's voice again.

"Gabe you asked for help with the bad men. You can't stop them all together but if you think real hard you can make rocks fall off the hills around them and trees fall in their path. Hopefully that will detour them but if not it will be up to Jason and his men to stop them. Understand?"

"Yes sir. I understand."

I saw Jason run to the telegraph office then run out again. He was going down the street talking to people. Then the people would run into a building or just go home. I turned back toward Johnson's ranch and there was a large cloud of dust about two miles away. I started concentrating on a rock ledge that was ahead of them. The whole side of the hill came crashing down around them. Three horses spooked and reared up and the men fell out of their saddle. The horses ran back down the road to the ranch. Then I did the same to a group of trees and they fell across the road but they just rode around them. I saw one more chance. It was a group of cattle I concentration harder and they moved and stopped in the middle of the road and on both sides for a hundred feet. I had to get to town and warn Jason. As I mounted I saw the men's horses scatter the cattle and kept riding. I had my horse at full gallop. I rode to the back of the marshal's office and jumped off and ran inside and locked the door.

"They're coming, about a mile out. About twenty men."

Tom said, "Gabe get me to a window. I need to get them."

I said, "Tom you know what the doc said. You stay in bed and out of this. If they brake in you have your gun beside you."

Doug said from inside the cell. "Now you're going to get it. They'll shoot this place apart."

I told Doug. "Boy don't you know that you're right in the middle of the building that you think they're going to shoot up."

All five men got down on the floor.

Tom said, "Jason see that big iron bar beside the door. Put that across the door into the slots it should fit perfect. Then shut the steel shutters over the windows. There are slots cut in the steel so you can see what you're shooting at but bullets won't penetrate it. We should be safe until another marshal and the federal judge get here."

Jason said, "They said in two days. We have enough food and water but I don't want to stay in here that long."

Johnson and his men came riding up the street like they owned the street and the dirt under their horse's hoofs. They tied their horses in front of the saloon and went inside. Johnson came out of the saloon with two of his men and walked to within twenty feet of the jail.

"Tom, Jason you have some of my men in there. Why don't you let them go?"

"Not on your life and it may come down to that. The judge, Doug and Jordan are locked up to and we left room for you."

"Now you know that you don't have any proof of any wrong doings."

"I just know you had me beaten. You came in that cabin in that hide away canyon. I pretended to be knocked out but I saw you and I'll show the proof to the federal marshal and judge that are coming who killed Billie."

"You're going to make me mad if you don't let them out. We'll have to come in and get them and leave all of you dead on the floor for the marshal to find."

Jason said, "Sam you just stayed around here too long. This time your scheme isn't going too pan out. And when the auditors get through with the bankbooks you will be dead broke. I told them at the bank that your bank accounts were closed until the audit is done. But that murder is going to get you hung out there in the square."

I said, "I didn't hear a reply to that. Are you sweating a little? By the way did you have a little trouble getting into town today? That was the doing of my boss. He doesn't seem to like people that take advantage of people and murder that will send you to a hot place. You better get used to that sweat rolling down your forehead."

Johnson said, "Gabe I don't know what the hell you're talking about."

"You'll find out one day soon."

"Tom, are you letting these strangers talk for you? We've been friends for a long time."

"Sam I might have given you the benefit of the doubt but that changed when you had me shot and then beaten. Twelve men in this town will judge you in front of a real judge."

Johnson turned around and went in the saloon. I know we hit a bad spot in him. It was near dark and we saw the lanterns come on in the saloon. We sat back and ate and one of us kept watch at all times. Tom had fallen asleep and I knew that would do him good. We lit our lanterns and Doug said.

"About time."

"Yea, so they can see to shoot at you better. You noticed that there is no steel over your window. They can come up and shoot you at any time. They might think you will tell what you know."

"We don't know anything and Johnson knows that."

Jason said, "You were on the road when they brought Billie's body out of the house. You saw that same as Gabe and me did."

"You saw that?" Doug said.

The judge said. "Shut up stupid. Everything they get you to say gets you in deeper. So shut your mouth before I shut it for you."

Jason said, "You think you're pretty smart don't you judge. We saw you come out of the house after Billie was brought out dead. You may have killed her."

"I'm not saying anything."

Tom was awake and called Gabe and me over to the bed where he was laying.

Tom said, "Don't say anything to them but I know the judge killed Billie. If you can when this is over get the judge's belt off of him its evidence. I went over and looked at Billie's body and she was strangled with his belt. I just said that Johnson did it so he might let his guard down."

I said, "How you know that Tom?"

"He's proud of that belt and showed it off when he got it to everyone. The same exact marking are on Billie's neck. He strangled her that hard and the undertaker saw them and I brought over doc to verify the marking. He's seen the belt. And the judge was beating me with that same belt and Johnson just stood there watching."

Jason said, "Then we got proof on all of them if we can get out of here alive by the time the marshal and the federal judge get here in two days."

It was fully dark by now and Tim called us over to the window.

"They're starting to come out of the saloon and Johnson is in front."

"You better let them out of there before we have to kill every one of you." Johnson said.

Jason said, "Does that include your so-called partners? You really want Emily's ranch all for yourself."

"Don't you worry about that I sent five men to take care of that pregnant bitch and her daughter. I'll give them to my men they'll take good care of them."

I could see that Jason was fluming but said very calmly.

"I'm not going to kill you right now. I'm going to wait 'til I can see the fear in your eyes and get my hand on you and beat you to death with my bare hands or wait and see you hang."

One of his men said.

"Bring those women in town and I'll do them right here in the street what we used to do to Billie at the ranch and I'll enjoy that young one."

"Well, what's keeping you Jason I'm right here."

When Jason heard that he exploded and shot a single shot that went right through the man's head and he fell dead in the dirt of the street. All of a sudden the street was empty and they began firing at the jail. The bullets just bounced off the steel plated windows. Jason said to Jay and Tim.

"Make your shots count."

Tom said, "Gabe get me over to the window and get me a rifle."

"Tom you stay right there. You're hurt too bad. We can stay here for three days we have food enough."

"Right now I'm your boss so if you don't get me to that window I'll hobble over there myself."

"Gabe help him over there. And Gabe keep down and keep an eye on that window in the cell."

Tom was up at the window and the firing went on for another five minutes. Then Johnson yelled from behind a wagon.

"Jason that was cold blooded murder."

Tom yelled back. "Sam he was just protecting one of our citizen that had been threaten by your man. You should know what murder is I saw Billie's body and did you forget I was there when you and the judge were beating me."

Johnson started firing at the window where Tom was and his men were firing. Then we heard noises at the back door. They were trying to bust it in but the iron bar was across the door. Jay had taken the horses to the stable while I was gone. Our men and Tom were firing back. Johnson's men were behind hay bales and wagons and some were around corners of the buildings and then there were some on top of the buildings across the street. Every once in a while we would hear one let out a yell and then fall into the dirt. Johnson's men were getting picked off one by one. The one's that were at the back door were still banging away at it and trying to shoot through the door. Tom said.

"You men out back. If I were you I'd get on my horse and ride out of here before the other marshal gets here or you could be put on trial for accessory to murder and attempted murder. Ask the judge here. That will get you at least twenty years in federal prison."

"Don't listen to him. I will protect you haven't I always seen that you go free." The judge said.

"He won't be the one on the bench. The federal judge is coming with the marshal. They already know of the trouble around here."

The noise at the door stopped. The night went by slow but by daybreak it was still a standoff. Johnson's men went and busted down the door of the saloon. The street was littered with bodies and we saw some more wounded men being carried in the saloon.

"Tom you should get some sleep and you to Jay and Tim and you Jason. I'll keep a watch."

"Gabe, I'm too worried about Emily, Lilly Ann and the men out at the ranch."

"Jason try to get some rest remember when they told you I was dead. This is the same ploy. He's trying to scare you into doing something that will get you killed."

I kept watch and they tried to get some rest. While I was watching the sounds coming out of the saloon grew louder. I sat back and concentrated on what was going on around the ranch. I could see Eugene and the men working in the mine with Bob on guard. Then Tab and Bo were at the house protecting the women. But Emily and Janet were walking the floors. I worried about Emily the most. I saw four bodies beside the bunkhouse and then the images were gone. Two hours went by and I saw the undertaker and some men from the town come out and take the bodies away during the lull in the fighting. The wounded were helped to the docs. I knew that he would treat them but would somehow keep them from returning to the battle. I thought of one thing that I could try when they came out of the saloon. I saw that Jason had woken up and came over.

"Anything yet Gabe."

"No, but I know that everything at the ranch is alright. The men Johnson sent are no longer going to be any trouble."

"How you know? Gabe sometimes you're strange."

"Jason you know better than to ask. Just say I'm in good with the man upstairs and leave it at that."

Johnson and his ten men came out in the street.

"Jason you ready to give up."

"Johnson, it's Gabe. Why should we give up it looks to me that you have lost half of your men? You men out there don't you wonder how those rocks fell off the hill when you were coming to town and all the cattle got in your way. Ask yourself how I know about that. Johnson how would your mother Joy feel if she knew that you killed Billie and you men how are you going to get paid if Sam there is hanging from a gallows next week after his trial. You ten might be in prison. It's all up to you."

"How you know my mother's name? It don't matter now she's dead and some supposedly good men did it to her."

"I know a lot about all of you. Over there, Ted you left Texas last year because your girl had married another man while you were gone to war. Pete, you came down from Virginia because your family farm was taken away and your mother and father were dead. I know things about all of you. War is bad and it was bad on Emily that you are trying to get her ranch for Sam here. I'll say again you will never see one penny of the money Johnson promised you. His funds at the bank are gone."

Jason spoke, "We're here to make sure that he doesn't get away with this murder and beating Tom."

"Look Jason some put up their guns and are looking around at each other."

Then the shooting began again but three had walked away and we saw them mound up and leave town to the west. The shooting woke up Tom, Jay and Tim. The men started firing back and two more fell in the dirt. Johnson was safe around the corner of the general store. We had been in the jail for a day now. We had enough food and ammunition to last. None of us were hurt yet. One man had tried to shoot through the bars in back of the cell but Jason shot back and wounded him. Our prisoners didn't like being in between the two firing at each other. Dan that had brought Billie's body to our ranch yelled.

"I'll tell everything I know, just get me out of here."

Tom said, "You stay put we already know enough to hang you all. So just shut up and sat down."

The tide seemed to be turning in our favor and against Johnson. He was down to six men and Johnson and three others were the only one's firing at us now. Mr. Jimson had refused to open the general store so they couldn't replenish their ammunition and Johnson's men refused to break the door down. It was now turning dark and the saloon didn't open.

Jason said, "I think in the morning I'll open the door and go face the ones that are left."

During the night the shooting had ceased and Jason had gotten some much-needed rest. Tom was resting and I didn't need much sleep at all so I stayed on watch. The men in the cells were walking the floors because the judge knew their reign of terror in this town was just about over and they all would be paying the price for their deeds. The dawn of a new day was on the horizon and everyone was awake. Jason had just opened the door of the jail and him, Jay and Tim had stepped out on the front porch of the jail.

"Johnson, it's time to get this over with. Step out and take it like a man or stay where you are and hide like you have been doing all your life. We'll put you on trial and you can take what you get or fight now and go to hell."

Two men came out and threw their guns in the dirt of the street and raised their hands toward the sky and walked towards the jail. Then out of nowhere came two shots and the two-lay dead in the street. Johnson had shot them. Then him and his last man stepped out from behind the bank building and were walking toward us.

Johnson said, "That's what happens to people that are disloyal to me."

"Like Billie that the judge strangled with his belt on your orders."

"Yea, but me and the boys sure had some fun with her before he killed her. She wanted to leave town and take some of my money that I worked so hard to get. We showed her didn't we?"

"Your money. That was the money of the hard-working ranchers that you and Jordan had ruined. Jay, you and Tim just take care of Jess I'll handle Sam by myself."

"Yes, boss. You can have him I wouldn't dirty my bullet on him."

"Any last words Johnson?"

"You really think you can better me? I'll show you. I've been around a long time."

Johnson and Jess drew at the same time. I saw Jay's gun come up as mine was already level and my slug was out of the barrel of my gun as I heard Jay's and Tim's gun's fire. Johnson's and Jess's had just cleared their holsters as our slugs entered their bodies. Mine in Johnson's head and Jay's through Jess's heart. They both were dead in the dusty street of Joplin, Missouri. It was not a day to celebrate but a time to look to the future of this town and great country. It would be so nice if this event never had to be played out again but as long as there were greedy men in this world there would be good men to take care of them.

Even if it was early in the morning doc came over and checked the two dead men.

Doc said, "They're dead I better get over and check on Tom."

Jason said, "Jay, if you and Tim don't mind Gabe and me will head to the ranch to check on everyone. We'll come in later and relieve you two."

Then Jay said. "That's fine Jason. There's not much left to do around here. We can get some sleep cause I don't think those men locked up are going anywhere."

We went in the marshal's office and doc was checking over Tom.

Jason said, "Tom, I'll have one of the men bring Janet in town. Gabe let's get to the ranch. I'll be in later to give Jay and Tim a brake. We'll take care of the prisoners 'til the marshal and judge get here. You just get well."

"Thanks for all the help cleaning up this town."

Jason and me headed out of town on the same road we came in a short two and a half months ago. The day looked brighter than ever before and now all I had to do is get Jason and Emily together for the rest of their lives. As we rode up to the front of the house Emily and Janet came down the steps and Jason took Emily in his arms and kissed her. I told Janet.

"Tom's alright, the doc is with him just to make sure he is healing alright. Bo would you take Janet to town and she can help take care of Tom. Emily there's no need to worry about any more attacks. Johnson and most of his men are where they belong my boss will see to them. Have no fear of that."

Bo helped Janet and took her to her husband. Lilly Ann came out on the porch and said.

"Gabe who is your boss? When do we get to meet him?"

"You never mind Short Tail and it will be a very long time until you meet him. Now do you have some breakfast ready today I'm even hungry."

14

The next morning there was a thin power of snow on the ground as Gene came riding up with the wagons full of equipment and Todd, the assayer. After they ate Gene took both wagons up to the mine and all the men helped unload the equipment and get it in place before more snow fell. The equipment was heavy and it took all the men and some horses to drag it into the mine. The mine was taking shape and Todd was over looking at the ore that had been piled up beside the mine. He seemed to be like Gene even snow and the cold didn't keep him from his job when it came to rocks.

Gene said, "Todd, I have all you need in my lab to run any kind of test you need to."

Jason and I were there but we didn't know much about all the equipment but Jason said.

"Gene now that there won't be any more attacks I'm going to spend more time with you up here and learn all I can."

Gene said, "I heard about Johnson. Maybe you can find out about his ranch and if it's for sell. I told you and Emily I had a few ideas to run across you two."

"The marshal and judge should be in tomorrow and we'll have a trial. I also sent for the bank examiner to go over the banks books. He should be here soon."

"Jason I'll talk to you and Emily at dinner about my thoughts on the future of the mine. I'm sure Todd will be glad to lend his two cents worth to the conversation."

Jason and me headed back to the house and Emily was already cooking dinner. Emily and Lilly Ann came out on the front porch and Jason asked Emily to sit with him awhile. He took her hands in his and looked her straight in the eyes and said.

"Emily, Gabe and I only came here two and a half months ago. With all the trouble that we have had I didn't know what the future might hold but now that is over and maybe we will have peace around here. I know that you and Lilly Ann loved John very much. I have grown to love you both very much and I hope you both have room in your hearts to feel the same about me. I want Lilly Ann here cause she's part of you and Gabe I think helped bring us together."

Emily said, "Jason what are you trying to say?"

"It's just hard to say cause I have never felt this way about anyone before. I would like to help raise John's baby and see to it that Lilly Ann grows up a fine lady. I know that you could do this without me but I would like to be a part of your family. Emily will you marry me?"

"Jason, I don't know what to say. Yes, I feel love for you and I will say that to anyone but look at me I'm so big." There was a tear rolling down her cheek.

"Emily, I think you are so beautiful that I almost didn't ask you. I don't see what you could see in me. I just felt that I needed to ask. I'll still help you run the ranch."

"Now that's not what I meant. I will marry you if you want me."

"Want you! Why that's all I've been thinking about for a month."

They hugged and kissed each other and I shook Jason's hand and hugged Emily. Then Lilly Ann hugged Jason and kissed her mother and was crying as she said.

"We are going to have a family again. Now when are you two getting married?"

That's when another big bell went off in my head and I knew I was one step closer to helping my friends start their new life together.

I spoke up. "How about Sunday with the whole town there?"

Emily said, "That's so soon. I won't fit into much of anything nice."

Jason said, "You're beautiful in anything. I think Sunday will be good. The people will get to see a new beginning for this town."

"Alright, that will be good." Now Emily was crying and saying.

"I didn't think I would ever feel this happy again."

She turned and wiped her eyes and hugged me again.

"Thank your boss for sending you to us when we needed help. Now come on Lilly Ann before the dinner burns. Jason, you and Gabe round up everyone for dinner and we'll tell them the news."

"Gene wants to talk to us about the mine's future."

I got some of the men together with Evan and we moved the food from the bunkhouse to the main house. We were going to have a small but fine engagement party with everyone that were now family. Everyone was seated around the table and Emily said grace.

"I welcome Todd to our ever-growing family and hope he enjoys his stay here. I thank the Lord for all this food that he has provided and all of you for the risk that you have taken the last few months and hope that is over. Amend I think Jason has something to add before we eat."

"Like Emily, I want to thank you all for helping with all the trouble that has come our way. That is in the past and now with Gene and Todd's help we are looking to the future. So I have asked Emily to become my wife and she said yes."

The cheers went up and the men were saying. "It's about time we could see you two were meant for each other."

Jason spoke. "We're getting married Sunday and we would like everyone to be there. Now let's eat before this good food gets cold."

Everyone was eating and talking about everything that had been happening and what the future might hold. It seemed the talk around the table was about Jason and Emily and I could hear Gene and Todd talking about the mine and the cowboys talking about the future of the horse ranch because of the mine. I spoke up.

"I am hearing you all talking about what might happen to the horse ranch because of the mine. I think Gene might have an insight to that. I know Emily wants to keep the ranch continuing."

"Jason and me want you to know that no matter what the mine will bring that the horse ranch will continue into the future. Now Gene if you could tell us about what you might have in store for the mine. These men have the right to know I feel we are all family around here."

Gene got up. "Todd and me have been talking and he has been looking at the ore that has come out of the mine so far. He will make further test but he thinks that this is a huge find and will last into the future. Jason is going to find out about Johnson's ranch. If Emily and Jason can purchase it we will have enough room for both enterprises. I'm thinking and Todd thinks it will be worth the investment to build a smelting plant here. The ore could be processed here and be sold for more money. This will be a large undertaking and will take a few years through different stages. We can start shipping out the raw ore right away until that happens Todd's company will buy everything we can ship."

That afternoon Jason and me went back to town to relieve Jay and Tim. As we rode up to the jail there in front was a man with a suit and another man with a star pinned on his coat and Jay was talking to them. Jay said.

"Jason this is judge Blackburn and Marshal Moore. They just got in from Kansas City."

"Good to see you so soon. This is Gabe Owens."

We all shook hands and went inside. Tom had already gone to his home with Janet and doc. Judge Blackburn walked over to the cell and look straight at the judge.

"William how could you have had a part in this. I once had the greatest respect for you. Your trial will be the day after tomorrow."

"Henry don't believe anything those two tell you. I didn't have anything to do with Billie's murder. It was all Sam's doing."

"You better shut your mouth. I hear there's one lawyer in town I'm going to have a talk with him right now. The prosecutor should be in from Springfield tomorrow and also the bank examiner to go over your books Mr. Jordan and we'll find out how much you and Johnson really stole from this town and its people. I think Mr. Jimson will have a very interesting story about his trial the day you were locked up William."

"That was all a mistake. Tell him Jordan."

"Save your breath Joe Billings the prosecutor will talk to him tomorrow and get the right story. Now Mr. Moore will hire some deputies to look after the prisoners. I'm going to the hotel. Jason, could you and Gabe come in tomorrow to discuss the case with Joe? He'll talk to Tom also before the trial."

"We sure can we'll be in early. The sooner we can get this bunch out of town the faster we can get back to normal."

Marshal Moore hired two of the local men on the spot as deputies and we four headed out of town for the ranch. When we rode up to the house Jane was out front doing the laundry for the bunkhouse.

"Jason, I'm staying the night. Emily and me are going to plan the wedding. You know five days isn't enough but we'll get it done somehow. I really think I should stay until the baby comes but Emily won't have any part of it. I've helped doc deliver babies before. There is not always enough time for the doc to get here."

"I'll talk to her I think that is a good idea. I wouldn't want anything to happen to her or the baby. I'm going to town tomorrow and I'll talk to doc about it and then she might change her mind. Stay here tomorrow and I'll let you know when I get back."

Gabe and I went inside and Emily and Lilly Ann were talking.

"Jason I'm trying to talk mother into Jane staying. She has admitted that she is bigger than when I was born."

"I just have eaten more than I should have."

Jason and me sat down by Emily.

I said, "Emily why don't you want Jane to stay here with you. She knows what to do if doc can't get here in time. I don't think you want me to deliver the baby."

We all laughed and Jason said.

"We'll pay her for her time."

Emily said, "She said she wouldn't take money. It's just that I have been taking care of this family for so long by myself. I hate to have to think about depending on someone."

"Emily, everyone needs help sometimes. If it wasn't for Gabe I might have never come here. He helped me make up my mind. I'm going to talk to doc tomorrow and if he thinks it's a good idea we're going to let her stay. Is that all right Emily? It's for the best."

"It will be fine. I need to be happier. I'm going to be getting married and have another beautiful baby. I'll tell her tonight when we talk about the wedding."

"I need to talk to preacher Simms tomorrow about Sunday. I forgot today cause we were talking to Judge Blackburn about the trial day after tomorrow."

After supper we all sat around talking about the wedding and the coming baby when someone knocked on the door. There was Zack and all the men behind him. Zack had a big wrapped bundle in front of him and a huge grin on his face.

"Miss Emily, this ain't to much of a present but we all wanted to show you and Jason how much we care about you. Me and Bob made this for you after you told us you were getting married."

Emily said, "Everyone come in please you're always welcome in our home."

I brought the gift in and everyone came in and Lilly Ann and Jane got drinks for everyone.

I said, "Well, open it you two."

Everyone yelled "Jason, Emily please open it."

They tore it open and there was a big handmade baby crib. It was a real beauty.

Emily said, "It's so pretty. But it's big enough for two babies."

Zack said. "I told Bob not to make it for a baby like he was."

Everyone laughed.

"Never mind Bob I love it and the baby will look beautiful in it."

Jason said, "Thank you men we will always think of Bob when we look at it."

Everyone laugh and Bob turned red as a beet and Emily went over and kissed him on his red cheek.

The next morning Jason and me headed to town in the bitter cold with a strong north wind blowing at our backs as we rode up to the doc's house. We talked to him awhile and he thought it was good to have Jane at the ranch because we didn't know what the weather would bring this time of year and Jane would know what had to be done. Then we went to the hotel but the judge was already gone to the diner. As we walked in we spotted him sitting with another man. Judge Blackburn introduced us to Joe Billings the prosecutor and we talked and I gave him the letters from the towns where Johnson and Jordan had other schemes. I turned over the belt that we had taken off the judge and told Joe of the same impressions on Billie's neck and that doc had seen them. He was impressed with the evidence. He was going to talk to Tom about the beating he had received at the hands of Johnson and some of the men in jail. We found out that the auditor had gotten in late yesterday and was in the bank early this morning going over the books. We headed to the church where we found Mr. Simms in the back room.

"Hello Jason, Gabe. Congratulations I heard about you asking Emily to marry you. It's about time. I've been expecting it for some time."

Jason said. "I was just waiting for all the trouble with Johnson to be over."

"That was bad. We buried him and the others this morning. I said a few words over them I thought it was my duty even if he was so bad. But not a single person from town was there. It was really sad that a man can go that bad."

"It is, but I'm here on a happier note. Emily and me want you to marry us here after church on Sunday. Gabe here will be my best man and Lilly Ann will stand up with Emily."

"Jason, me your best man. I don't know."

"Who else? You help get us together and got me to come here. You are my true friend."

Mr. Simms said. "Jason that's a good choice. Sunday will be good everyone in town will be here. I think everybody in town are your and Gabe's friends. I think they have learned not to listen to rumors. You'll have your hands full with a new bride and a baby."

"That I will but I'm looking forward to it. We'll see you Sunday. Now Gabe let's get over to the general store and pick out some rings for the bride and me."

We left the church and went in the general store.

"Mr. Jimson, it's nice to see you here and not in jail."

"That it is. I tell you I was a little worried there until you two showed up. You know I think you seem to always show up where people need help. Now what can I do for you two?"

Jason spoke up. "I'm looking to buy two wedding rings."

"It's about time. You and Emily will be a fine couple. What size do you need?"

"Well, here's my finger. I don't know about Emily's."

I said, "Here Mr. Jimson I think her ring will fit me."

"How you know that?"

"Mr. Jimson, I've learned not to ask. Somehow he always knows."

"Here's two of my best. These are only fitting for the two best people in this town."

I said, "Those look fine and they fit perfect."

"Gabe, I just knew somehow they would."

"You know Jason don't asked."

"Anyway how much do I owe you?"

"Why, nothing at all. It's a wedding present from my wife and me. If it weren't for you I wouldn't have this store. Just have a happy life."

"I just don't know what to say just thank you from the bottom of our hearts and we'll see you Sunday. That's when we're getting married after church. So stay around."

"We'll look forward to it."

We mounted up and headed out of town. It was hard going against the strong northeast wind but we finally turned into our road and made it to the barn. As we unsaddled the horses Zack came up to us.

"Mr. Jason, I need to talk to you and Gabe. I want to thank you two for all you've done around here. I am so happy that Miss Emily and Lilly Ann are going to have a man like you to look after them. I feel I'm no use anymore around here with this one arm. I think I'll be having to mosey down the road."

"Zack, I thought we talked about this before. We are going to have an important job for you when we start shipping ore out of the mine. You will be our shipping manager and keep track of the wagons going out with ore and coming in with supplies. It will be happening soon just hold on awhile. You can't miss our wedding. We just won't stand for it. You will be very important and we know we can trust you. It will be a small job at first but in a couple of years when we get the smelting plant built you will have men working under you loading the wagon and we'll pay you a very good wage. You might even find a good woman to marry and raise children around here."

"Could it work into something that big?"

"It will, just ask Gene about it. We have to keep track of all that goes in and out. We may even have Tab or Bo as head of security. It's nice to have close family we can count on and you are close family to Emily and me."

"If you're sure I'm not in the way then I'll stay."

"You are not in the way. I don't want to hear any more talk like this."

"You won't, I better get doing something before you change your mind."

We saw Gene coming in from the mine with Todd, Eugene and Guy. They were unsaddling their horses. Gabe and me went over to talk to them.

Jason asked. "How's it going at the mine?"

"It's going good, so good that Todd thinks he should take a couple of wagons to St. Louis where his company has their smelting plant. We can rent some wagons at first. He's sure once his bosses get to look at the ore they will be sending wagons from the plant to pick up loads. I think after your wedding we'll take off and I can talk to the company for Emily and you and get a good deal after they see what we have."

"I'll talk to Emily tonight but I'm sure it will be alright. You know about the cost and what you should be able to get than we do."

"I sure wouldn't cheat you. I've seen you draw that gun." He laughed.

"I want to tell you that Zack is a dear friend of ours. He lost his arm in the war fighting for the union. Emily and me want to make him shipping manager. I know there won't be much work at first but there will be later. If he asks you about it you can tell him that he will have to keep track of what goes out and what comes in and keep it written down. You know, I just had an idea we might need to build an office up at the mine to keep your things you need up there and Zack can have an office in there."

"I'm glad you told me because I was wondering how I was going to handle everything by myself. He will be a big help to me. Have you found out anything about Johnson's ranch? If you can get that we will have a sweet set up for both businesses."

"I may find out something at the trial tomorrow when the auditor testifies about Jordan's dealings at the bank."

"We better get to supper before the men eat everything. I'll talk with Zack and I know he can handle the job. I've talk with him he's a smart man. All learning doesn't come out of books. He worked in the house and the daughter thought of him as one of the family and she taught him to read and write."

Jason and me headed for the house for our supper. Tomorrow was going to be a long, rough day at the trial. We went in and Emily and Lilly Ann had supper on the table. Jason and Emily both said prayers at eating time now.

"Emily, tomorrow is the trial and Gabe and me and some of the boys may have to testify about what we know. We might not be back 'til supper. It might take two days I hope not."

"At least we're rid of that scum out of this town. It still makes me mad that I trusted that man for so long."

"You didn't know and the towns people didn't know. Jane we would like it if you would stay here 'til the baby comes doc thinks that is great because of the weather around here."

"Can one of the men take me to my place tomorrow to get some things and let the diner know. I think they can get by without me for a couple of weeks."

"Sure, I'll get Bob to take you. I'll send two more men with you. Gene needs two wagons to start loading ore to take to St. Louis. He's going to leave on Monday after our wedding."

Emily acted surprised. "Jason, you mean it. This is really going to happen?"

"Yes, I believe so. I told Gene that we wanted Zack to be the shipping manager for the mine and he agreed that he would need the help. You know Zack was about to leave cause he thought he was useless around here. He brightened up when I told him about his new job. It will take a while to get going."

"I will have to talk to him. I do need him. He was the only one we had for four long years."

The morning came fast and we had breakfast and headed to town with some of the boys and Bob with Jane in the wagon and Steve and Mat from the mine were going to rent wagons and head back to the mine and start loading ore. As we came into town we saw the courthouse was filled and overflowing out into the street. As we dismounted we saw the prisoners being led out of the marshals office with cuffs around their wrist and ankles. They entered the courthouse with us right behind them. There was room for the witnesses in the front roll seats. Marshal Moore sat the prisoners down across the aisle from where we were with their attorney in front of them and Joe Billings the prosecutor was in front of us. All was called to order and we stood up and Henry Blackburn the judge came out and set on the judge's bench in front of everyone. We all sat down and Judge Blackburn read all the charges against each of the defendants. The worst was murder against Judge William Deets.

Blackburn picked twelve men from the crowd behind us and swore them in as the jury and then told Billings to call his first witness. He called Tom and showed him the belt that belonged to Judge Deets and enter it into evidence and about his beating at the hand of Johnson and Deets. Then he called Doc Wade to tell about the patterns on the belt were the same as around Billie's neck. Then he called Jason and asked him about seeing Billie's body being brought out of Johnson's house and took to Emily's ranch. Then about the telegrams from towns around the state and how Johnson with the help of Judge Deets and Doug and Jordan had swindled the ranches out of their land to make a big ranch. Then it was my turn and I told the same story as Jason and how we found Jason beaten at the hands of Johnson's men and Tom was tied up and beaten. Then came the auditor about the banks books. He told how Johnson didn't own any land it was just carried on the banks books for many years. He never made a payment on any of it. The ranches he had stolen from their owners were paid out to the former owner before they left town by the bank where Jordan would hide it as expense and nothing else. The same was done to several business around town. Then he called Mr. Jimson and asked him about his trial a few days before. After that Billings rested his case and Blackburn adjured for lunch. We went to the diner with the men and ate.

"Jason, did you hear about Johnson ranch. I think you need to find out about how much it will take to buy all of Johnson's ranch."

"I heard that. After this is over I'm going to find out from the auditor what it would take to get it all. It sounded like all the former owners had been paid for the land so I don't know. We'll have to find out. Let's get back to court and see what defense they will put on Deets being a judge you never can tell."

The defense opened with Don Turnble their attorney calling the honorable Judge William Deets to the stand. He told of how he was tricked by Johnson into helping him and it was Johnson that had killed Billie with his belt and Johnson and his men had abused Billie and raped her to the point that he was sick but couldn't do anything about it because there was just to many of them. Then Billings asked how his belt had also been used to beat the marshal and his belt had been taken off of him in the jail and why he didn't go to Tom and tell him. He also was seen laughing at the scene of the murder. Deets said that was just a pretended laugh. That he was in fear of his life. Then Billings asked him if he was in fear of his life when he tried to send Mr. Jimson to prison for having merchandise in front of his store. Deets said that Johnson would kill him if he didn't do as Johnson said. Then Jordan was called to the stand and told about the same story. Billing asked why he went along with Johnson to so many towns to get more money out of people. Jordan said that Johnson would have killed him if he didn't. Then he asked him why he didn't go to the law in the many towns that they were stealing money. He gave the same answer that Johnson would have killed him. Then Billings said.

"It seems to me that these two blame everything on a dead man even though they were getting rich from all the deals."

The case now went to the jury. We waited for the outcome.

15

We were sitting there in the courtroom where just a couple of days before Judge Deets was trying to take away a man's business and send him to prison. Now that same judge was on trials for murder and we were waiting to hear what would happen to that judge and his partners. The people in the courtroom and those outside were all talking about different aspects of the case and what the outcome would be. Judge Blackburn had retired to his chamber for he knew he was going to have a tough decision to make if a guilty verdict came in. The people seemed to have an option that there was no doubt of what that decision should be. But it was up to the judge to sentence the lot of bad men but it would be hard to do what he knew had to be done to a fellow judge. He also knew that the law had to be equal for everyone in this country especially after the war that had just been fought for the rights of human beings in this country. An hour went by and then two hours. I saw Jason go talk to Billings and come back and sit down.

"I wish they would hurry I'm worried about Emily. Our baby could come along at any time."

"Don't worry about Emily, she is in the best hands. I know that she will be fine you just wait and see. You'll make a great father to both of your children. What did Billings have to say?"

"He thought it was cut and dry what would happen but the jury is taking this long he just doesn't know."

In less than thirty more minutes Judge Blackburn came out of his chamber and everyone rose and he hit his gavel on his bench.

"Please come to order. The jury is coming out with their verdict in a minute. They will read their verdict and if a guilty verdict is rendered I will sentence them right away. If they are found not guilty they will go free."

Boos could be heard all around the courtroom.

Blackburn said, "Now I'll have none of that in this court."

The jury filed out of the jury room and was seated.

"Would the defendants please stand? Do you have a verdict in this case?" Blackburn said.

The first man in the front roll stood up and spoke.

"Yes we do your honor."

"Is this the decision of all of you?"

All of the men in the jury said at the same time.

"Yes, your honor."

"Would you please read your decision out loud so everyone can hear it?"

"We fine the defendants in this case before us guilty of all charges brought against them. Judge may I say something else."

"Yes, you may please continue."

"We found it hard to make this decision on men that we have known for years and trusted them sometimes with our life's. But now with the war over we have to show people that we are a country of laws and not anyone no matter their standing in the community can break those laws. That is all judge."

"Well said and I applauded your decision. I feel it was a just decision. Now I will sentence each of the defendants. Judge Deets I sentence you to hang by the neck until you are dead tomorrow morning at seven. Mr. Jordan you will be hung by the neck until you are dead at the same time. The other three will be sent to federal prison for the rest of their natural life with no chance of parole. Your reign of terror is over in this town. I to want to say that this was a hard decision to sentence a fellow judge to death but it's my duty to treat everyone the same by the law. If we have four or five carpenter in this courtroom the court will pay you to work all night to construct a gallows in the town square and tear it down after the sentence has been carried out. I will remain in town until the sentence is carried out. Now the jury is excused and the defendants will be taken to jail to await their sentence. Mr. Moore will escort the other three defendants to federal prison in Kansas City after the hanging. The deputies that were hired will stay on duty until Tom is well enough to take over and they will administer the sentence. May God have mercy on your souls. Court is adjourned."

Everyone waited for the prisoner to be taken out of the court and then we all filed out. There was not much talking to be heard through the crowd for it was hard to hang men even if they deserved it. After tomorrow morning it will all be up to my boss. As we started to ride out of town we could see the lumber being taken to the town square and the carpenters were starting their work. Jason pulled up when he saw Mr. Wright the auditor.

"Mr. Wright may I talk to you a minute." We dismounted.

"Yes sir, Mr. Benning isn't it."

"Yes sir. I was wondering what will happen to Johnson's ranch now."

"Since it wasn't really a part of the banks books it will probably be sold for the taxes owe on it. Mr. Johnson never bothered to pay them for the five years he lived on the land."

"Thank you Mr. Wright. You two wait here, come on Gabe, we'll be back in a while."

We went back in the empty courthouse and right in the tax office.

"May I help you Jason."

"I would like to know how much is due in taxes on the old Johnson ranch."

"Well, let me see. There are six different ranches involved with his dealings. I'll add them all up and here is the total due. It is $3,546.45 that's for five years."

"Can we pay it right now and it will be ours."

"If you can come up with that much."

"Gabe, I know that you seem to have what you always need in your wallet. So do you have that much now?"

"I'll see." I pulled out my wallet and opened it and there was, I counted it, $3,600. I looked up and said.

"Thank you Lord. Jason here it is."

Jason handed it to the clerk.

"You make out the deed to Mrs. Emily Truman."

The clerk went to the other room and came back with the deed made out in Emily name. We went out and headed out of town down the road to the ranch.

Jason had something on his mind. He was so quiet and we were riding so slowly. It was past suppertime but I gave him time to think to himself. Then as we rode up the road to the house Jason said.

"That was harder than I thought it would be. I know in my heart it was right but it was still hard. I just can't imagine how those men on the jury were feeling and the new deputies that have to hang them. I pray that they can handle it well. I will not go to the hanging in the morning but I won't stop anyone on the ranch from going. Tim, Jay you make sure everyone knows that."

"Yes sir we will."

As we came in sight of the house there sitting in the swing on the front porch was Emily, Lilly Ann and Tab. Emily came down the steps as we rode up and Jason dismounted and held Emily in his arms.

"It's good to be home. Is there any supper left I think even Gabe is hungry tonight?"

"There sure is I'll just heat it up a little. Come on in all of you. I think Evan put everything away in the bunkhouse so you eat here." "Thank you Emily. It was a long hard day. I think I'd rather be working." Jay said.

"You're right it was hard but it had to be done. It will be over in the morning."

We went in the house and Lilly Ann and Emily set some dishes on the table for us as Jane warmed up the food. Jason disappeared into the next room and came out with a hand full of money and handed it to me.

Emily said. "Jason what's that for?"

Jason handed Emily the deeds and raised her high in the air.

"Jason, put me down you'll hurt yourself heavy as I am. Now what is this?"

Emily opened the folded paper and looked at it.

"Emily, it's made out in your name. You own all of Johnson old ranch and that is the money that Gabe let me borrow to pay the taxes on it. The bank had no claim to it. Look how many acres it is."

She looked and said.

"3,895 acres I don't believe it."

"Believe it my dear."

We sat down to eat and I said the prayer tonight.

"Thank you Jesus for this food and all the joy you have brought to this table. I know that you will see to it that these two loving people will be happy along with their daughter Lilly Ann for rest of their life's. Amend."

Emily said to Gabe. "That was very nice of you. But I don't know about this land so many people have died for it."

Jason said, "I know Emily it's hard but I have thought about it and I promise that we will do nothing but good with the money we make off of this land. We will provide many jobs for the families of this town and all over the state."

"Alright, but we will put all of this land and the mine in mine and your name after we are married. Mr. and Mrs. Jason Benning. That has a nice sound."

"Jay, you and Tim get everyone tomorrow and start tearing down the old fence to the old Johnson ranch and the new Truman ranch."

"Yes sir."

"Tim, I want you and Tab and Bob to go on our new spread and get a rough estimate of the total number of cattle we have inherited. I know this is a horse ranch Emily but it is big enough to have both or we can round them up in the spring and have a cattle drive."

We finished eating and Jay and Tim headed to the bunkhouse and Jason sat in the front room with Emily and Lilly Ann. They were getting married in two days and as the best man I had the rings right here in my pocket. Jane woke me out of my thought when she said.

"Gabe, it will be nice when those two are married in two days. What job will you have with the new mine?"

"Job! Why my job is just about over and I will have to leave to the great beyond. Look at them they are going to be so happy when the baby comes." I continued.

"That will be soon I can tell and there may be a big surprise in store for them."

"You can tell that?"

"I know there will be on the word of a great authority. You know you should get Gene to find you a job in the mining office. He said that he was going to need help in the future."

"I may do that but right now I have one job to make sure that Emily doesn't have any trouble when it comes her time to deliver."

"You are very nice company but I better get to the bunkhouse. Goodnight Emily and you short tail. I like that nickname. I don't know why but it suits you. See you in the morning Jason."

In the morning Jason and me sat down with Gene at breakfast in the bunkhouse.

Jason said, "Gene we have what you ask for. Start making plans for the new smelting plant. We have the whole old Johnson ranch for the horses and cattle."

"That was fast. We leave Monday after your wedding. I'll contact the people in St. Louis that will know about starting to build the plant. It will have to be a good distance away from the mine cause we don't know how far down or through that mountain the ore goes and then there is that smaller mountain back over yonder. I assume that there will be enough land."

"With this ranch there is nearly 4,000 acres. We're tearing out the old fence today. Do you think we need to put up a fence around the site of the mine and new plant?"

"I don't think so the horses have been doing fine. I don't foresee any trouble with the added cattle for now. I haven't looked over all of

Emily's property just around the mine very close. I'll take Bo and Tab and have a look see today."

"Men let's get going we have a fence to tear down the same one that Johnson wanted to get rid of all these years."

Bob said, "Boss, I'm going to the hanging and see the other three get out of town alright. I don't like hangings but I think that one of us should make sure for ourselves. I hope you understand."

"That's fine Bob. I guess it's fitting that someone from the ranch is there. Thank you. We'll see you later."

Bob headed to town and the rest of us headed to the mine and to get that fence torn down that had been the cause of many men's death. It was going to be a thing of the pass. It was early so Jason didn't stop by the house. Emily had been sleeping in more now that her time was approaching. Jane would make sure Emily was all right and send for us if we were needed. Short tail would be returning to school Monday after the wedding and be out before Christmas. She should have time to spend with the baby before returning to school in January. It was now cold every day as winter came closer. Some of the plans for the ranch and mine would have to be put off until spring. As the men were tearing down the fence Jason said.

"Gabe, you remember that night, it seems like ages ago, when Johnson's men were trying to steal the horses and I thought they shot you off your horse and all the horses ran over you."

"That was a close call. I guess we won't have to worry about that again."

"I'm sure glad I met you old pal. I really think I love this ranch. I hope Lilly Ann and the new baby will love it as much as Emily and I do. When we're gone it will be theirs and their children's."

"You sure are thinking a long ways in the future. I know they will."

"Look how wide open it looks now and the horses and cattle are already crossing the old fence line. Men try to fill in the postholes we wouldn't want a horse or any cattle breaking a leg. James go bring the wagon up here and get all the post and fencing stacked behind the barn for future use."

At noon everyone went in for dinner and Jason and me went to the house and Jane was fixing dinner with Emily's help and Lilly Ann was setting the table.

"Well, Emily the men got most of the fence down. They'll finish this afternoon and get it stored behind the barn."

Emily said. "Just a few months ago we wouldn't have thought of taking down that fence and I wouldn't had thought we would be getting married tomorrow."

Jason went to her and hugged her and patted her stomach. "And in ten days or so we will be having an addiction to the family."

"Oh, Jason you'll embarrass me. In front of Jane and Gabe."

I said, "You sure you two aren't getting nervous about tomorrow."

"Not me, are you Emily?"

"Just with the baby coming so soon we can't have a normal honeymoon and I think it's going to get a little crowded with just two bedrooms. You me and the baby in one but how about when he is older."

"Listen to that Gabe, she's already has the baby grown."

"You know what I mean."

"I do and I have been thinking about that. First by next summer the mine will be up and going and when Lilly Ann is out of school and the baby will be bigger. I think our whole family should go and spent two weeks in St. Louis and while we're gone the men can get started on adding two more bedrooms to the house and enlarge the front room. We'll have more room to fed everyone on special occasions."

Emily said. "With the ranch bigger and the mine will be bigger we will have to hire more men."

We sat down and said grace and ate a fine meal.

"Gabe, we better get back to work old friend. That was a fine meal you three. Maybe a couple of suppers a week we can have Tab come eat with us. What you think of that Lilly Ann."

"Oh yes. I would like that. He is so good looking."

"Well you get your mothers okay and then I'll ask him."

"Thank you Jason. Ma, after tomorrow you think that pa would mine if I called Jason dad. I've been thinking about it and I think I'm closer to him than calling him Jason."

"That's up to you. I don't think your pa would mine. I think John somehow sent Jason. What do you think Gabe?"

"That just could be. I have no first-hand knowledge of it but it could be."

"How would you like that Jason?" Emily said.

"I just don't know what to say Lilly Ann but I would be honored."

Jason went and hugged Lilly Ann.

"I do hope that we will become real friends and I do love you like a father would."

Then he hugged and kissed Emily and said.

'Gabe, we better get now the men are already back out there and we'll see you two later."

We mounted up and headed out to the range when Bob rode up to us. All he said was.

"It's done boss and they are already tearing down the gallows so you two won't see it on your wedding day tomorrow." Then he rode off to work.

We spotted Gene and rode up to him and Bo.

"Jason over here. We staked out this flat spot. It's about a quarter of a mile to the east of the mine. I don't know it will probably need to be enlarged but I think this is a good spot. If you look toward the mine you can see how it slopes down this way and flattens out about an eighth of a mile from the mine. I'll know more when I talk to the mining people in St. Louis."

"You know your business just make it large enough to handle the load."

"It will be and maybe bigger where we can handle other mines ore. We'll make a little less but it all mounts up."

"I'll see you and Bo tomorrow morning before church."

"Yes sir the big day. I'm glad to see you two together. I think I'm married to these darn rocks." He laughed.

Gabe and me were laughing as we rode away. I said to Gabe.

"You know Gabe that place we found Tom at. I think that will be a nice place for Emily and me to get a way once in a while and I'll tear down that old cabin and build a new one. No one but us will know about it. Just a special and beautiful place."

Jason and me helped the boys load the wagon and I drove it to the barn to unload. We had to make three trips. The last day that Jason would ever be alone was fast coming to a close. Tomorrow would bring a whole new way of life for both of them.

At supper the talk was about the wedding. The women had taken over the whole celebration. Jane was saying.

"Evan and me are baking some cakes and pies for tomorrow. There is a room behind the church and the reverend said that we could use it after the wedding with the cakes and pies and Mr. and Mrs. Jimson are fixing two big bowls of punch and they will also bring the knives and forks to cut and eat the cake. He said he would furnish just about anything for keeping him out of jail."

Emily said. "I will help you Jane tonight."

"I wont have it Lilly Ann and me and Evan will do everything. Tomorrow is your day."

I heard Jason say and I knew he was going to get in trouble for saying it but I didn't have time to stop him,

"We'll load everything in the wagon when I take everyone to church in the morning."

Jane and Lilly Ann both said at the same time.

"No you don't you and Gabe will ride your horses into town. We'll have Tab drive the wagon. We'll show up after the reverend is done with his sermon. Jason you should know you can't see your bride before the wedding."

"I'm sorry, it slipped my mind. Maybe I lost my mind. But I found it now."

Emily was laughing and holding her stomach.

"I hope being married to you is as fun as this. But Jane I haven't had time to get a new dress."

"I took care of that when I was in town yesterday. Don't worry I'll show you later when Jason is gone and Mr. Jimson knew Jason's size."

Jane handed Jason three boxes. Then she handed the same to Gabe.

"These are for you to wear to your wedding. A new suit and shirt with the boots and hat to match and do wear them. You'll be very handsome. Gabe these are for you. You should be dressed nice you are the best man."

Jane brought out another box and handed it to Lilly Ann and said.

"This is for the Maid of Honor. There is new everything from top to bottom and in between. I told you Mr. Jimson and his wife was very grateful for what Jason did for him. I got me a new get-up to."

"I can't wait to see mine. Jason you mind if we say goodnight now. We'll be together tomorrow and for the rest of our lives."

He kissed Emily goodnight and told Gabe.

"Come on Gabe I know when we aren't wanted."

We were laughing as we went out the front door and into the cold night air. We walked in the bunkhouse and the yells and howls went out and all the men were there shaking Jason's hand and patting him on the back. Evan had cakes all over the table and some beer from the saloon.

"Gabe you knew about this didn't you. My old friend."

Evan said. "Drink all the beer you want but leave some cakes for tomorrow after the wedding. I've already done enough work today."

Jason laughed and patted Evan on the back and said thank you.

"Don't thank me it was Gabe's idea I just had to do the work." He laughed and continued. "Really I owe you this and a lot more for giving me another chance in life."

All the men raised their glasses of beer and said at the same time.

"That goes for all of us, to Jason."

Gene said. "You know Jason when you came to talk to me in Kansas City I was mad and ready to give up. That is why I came with you so fast. It was a chance to realize my dream. Here we are my gang of rock hounds and me. We are very grateful to you."

Jason said. "You all have it backward I couldn't have done all this without you. Especially you Gabe you set me on the right path."

This went on for three hours and each man came up to Jason and shook his hand and each said goodnight. Then Zack came up and said.

"I have the most to thank you for. All I can say is that everyone here is a true friend to me and treats me like a man should be treated. I remember that first day you and Gabe came. I wanted to kick you two off the ranch." Everyone laughed.

Everyone was gone off to bed and it was just Jason and I there.

"You know Gabe I want you to know that Emily and me know just how much you have really done for us and I just want to thank you for it all. I'll see you in the morning. We have to get ready for a wedding."

16

I could see the sun coming up in the east as I opened my eyes. My days on earth are numbered now that Emily and Jason are getting married. I prayed to God to let me stay until after the babies come. That will make me happy. Jason came over.

"Get up Gabe this is an important day. You are the last one up. We all took a bath and I have some fresh water for you. You should be clean for your new clothes. We have to be there before Emily."

"You're right, I'll get up and get ready. Are you getting nervous, Jason?"

"I don't think so. All right I'm more nervous than that day I met you on the road coming here."

"That's right, tell the truth. This is the best day for it."

"I think I'm more nervous about being a father. I'm going to have three people depending on me for the rest of my life. Not to mention all the people that work here."

"Now, I'll get ready and we'll be on our way. You'll be a great father." Jason called Tab over.

"Tab you're going to take all the things for the party into town. Emily, Lilly Ann and Jane will come with you in the wagon and be sure to take it easy, go slow. The doc doesn't even want Emily to be in the wagon. So please take it easy."

"Jason I will. I wouldn't let anything happen to your bride. You quit being so nervous. It will be all right. You and Gabe and the boys better get going I'm taking the wagon to the house and load all the goodies."

Then Gene came over.

"I just wanted to tell you good luck and that we have the ore loaded in the two wagons and we'll be leaving tomorrow morning early. I didn't want you to worry on this special day."

"Thanks Gene for everything."

"Gabe, are you ready yet. We're waiting for you. The men have our horses saddled and ready to go."

"I'm coming, keep your shirt on. I'm sure Emily will wait for you."

As we mounted and left for town I could see Tab and Lilly Ann loading the wagon. Lilly Ann was all dressed up. What a beautiful young lady she is going to be. I could tell that Tab thought so to. I checked my pocket to make sure I had the rings and they were there. It was a clear blue day but the fridge cold was in the air but the wind was blowing only a might. It was a nice day for the wedding. We rode up Main Street and the first thing I noticed was that the gallows had been completely torn down. Jason said.

"Look over there, Tom is up and around."

We rode over to Tom and Janet.

"Tom what are you doing out of bed?"

Janet said. "I just couldn't keep him put. The doc said it would be alright if he went right back to bed."

"Why you didn't think I would miss your wedding after you and Gabe saved my life. I'm staying for the party to. Can't dance but I can watch."

"We better get in the church. Emily is coming with Tab in the wagon. They wouldn't let me see her. She'll be in after the sermon."

We took off our hats as we took our seats in the front roll of the church. It looked as if everyone in town was showing up today. As the preacher started his sermon I noticed that Jason kept looking back at the door but there was a partition in between the outside door to the church and the congregation. I'm sure that Jason didn't hear anything that Mr. Simms said even when he told everyone how nervous Jason looked. The whole place laughed and I said to Jason.

"Jason she'll be here. I'm sure that Tab will let us know when they get here."

"I just worry about her in her condition."

"It will be over soon."

I then saw Tab look around the partition and Mr. Simms stopped and Evan got up and went to the back of the church. Then Mr. Simms said.

"I'm cutting the sermon short today. It seems we are here for a special reason today. I just want to say before we begin that I think these two people that I am going to join today are so well suited for each other."

Tab escorted Lilly Ann to the front of the church and Tab sat down. Then Mr. Simms said.

"Jason if you would please stand to the left in front of me and Gabriel to the left of Jason. Please begin the wedding march."

The music began and Jason and me turned toward the back of the church and out from behind the partition stepped Evan with Emily on his arm. All eye were turned toward the bride now as they slowly made their way down the aisle to the front of the church. Emily was wearing the most beautiful beige dress with a veil over her face. The dress had lace coming over her stomach in different layers. Jason's eyes were focused on nothing but Emily. Evan and Emily stopped in front of the preacher and to the left of Lilly Ann and to the right of Jason and me.

"Who gives this bride away?" Mr. Simms said.

Then Evan said. "I do."

Then Evan kissed Emily on the cheek and stepped away and sat down next to Tab. I saw Jason look at Emily with so much love in his eyes that there seemed to be no one in the room but them. Then Mr. Simms broke the silence.

"We are gathered here in the presents of God to join this man, Jason Benning and this woman, Emily Truman in the bounds of wholly matrimony. Jason you and Emily join right hands. If there is anyone here that has a reason that these two should not be joined speak now or forever hold your peace. Now do you Jason take Emily to be your lawful wedded wife to honor and obey in sickness and in health until death do you part?"

"I do."

"Now Emily do you take Jason to be your lawful wedded husband to honor and obey in sickness and in health until death do you part?"

"I do."

"Who has the rings?"

I said. "I do." I took the rings out of my pocket.

"Jason place Emily's ring on her left hand and Emily you place Jason's ring on his left hand."

Jason said. "Mr. Simms may I say something."

"Yes you may."

"I want to promise you Emily in front of the whole town that I will always take care of you and Lilly Ann and the new baby on the way. I pray that John is up there looking down on us with his blessing. He was your loving husband and my best friend that I have ever known. There will always be love for John in our home. Thank you reverend."

"Thank you for that. Now with the power vested in me by the Lord our God and the state of Missouri. I now pronounce you husband and wife. Jason you may kiss your radiant bride."

That's when another bell went off in my head. This time it was even louder than before and lasted for ten minutes. Then Peter's voice came to me.

"You have almost completed your assignment. You can stay until the babies are born."

Everyone stood up and the applause was so loud. I'm sure they heard it in heaven.

Jason took Emily in his strong arms and gave her a long kiss in front of the whole town. Then he shook Mr. Simms hand and Mr. Simms kissed the bride and then all the men from the ranch shook Jason's hand and kissed Emily on her blushed filled cheek. Then Lilly Ann hugged and kissed her mother and kissed Jason and said.

"I'm glad to have you for my father."

Mr. Simms said. "Everyone is invited to the party in the hall behind the church. We have food and drink and a lot of fun and dancing.

Everyone get to know the new couple because they are going to put this town on the map."

Jason and Emily were married on December 14, 1865. Everyone stayed and danced to the music of three men in town that had fiddles and one had a guitar. The man that played the piano at the saloon was there playing up a storm. Jason and Emily had the first dance and then everyone joined them on the dance floor. Lilly Ann danced mostly with Tab but did dance with some of the boys from school. Emily danced with all the men from the ranch. Even Zack was a real smooth dancer. Tom and Janet were sitting to the side of the dance floor. I went over and ask Tom.

"May I dance with your lady?"

"Why sure if she wants to."

I took Janet in my arms and we danced around the dance floor for two whole songs. I told Janet.

"Don't ask how I know but you and Emily and Jason and Tom are going to become really close friends. Time will be good for both families. It doesn't seem possible now but you and Tom will have a child like you always have wanted."

I took her back over to where Tom was sitting and she just sat there and looked at me with an unbelievable stare. I heard Tom say.

"What is it Janet?"

Then I went over and danced with Emily.

"You look so happy this afternoon. Let me tell you Emily, you and Jason are going to be so happy for the rest of your life and you are going to have a big surprise when you give birth. You'll have a bigger surprise later. You'll have Jason's child. The Lord has blessed you and Jason. Don't ask me how I know but I do. And Tab will be the right man for Lilly Ann. They will find their way in the future."

"Gabriel, sometimes you just puzzle me. I know because of you my life will be full. There is only one thing that will make me happier than I am at this moment and that is when I have this child and when I do have Jason's."

That's when I saw Jason dancing with Lilly Ann. I could hear her say to Jason.

"I haven't seen mother this happy since before father left for the war. I know you will make her very happy."

"You can bet I'm going to try my best. I hope I can make your life happy as well. I do love you as if you were my daughter. Don't ever forget if Emily and me have more children you will still be my daughter."

Jane was also having a fine time dancing with all the men from the ranch.

The party had been going on for three hours when I saw doc go over to Emily and Jason. I heard doc say.

"I hate to take you away from your friends but Jason I think it's time to get this little lady home and in bed to rest."

"Doc I'm fine I am having a good time."

"I know but we have to think about the baby. This puts a strain on you and the baby and I want you to lay down in the wagon all the way home."

Jason and Emily got up and the music stopped.

"Doc just told us that he think Emily should get home and rest. We want to thank you all for coming see us get married. You all stay and have more fun for us. So goodnight."

Then Emily said. "I want to stay but you know doc he thinks he knows best. I think this time he is right I do feel a little tired. So good night."

Jane came over.

"I'm going to stay and give you time to be alone with Jason."

Everyone saw Emily and Jason out into the late afternoon cold and hurried back in the warm building for the fire was blazing high in the fireplace. I stayed for a while and then headed to the ranch and the warm bunkhouse. Tonight Jason would be staying in the house with Emily. It was way after dark when the men started coming in and Evan fixed a small meal for them. Then I saw Tab bring Lilly Ann and Jane, in a buggy, to the house where the lanterns were lit and I could tell that Jason had gotten the fireplace ablaze for it was freezing outside. The women went in the house and Tab got his horse saddled and I went out and saddled mine and we tied them on to the buggy and we went back to town.

"It was kind of you to come with me. I like the company."

"I would like to talk to you."

"What is it?"

"I can tell that you and Lilly Ann are going to be very much in love. I can see a great future for you two. You will be greatly involved with the work in the mine. You and Bo will learn a lot from Gene. Learn all you can Gene will be willing to teach you two."

"How do you know all that?"

"Don't ask I just do."

We got doc's buggy back and got back to the ranch late. Everyone was already in bed.

The morning brought a bitter cold from the north. It was now December 15, 1865. Gene had the wagons pulled in front of the bunkhouse. Todd was up on the seat with Gene. They both had their coat collars pulled up around their neck with a winter scarfs tied under their chin up above their heads under their hats. Jeff and James were on the other wagon. Guy and Eugene were left in charge of the mine with Steve and Mat and two others to work the mine. Jason came out of the house to see them off. Gene said over the howling north wind.

"Jason this looks like a bad time to leave. We may take longer than I expected. We may get some snow up the trail. Keep an eye out for a telegram to let you know what's going on."

"Just be careful and if you need to hold up just let us know if you can. You sure you don't need any money?"

"I think this ore will cover any expense we might have and we have the extra money you gave us until we get there. We better get going before we freeze. Tell Emily good luck with the baby."

"Thanks Gene and you Todd for everything you have done." They headed down the drive to the main road and then turned northeast toward St. Louis. Jason and me went to the house for breakfast. Jason was whistling and I said.

"So it sounds like you had a good time last night. How you like being married."

"It's great Gabe you should try it one day. We lay there all night just talking about the future. I know that I can tell her anything that is on my mind."

"Wait until the babies come you'll have another reason to stay up all night."

"What did you say? Babies!"

"I'm sorry just a slip of the tongue. You know how that is. We better hurry inside and eat some nice hot breakfast before we freeze."

"I sure hope the boys are alright on those wagons."

We walked in the house to a nice warm greeting. I think I'd better get down some hot meals for I may not get any for a while. My time in this world is limited.

Lilly Ann and Jane were serving us three and then seated themselves. Then Lilly Ann said.

"Mother we heard you two talking all night. How you think of that much to say?"

"Just about the baby and your future and the future of our family."

"Don't you have something better to do. Like sleep."

"We have our whole life to sleep and enjoy each other. This was our wedding night and we won't have another one."

Jason said. "Emily you have said that doc told you that you are bigger than with Lilly Ann."

"I just eat too much that's all."

"I don't know. You know how Gabe says things that we don't understand."

"Yes, what did he say now?"

"Jason, I told you it was a slip of the tongue. That's all it was."

"I don't know."

Jane said. "Jason, tell us what he said?"

"He just said when we have the babies."

"What! Gabe I know you know things. I don't know how but we know you do."

Then Jane spoke up again. "You know I have the same feeling."

"Jane you don't mean it."

"Well, we'll just have to wait and see. Anyway I'm here I think I can handle it if two babies show up."

We left the house and went to the mine. As we walked in the mine there was a noticeable change in the temperature. It was a lot warmer inside. We walked way back and there was Eugene and Guy without a coat on.

"Eugene, it's warmer in here than outside."

"That's the way it is working like we do we don't even need our coats but we freeze when we go out. As we get deeper it will be even warmer and in the summer it will be nearly unbearable with the heat. We don't mind the heat, for a find like this only happens once or twice in a human's life time."

"We'll leave you to your work. Gene got off all right. Is Tab and Bo back there?"

"They sure are they came out this morning asking all kinds of questions. They seem to have a real interest in everything we do now."

"They're young and might see that they could have a real future here." I said.

Jason and me headed to the old Johnson ranch and on the way we spotted Bob and Jan checking on the horses. We rode over to where they were.

"How the stock doing?" Jason asked Bob.

"They're good. The horses and cattle seem like they always have been together. Right now they seem to spend their time looking for the best grass. It will be like that 'til spring."

"You and Jan come with us I have a little job for you to help us with."

I said, "Where we going Jason?"

"You should know where we found Tom."

We rode on to the northern part of now the Truman ranch back in the hills. It was a ways off any trail that was around. We rode up to a shear face of rock that shot up a hundred or more feet. This is the first time we have seen this place in the daylight.

We dismounted and Jan said.

"Boss, why are we here?"

Bob said, "I was wandering the same thing."

"I don't want you ever to tell anyone about this place except our people. Alright!"

"Sure boss."

Jason and me pulled back some old dead sagebrush that had been piled up and Bob and Jan's eyes lit up with amassment as we mounted up and rode through the large crack in the face of the wall of rock. We rode on until we came out in the valley. It was still somewhat green and we rode on until we came to the creek. It still was running full this time of year and wasn't frozen yet. The cabin could be seen a ways in the distance.

I said, "I wondered why you put these tools in our saddlebags."

We rode up to the cabin and looked around. Then Jason said.

"We're going to take it all down and stack it over there and burn it. Now let's get busy and warm this place up."

By noon we were so far along that we keep working.

Bob said, "Boss how did you know about this?"

"Gabe and me were looking for Tom and we followed two of Johnson's men and they led us here. This cabin is where they beat Tom so badly."

"I understand why you want it torn down."

"Jan start what we have on fire and we'll add to it as we tear it down. Next spring we're going to do the same thing to the old Johnson's ranch house. We might keep the barn to store hay for over this way. Tomorrow I want you two and get Jay and Zack and get some timber cut around the mine and bring it up here and start building a new larger house with a porch and while you're at it cut enough for two more bedrooms on our house just in case Gabe is right about more than one baby. You two and Jay will work up here and Gabe and Zack and me will work on our house. Gabe I think we should enlarge the house now with the baby coming."

"If the weather holds out with no snow we should be done in no time. You know boss it sure is nice not to have to look over our shoulder all the time for someone trying to kill us."

"That is nice but don't take down your guard always keep it in the back of your mind. Cause you never know what will happen."

We got it all burned and the fire out by mid-afternoon and we headed back home. Emily was worried about us when we didn't show up at noon.

"Emily, I should have told you but I didn't think about it 'til we were at the mine. We went over to our new property and tore down an old cabin where they beat Tom and next spring I'm going to do the same thing to the Johnson's old house. I still have a ranch to run."

"I know I just worry about losing you."

"Don't worry dear you'll have to chase me away with a stick to get rid of me and that may not do the trick." They all laughed.

That night after supper we sat around the front room and just talked. Emily was lying down on the divan with her head on Jason's lap. She looked so relaxed and happy and secure. Jason told Emily.

"Tomorrow we are going to start on enlarging this house with two more bedrooms. We'll cut the timber up by the mine and bring it down here. We'll have to take out a wall and make a hall to the other bedrooms. I'll be no further than the mine. I don't want you to worry and if you need me sent Jane for me until Lilly Ann gets home from school. Lilly Ann have you met any boys at school that you like."

"Father, those are just boys not a man like Tab. You know I'm almost fifteen and I just have one more year of school after this."

"I just thought I would ask. I know Tab is working really hard at the mine trying to learn everything he can. I think he may have plans to stay around here."

Jason was running his hands through Emily's hair and she had her eyes closed and she loved it.

"You mean it. You think he will stay here." I spoke up.

"I do young short tail but I think he may have another reason for working so hard."

"Why do you insist on calling me that little girl name that my pa called me when I was four or five?"

Emily said, "Why young lady your pa called you that until he went off to war. I like that name."

"I'm sorry ma. I didn't mean anything by that. I'll never forget that's what pa called me and how I thought it was really special. Gabe you never said how you knew that name."

"I tend to forget but I think I met John somewhere. I'm sorry I really don't recall. That's the truth Lilly Ann. I may remember someday."

Jason spoke up. "Emily, we better get to bed you need all the sleep you can get and Gabe and me have a lot of work tomorrow."

The next day we fell all the trees that were needed for all the work and they were taken to the different work sites.

Jason said. "Zack, you and Jay take the wagon into town and get enough tin for both roofs from Mr. Jimson. If he doesn't have all we need get him to order it. Get some paint and more nails. We'll do them up nice and tight so the wind won't blow through."

The next day we had everything we needed and we went to work. Zack was a surprise to me how fast he could work with one arm. He didn't let it slow him down.

We got the back wall of the house knocked down. Jane had the fireplace and the stove fired up to try to keep the house warm. By the end of the day we had the new peers in place and the back wall with the sidewalls up. The men at the mine with Bo and Tab helped us get it all closed in with even the roof on for the cold night.

Emily said. "I don't believe how fast you got it up."

"That's cause of the extra help. It will take a few days longer to get the inside done and paint the outside and inside. Jay tomorrow you and Jane go to town and she will know more about ordering furniture than you do. We'll just have to make do 'til it comes in after the baby comes. Don't worry Jane I'll be here with Emily 'til you get back."

"If she starts hurting in any way you don't wait. Send someone for me and doc right away."

"Jason, how are the men doing on the house in the peaceful valley?"

"Gabe, be quiet that way supposed to be a surprise for Emily after the baby. Well, now that she heard you they are coming along fine. When we get this house done I'm sending Jay and Zack out to finish it up and get it painted for the winter. But it is warmer in that valley so there might not be much of a winter."

Emily said, "Jason what are you talking about? You already have a secret from me."

"No not really. It's just a place we found when we were hunting for Tom. It's hidden away where no one could see it. It's on your new land and I knew you would want to see it and you can't right now so the men have been fixing it up for us to get away by ourselves once in a while. I was going to surprise you after the baby is born. Jane now that my surprise is out you might get Mr. Jimson to order furniture for another home about the size of this one. It will need everything cause it is bare."

"You mean our land. When we married all the land and the mine became yours and mine. Later when Lilly Ann gets married we can give her a piece of it. Later on the baby will get some and any more children we might have."

"More children, I didn't think we would have any of our own."

"Why not we can have at least one more of ours. If we don't we'll have fun trying after the baby comes."

Jane and I were laughing.

"Emily, how could you say that in front of Jane, Jay and Gabe and Lilly Ann?"

"They are our good friends and the Lord didn't expect us not to know each other in that matter forever just until after the baby arrives. I've explained to Lilly Ann how a baby is made. Young ladies need to know things like that. It's what life is all about."

"All right I give up to your womanly know how."

The next day Jay and Jane went to town. It was now December 18th and we were only a week away from Christmas and Emily and Jason's new arrival. I think they are doing fine and I hope the Lord have more good people for me to help. It will become a little easier if God see fit to give me my wings. Seeing their babies born will fulfill my prayer.

Jason, Zack and me were finishing up the new additions to the house and then we were ready for painting the whole outside and the inside just when Jay and Jane came riding up with some things in the wagon. Then Jay helped Jane down and Jane said.

"Mr. Jimson had the beds and rugs in the back room. He was wondering how he was going to get rid of them. He had to order the dressers and some other things not much more. Depending on the weather they could be here in a month." Then Jay spoke up.

"Boss, we had to make a decision. Mr. Jimson said Billie had ordered them when she had the idea that she was going to marry Johnson. We finally felt that since they were never in Johnson house it would be all right. Mr. Jimson didn't ever think that Johnson knew anything about any of the furniture. It was just a foolish woman's hope."

"That should be fine don't you think Emily."

"I do, they are new so now you men need to get this house painted so we can put the new furniture in here. Jay will you take the wagon to the barn and leave the furniture in the wagon. Maybe by tomorrow you men can unload it in the new rooms. Come on Jane here comes Lilly Ann up the drive from her last day at school before Christmas. We'll have supper ready in no time."

We worked until an early supper and we got all of the painting done inside. We just took a break to eat. Jay and Zack ate with us so we could get started on the painting of the outside. During the prayer before supper the fumes were really bad from the painting so Jason opened both doors and all the windows. It was better as we were eating but it was cold. The fireplace was going full blast. As we got started painting the outside Emily and Jane went to the bunkhouse and stayed in where it was warm. The men were done with their daily chores but they came and lent a hand so we could get done before dark. The house was now just about double in size and all painted.

Emily said, "You men don't mine if Jason and me move in with Jane and Lilly Ann tonight. That paint in the house just needs to be aired out for a night. It's so cozy in here."

Evan said, "My room behind the kitchen I think will be enough room for the four of you for one night if you don't look at how messy it is. I can sleep in Jason's old bunk."

"Thank you Evan that will be fine."

We worked until late and were done with the whole job.

17

The next morning everyone ate in the bunkhouse and Jane and Emily helped Evan with breakfast. Evan said to Emily.

"You sure you're not doing too much. No disrespect but you look like you could have that little one any minute."

"Thank you for your concern Evan but I may look terrible but I feel fine."

"No ma'am you don't look terrible. Ever since I saw you I thought you to be very pretty. Walking you down that isle to be married was the greatest honor in this old man's life. Jason I hope you don't take that the wrong way."

"No Evan I thought that the first time I saw her. I understand what you mean. That just means I was right I have a beautiful wife. You did a great favor bringing my darling to me in the church."

The men drifted off to their regular jobs around the ranch and the mine. The five of us went to the house and the odor was all but gone so I helped Jason get the fireplace going and Lilly Ann and Jane got the stove hot as could be. Today was a little warmer but there had been frost on the ground early in the morning. About mid-morning a rider rode up. It was one of the new deputies. He removed his hat as he spoke to us.

"Good morning I'm Pete, Tom's new deputy. Tom's still at home but is doing well. This telegram came for Mr. and Mrs. Jason Benning. Toby at the telegraph office brought this to me and Tom said to bring it to you fast it might be important."

"Thank you Pete, would you like some coffee."

"No thanks ma'am. I better be getting back to the office. Tom's is counting on me to keep the peace until he gets back to work."

"Thank you Pete and keep up the good work."

He took off down the road to Joplin.

I said, "That was refreshing, sure is different than Doug."

Emily handed the telegram to Jason and he opened it.

"Emily, it's from Gene they got there this morning and are waiting for the offices to open. They will let us know when they find out more. They hit light snow about half way there but it was done in a few hours."

I said, "At least they're there if they get caught there all winter we know they're safe."

Jason said, "I'm going to get the wagon hooked up and get the furniture unload in this brand new pretty home. Jane now you and Lilly Ann can have your own rooms and one for the baby when it's big enough. Come on Gabe you can help me."

As we were bringing in the furniture, Emily and Jane were directing us where to put each piece of furniture. By dinner we were done and sit down to a nice meal in a nice warm house. Things were back to normal until the baby's arrival.

After supper Jason and me went to the bunkhouse to talk to the men.

"Tomorrow I want all of you except the men working in the mine to go out with Bob and get the other house finished as fast as you can. Take the wagon with all the paint and other things we had left here. I would go but Emily is nearing her time and I want to be near."

"We understand daddy. We just hope the baby looks like Emily." They all laughed and patted him on the back.

Jason said, "You're all fired." Then he laughed.

"Thank you men you are really all part of our family. By the spring we're going to have to hire some more men cause of the new land and cattle. I want you all to know that you helped save this land and Emily and me will always be grateful to all of you."

The next morning everyone but Jason and me followed Bob out to what had come known as "Peaceful Valley" even if it was used for evil in the near past. I was sure it would never be used for that purpose ever again. We got our coats on and cleaned up the yard of all the debris from the work that had been completed. The men came in that afternoon with the news that the house in "Peaceful Valley was done and ready for the new furniture.

This new morning was December 21st and the first day of winter. Emily was so patiently waiting for the baby to come but Jason, I could tell was on pins and needles.

It was all I could do to keep him still. Emily finally said.

"I love you Jason but you are driving me crazy. Gabe you take him out to that "Peaceful Valley" and make sure it's done right. Jane is here and Evan is always at the bunkhouse. We can send him for the doc if need be."

"But dear I want to be here when the baby comes."

"Jason you will be. I can tell it is a few days off. I'll be all right."

I said, "Jason let's get out and go up there and check and see if there might be another way in there. You know we never looked all around. There might be another way to get in."

We saddled up and left the barn. It was cold out in the open. We rode on for two hours without anything being said just the cold wind in our faces. The crack in the face of the cliff was in front of us and we rode through. Once inside the valley we rode along the inside of the cliff looking for another way in. We found where the creek came up out of the ground that fed the small lake a short ways from the house. Then we came to the house and went inside and looked around.

"This will be fine for us and maybe for Lilly Ann and Tab one day if they get married. It's nice and warm in here even without a fire."

We went outside and continued to look for another way out. Then we came to where the old cabin and barn had been and I saw something against the rock wall. We weren't but a hundred feet away from where the house stood now.

"Look Jason, over there against the wall where the cabin was."

We got off the horses and went up to the rock wall and there was a breeze blowing out of the wall. We removed all the sagebrush and there was an opening. It was smaller than the other one.

I said, "Let's try to get through and see where it comes out."

Jason looked around and said.

"You know if we can get through with the horses this would make a good place for a barn with a secret door in the back wall of the barn. If anything happened we could escape through the barn and any attackers wouldn't know until we were long gone."

We started through and there was less light than the other passage but we managed to go all the way to the outside. We had stayed on our horses except in one place for about fifty feet we had to walk. On the outside about a hundred feet was our fence on this side of the ranch. The fence had a gate in it and there was a trail on the other side. We followed the cliff around to the other entrance. It was a good ways and not in a straight path but wound around large trees and plenty of brush to the north and the south. Right now Jason's mind was occupied but as we came to the old entrance. I could see him returning back to thinking about Emily.

"He said, "We better get back the sun is getting low in the west."

"I know we have to get back, but did you see that gate on the fence line outside the new entrance. There was a trail on the other side of that gate. Just keep it in your mind and one day see where that trail leads."

"I saw that, could be a short way to town if we're up this way. We need to get back, I'm not leaving Emily again 'til the baby comes."

"Come on daddy let's get going." We turned the horses toward home.

We were in the barn just after sundown and Jay came in.

"Where you two been all day?"

Jason said, "Why is something wrong with Emily?"

"No Jason she's all right. She just was looking for you cause supper is on the table. She sent Lilly Ann to find you two."

I said, "We just went to check on the house in "Peaceful Valley". We found a new way to get in and out. Jason wants to build a barn right where the entrance is for an easy escape. Jay I'm telling you so you can remind him of it. He's just not in his right mind now. When we went out that way our fence was a hundred feet away and there was a gate in the fence and a trail on the other side leading somewhere. We had to get back. Just remind him of it later on one day."

Jason said, "Come on Gabe we need to get to the house. I just hope Emily is all right."

"See what I mean Jay. Just remind him after the baby comes. Come on daddy let's get to the house. See you later Jay."

"I see what you mean Gabe. I'll remind him."

We went in the house and Jason took Emily in his arms and hugged and kissed her.

"Are you alright, I missed you."

"I'm fine Jason now sit down and eat."

"I'm not leaving you again."

"Alright, Gabe has he been like this all day."

"Just about. I tried to take his mind off of you but it didn't work for too long at a time."

"Dear, this will be over soon I promise."

"I sure hope so. I wasn't this nervous in the war or any gunfight. I hope being a father will be easier than this. Gabe, when you go to the bunkhouse would you get Jay go to town in the morning and see if we have another telegram from Gene. I just wanted to tell you before I forget."

"I will, I won't forget. Jane what are you doing after the baby is born and Emily can take care of it. Are you going back to the diner?"

"I really haven't decided. I may go back to the diner."

"I have a feeling that Gene will need someone to help him in the mining office with all the paper work. If I know Gene he won't like being stuck in an office all day. Zack is going to be in charge of the shipping. He will need help also."

"I'll keep that in mind. That would be great. After that party I sure like some of the cowboys around here. Most are good dancers."

The next morning Jay went to town and came back with a telegram and some other news. We were eating breakfast.

"Tom's back at work. He's letting the deputies do most of the duties around town. He's sitting in the office and taking it easy. The bank has a new manager and there is a new judge in town. He was in Tom's office and wants to meet you someday after the baby. People are out on the streets buying for Christmas. Mr. Jimson is having a good old time. He says it is going to be the best Christmas since before the war. Doc asked about you Emily. He said it should be any day now."

Jason opened the telegram and read it out loud. It read.

"Todd and me met with his bosses the Harris Brothers. They were going to send another man to look at the ore but Todd told them that they needed to see it their selves. They did with another company man. They looked surprise at the quality and quantity of the ore and were pleasantly surprise when they heard how deep it might go. They will be sending wagons to pick up the ore starting in the spring and if we build a smelting plant they want all of that. I think it is a good deal and I would hire more men and get all the ore we can mine this winter. They will pay $1,000 per wagonload and they will send twenty wagons. We already have enough for ten wagons piled up outside the mine. And when we can refine it they'll pay $3,000 a load. I contacted Wright's and Son's with a note from the Harris Bother and they will be sending some men to talk to you and Emily and measure how big a plant you will need. They will come along with us when we come. The plant will cost different prices according to the size. We may take longer to get back for there was a big snowstorm here. Hope it's not coming your way. Hope Emily is doing well.

Your Friend
Gene Bailey

Emily told us. "This is hard to believe and then you are going to drive cattle to Kansas City to sell and the horse ranch will be going strong."

Jason said. "I will hire more men for the mine after the baby is born. In the spring we'll need more men for the ranch. Then more men when the plant is built and someone that knows how to run it and teach men what to do and Jay you might get with Gene and Bo and Tab and learn all you can. Looks like they'll be all kinds of work around here. We should build a bunkhouse up by the mine and hire another cook for up there."

"I think we can wait on that awhile. Gabe we finally got his mind off the baby. " Emily said.

"Emily, I'll never forget that. It's just now there is a real bright future for us and our children and the people in this town."

We sat around talking about the future and ate in between. As the day went on the dark clouds began to gather. The sun hadn't been seen since noon or before. It was just a gray winter day. At supper Jason said to Emily.

"You know tomorrow is the 23th of December. I thought you might have had the baby by now."

"Doc said it might come before Christmas but that's not up to us. We just have to wait."

"Well, I said that I wouldn't leave you but Christmas is just two days away. Could I take out some money and go get Christmas presents for every one of the men and us."

"You don't have to ask me for money we're married what's mine is yours. Anyway you never took any pay for the last four month. It's been so poor around here the last four years I just didn't think about it. You take Gabe with you and get everyone something. I'll be fine with Jane and Lilly Ann here and all the men are around one place or another."

So the next morning Jason and me headed to town. Mr. Jimson was the only place in town that had a great variety of things. The day was still over casted and downright cold. The sun couldn't be seen through the low hanging gray clouds. The winds were still not blowing very hard and they were out of the southeast. We made it into town early enough so there wasn't too many people out yet. We did see Tom going in his office. He didn't stop to talk cause of the cold. Then as we got down from the wagon doc was coming out of Mr. Jimson store and said.

"You come for me. I've been expecting you any time now. I've been praying that this weather might hold off until that young one arrives. It sure looks like a bad storm might be coming."

"No doc, Emily is about the same. Jane is with her. We decided that everyone on the ranch needed a good Christmas after all the hard times. We're here to buy presents for everyone."

"That's what I'm doing here this early before the Misses gets up. I better let you get through so you can hurry back to that pretty wife of yours. Send someone for me when it's time."

"Will do doc."

We got inside out of the cold and started looking around when Mr. Jimson came over.

"Jason, Gabe how are you both and Emily. I thought you might be in now that you have a new bride and Christmas is so close. Can I help you find anything special?"

"We were hoping that the baby would come by now. That's why we waited so long. We need to find something for everyone on the ranch. If you don't mind we will just look 'til we spot what we need."

"Why that's a lot of presents you're looking for. If you find what you need just put it on the counter and it's yours?"

"No sir, Mr. Jimson we will pay. You've done way more than enough for us already. No argument."

"All right, but I can never repay you for what you did for me and my family."

We looked around for a while and found things for the men. They were not expensive but they would appreciate what they received. For Evan we picked out a new-fangled potato peeler and Jay a new belt buckle and for Zack a new shirt and tie for church. I could tell that Jason was having a hard time finding something for Emily and Lilly Ann. Emily had told me to find something that Jason would like. I finally decided on a belt with a very manly buckle on it. I said.

"Here Jason try this on see if it fits you. You better act surprised when you get it because Emily told me she was tired of seeing that old army belt that's been through the war. She said it was time you had something nice."

"Alright, but I like my old belt."

"You can just tell her you'll wear the old belt to work in and the new one when you're not working."

"That's good thinking. But Gabe I'm having a hard time finding the two special women in my new life anything. Jane I got this perfume but I want something real special for them. It's our first Christmas together."

Mr. Jimson came over and looked at me.

"Come over here I think Lilly Ann would like some of these do dads over here. She's becoming quite a young lady. They always like these things."

I looked over the things with Jason.

"Here's some ribbons for her hair and a nice brush comb set and these to hold her long hair back if she wants to."

"Look here Gabe a nice pair of new boots for riding and a new outfit. All of that Mr. Jimson that should be enough for Lilly Ann and you know her size from the wedding clothes and now that leaves Emily."

Mr. Jimson said. "It's been a long time since Lilly Ann was a baby and it may be a boy. The baby will need some clothes and diapers with blankets for the cold. You know babies should be kept warm. The women around here give Emily some baby clothes but a baby can always use more."

"Jason you forget there may be two if I'm right and maybe a boy and a girl."

"Gabe you just don't give up. All right Mr. Jimson we'll take two of everything. A small size for sure. Now what for Emily."

I spotted just the thing that a woman would like.

"Over here Jason in this display case."

Jason and Mr. Jimson came over and took a look.

"Here I have the key right here. That's good just some personal things just for her not something she would use every day. Not very practical just pretty to look at and that means everything to a woman at this time of year."

"Alright I'll take one of these and this and this one to."

"You know those things have some diamonds in them that's why I keep them locked up very expensive and elegant and they will last forever. I think these are just the right choice."

Jason said, "I think that's it. Oh no I forgot about you Gabe my best man."

"No Jason I don't need anything. Really!"

"Nonsense let me see. Something you can keep forever and that can go where ever you are. Here it is. Now Gabe, you don't look 'til Mr. Jimson gets it wrapped up. I hate to do this but could you wrap everything separately."

"I sure will and let me see. That will be I'll make it an even $300."

"You sure even with those diamonds?"

"Don't argue with me I know what my merchandise cost."

"Yes sir, I wouldn't doubt your word."

"That's better now give me a little while and I'll have everything ready."

I went over to the door and looked at the sky.

"You know Jason it doesn't look to good outside. Good thing we brought that canvas to cover up everything and tie it down. The wind seems to be picking up."

Mr. Jimson had everything wrapped and ready to load up. We had everything loaded up and ready to go. Mr. Jimson came out to see us off.

"Tell Emily and Lilly Ann and everyone to have a Merry Christmas for me."

We said good-by and headed for home. The wind had picked up tremendously. It must be blowing forty miles an hour or more. It was hard going and it slowed us down as the horses fought against the strong north wind and then about half way home it started to snow and not the light power snow. This snow was wet and heavy. I thought to myself.

"I wonder if I have any new powers since I'm so close to completing my mission." I thought hard about the clear road how the road in front of us was clear and how the snow above would fall around but not on us.

Jason said, "Look Gabe the snow is parting in front of us and making it easier to go through and look behind it's going back over the road. It's snowing all around us but not on us. Gabe did you have something to do with this."

"Well I'll be. Jason I really don't know but let's get home fast before this miracle decides to stop."

As we turned up the road going to the house it kept happening and then we reached the barn and Zack happened to be there to open the barn doors. Jason drove the horses all the way in the barn and Zack closed the doors.

"Why Mr. Jason how did you come through all that snow? It must be five inches already. Miss Emily must be worried. Why were you out there when it looked so bad."

"You'll find out tomorrow and don't dare look under that canvas. It's a surprise for everyone for Christmas. Now Gabe would you and Zack get the horses taken care of. I better get to the house if I can."

"You will make it to the house. It will be the same as on the road."

"Gabe, you did have something to do with this."

"Jason just get to the house now."

I saw Jason enter the house and Zack and me finished with the horses and he headed to the warm bunkhouse and I to the main house.

"See you later Zack. Stay warm."

It had to be almost dark when I opened the door to the house. It was very hard to tell the way the wind was blowing the snow around in the sky. I turned as I closed the door and I had four pairs of eyes staring at me.

"What is it? What did I do?" I said.

Emily said to me. "Jason told us what happened out there. It's hard to believe."

"I know it was a real miracle. I just thought about that happening and it did. That's the real truth and I can't lie. It's not in me to tell a lie."

"Whatever it was I thank you once again."

Emily and Lilly Ann came over and hugged me and kissed me on the cheek.

Jason said. "Gabe, I might hug and kiss you to but that might look funny so I'll just shake your hand and say thank you for the prayer at the right time."

We ate and sat around in front of the fireplace and talked for hours. The snow just didn't want to let up.

"I said, "I hope the horses and cattle are all right in this."

"I know the horses have a little valley that they get in up past the mine. John told me about it one winter before the war started. I don't know about the cattle. They must have a place over on the new land that we don't know about. They seemed to have made it through other winters."

"I guess we'll find out once we can get out there again. I just hope Gene and those men from the smelting company can make it back. We also need to get in the mine."

I said, "This won't last but one more day. It should be gone by Christmas Eve Night."

Jane said, "I sure hope so or I may have to deliver this baby."

"If doc can't get here you can help Emily do it." Lilly Ann said.

Emily said, "Daughter you might have to help. It will do you good to see what we women have to go through."

"You mean it mother. You trust me that much."

"Yes daughter I do."

It was late so I went to the bunkhouse. The four of them were watching as the snow stopped in front of me and started falling again behind me as I opened the door to the bunkhouse. Some of the men were watching as I went in and had their mouths hanging wide open. They just looked at me and shut their mouths and didn't say much about what they saw.

18

The next morning was Christmas Eve December 24, 1865. Not anyone but the men in the bunkhouse knew that Evan had planned an early Christmas Day dinner. It was only eleven in the morning when the men gathered up all that Evan had been preparing all night and headed to the house with me in the lead. The snow had let up some and we went in the front room. Everyone yelled.

"Surprise!"

The men looked to see Jason and Emily looking at them with amazements to see us in the front room with our arms full of our dinner.

"What is this?"

As the men put the tables together and laid out the tablecloth on the table and laid out all the food I said.

"This was Evan idea."

Evan said, "You maybe too busy tomorrow so I thought we could have Christmas today."

Emily said. "I like that you're all welcomed."

We all removed our coats and hats. Then Emily said her dinner prayer and we sat down to a good old fashion Christmas dinner. After dinner Jason said.

"We might as well do it up right. Gabe, get some of the men to the barn and get all the presents out of the wagon. Gabe is going to be Santa Clause this year."

Four of the men and me went to the barn through the snow again and came back with our arms full of wrapped presents.

Gabe said, "It looks to me like Santa Clause made it to town yesterday."

Gabe started passing out gifts with the mens names on them. All the men were opening their gifts. I opened mine and Jane opened hers with Lilly Ann by her side opening hers and then Lilly Ann got up and hugged mine and Jason's neck and had a tear in her eyes as I handed Emily's her present and the baby's present. She opened the baby's first. She was amazed at all the things and then said.

"Why two of everything and two different colors."

Jason said, "Dear you know Gabe has insisted and me and Mr. Jimson didn't argue with him about two babies."

Emily then opened her present. There was the necklace and bracelet with a pair of diamond earrings. Emily looked and was crying and saying.

"How beautiful they are! I don't know what to say but thank you my love. I never thought I would ever have something this beautiful." It was two in the afternoon and we were having a good old time laughing and telling stores of pass Christmas's when we were young. That is when I looked over and saw Emily's expression on her face.

"Jason grab Emily."

Jason caught her as she fell to her knees and Jane said.

"Jason get her to your room now hurry. I think it's time Lilly Ann get some water boiling and bring some clean towels. Bob, you and Tab try to get to town for the doc. That snow better move for them this time Gabe."

Bob and Tab hurried to the barn and were gone in a few minutes. I concentrated for the snow to stop. We looked out and it had slowed down to a few flakes but they still had a time with the six inches of deep snow. The men were asking.

"What can we do Jane?"

"Just pray for the doc to get here and for Emily and me. Then stay out of the way. I don't know how long this will take."

After Jason had taken Emily in their bedroom Jane had run him out saying.

"I'm sorry Jason, but this is no place for a man right now unless you are a doc."

Lilly Ann had gotten the water hot and took it and some clean cloth into Jane and she stayed to help. I tried to calm Jason down he was beside himself with worry. I told him.

"Don't worry Jason doc will get here I am sure of that. Until then Jane knows what needs to be done and if need be I know Jane can deliver them. You just need to be strong and keep the faith and it wouldn't hurt to pray for the Lord to guide Jane through this and for Emily and the babies to be fine."

Every once in a while we could hear Emily let out a scream of pain and this would set off Jason again. The men had gone to the bunkhouse an hour ago saying they didn't want to be in the way. I think it was that they couldn't stand to hear Emily crying in pain. They said.

"If you need us for anything just come and get us. We'll be waiting."

I told Jason, "Those screams are really Emily's cries of joy. Women were made to go through this. It is hard but this pain will provide a woman with everlasting love for her child. It doesn't matter what the child becomes her love will always be present in her heart."

"Gabe, it is just so hard. I feel helpless cause this is one time I can't protect her from pain."

I sat and Jason walked from the front door to the bedroom door and back again. He would stop at the bedroom door and listen. Then he would hear Emily yell sometimes less and sometimes more and he would turn around and walk back toward the front door. This went on for three or four hours. Jane would come out and ask.

"Any sign of the doc."

I would tell her, "No, not yet."

Then Jason would ask, "Is there anything wrong."

Jane would say, "No, Jason everything is coming along fine. It's just that doc has more experience with this but it will be all right. Emily knows what it's all about. Lilly Ann is keeping her focused and calm."

I tried to see into town and a picture came to me. Bob and Tab had made it to town and the doc was saying as he got on his horse for the snow was too deep for his buggy.

"I don't know how you two got in here but let's hurry and get back. I told my wife not to worry I would stay until it was safe to come back to town and you two would see me back."

"We will doc, now let's get to the ranch."

I could see that the snow was piled up but the snow had quit falling so I thought in my mind about the road being swept of snow to the side of the road. I could see it happening in front of the riders. Doc didn't seem to know how this was happening but they were coming faster now and that's what counted at this moment. Emily's scream brought my mind back to this room. I called Jason over to the window and he said.

"Gabe, look the men are mounted on their horses and are headed down the road. The snow has stopped and they're getting off and shoveling the snow to the side of the road. They have the lanterns lit. I didn't realize it was dark already."

I said, "It's eight already and look they're to the end of our road. Doc should be here at any time."

We kept watching and the men were doing the same to the road going to town. I know that they had felt powerless in this house but outside, that was their life fighting for survival. Jason would remember this for all his life what friends could do for you. Then about thirty minutes later out of a cloud of snow on the road came three horsemen and all the men let out a yell that we could hear them yell from inside the house where we were. It was doc, Bob and Tab and all the men were behind them. Doc hurried up the porch steps as the snow was swept away from the steps. Jason ran to the door and opened it and took doc's hat and coat and doc hurried to the bedroom where he heard the yells coming from. It was now nine o'clock and doc was in there for an hour before he came out.

"Jason, Emily is doing fine. Jane and Lilly Ann did a fine job. All we can do is wait. It just takes time for some women and Emily is one of them. I seem to remember that Lilly Ann took I think about ten hours to come into this world. So don't worry everything is fine. Try to get some rest."

"Thanks doc."

Jason put on his coat as I did and went out on the porch. He told them.

"I saw what all of you did and I thank you. Bob, you and Tab risked your life for Emily and the baby. If there is anything that I can help you with don't hesitate to ask. I will let you know when the baby arrives. If you want to wait in the house you are welcomed anytime."

"Thank you boss."

Ten and Eleven o'clock came and went and Jason was back pacing the floors and I was just sitting and waiting for God to call me back upstairs. I needed to talk to Emily and Jason after the babies were born. I told Jason.

"I may not have much time left here but I need to talk to you and Emily and Lilly Ann after the babies are born."

"What you mean, you can't leave us we'll always need you."

"Just wait after the birth I can tell you everything you need to know. Now I know he will let me tell you."

The time was now 12:01 on Christmas morning when we heard a small cry and a smile came to Jason's face. Lilly Ann came out.

"Father, mother had a baby boy. But doc said to wait."

She went back inside and we waited for about five more minutes and there were two small cries now in the world. This time Jane came out and cried.

"Jason, Gabe was right you and Emily have a beautiful baby girl and a handsome baby boy. Doc said come on in."

"You come to Gabe I know you have something to tell us."

We went inside the bedroom and doc came out and I saw Jane get him some coffee. There they were. I took hold of Emily and Lilly Ann's hands and looked at the babies.

"Jason come here, I wasn't able to tell you anything before, God wouldn't let me but now I can. I was sent to earth on an assignment and you three were my assignment. I was to see that you three became a family and see these two born and to see that this ranch was saved. I had no wings when I came here but now I have earned them it took me a long time because I was killed during this time but it is now one hundred and fifty years from now. I was sent back to this time because I couldn't get any of my assignments right until now. I now know something that I didn't know when I was sent here. Emily, I am your John and Lilly Ann I am your and the new babies pa. Jason you have become my best friend and I leave you in trust of my family. I can tell you the ranch and mine will prosper with all of your hard work and love for the people that work for you and this community. So God is calling me back now. You are now my reasonability until you come to us. I can hear God calling I have to go." I had changed in a matter of seconds to an Angel with white flowing garments and the last thing I heard was Lilly Ann saying, with tears of joy running down her cheeks, as I went out of the house and into the heavy falling snow was.

"Thank you Lord for these two little babies on your son's birthday. Look father, mother at pa he has his wings and is flying home to heaven."

THE END

CPSIA information can be obtained
at www.ICGtesting.com
Printed in the USA
JSHW081627210323
39023JS00001B/3